HAT TRICK

FAKE BOYFRIEND BOOK 5

EDEN FINLEY

HAT TRICK

Copyright © 2019 by Eden Finley

Cover Illustration Copyright ©
Kellie Dennis at Book Cover By Design
www.bookcoverbydesign.co.uk

Photographer: Wander Aguiar
Model: Preston T
www.wanderbookclub.com

Edited by Deb Nemeth
http://www.deborahnemeth.com/

Professional beta read and line edited by Les Court Services
https://www.lescourtauthorservices.com

Copy-edited by Kelly Hartigan @ Xterraweb
http://editing.xterraweb.com/

All rights reserved.
This book or any portion thereof may not be reproduced or used in any manner whatsoever without the express written permission of the publisher.
For information regarding permission, write to:
Eden Finley - permissions - edenfinley@gmail.com

TRADEMARKS/DISCLAIMERS

This is a work of fiction. As such, the views in this book in no way reflect the views and principles of the NHL or any of their real teams.

Names, characters, businesses, places, events, and incidents are either the products of the author's imagination or used in a fictitious manner. Any resemblance to actual persons, living or dead, or actual events is purely coincidental.

CHAPTER ONE

SOREN

Whoever's idea it was to get away and recharge in Fiji is a dumbass. Oh, right. That dumbass is me.

Nothing emphasizes your loneliness quite like a beach vacation with four couples.

Laughter echoes through the night, coming from the open-air hut behind me where the rest of the guys are still having dinner.

The winter wind is cool and smells like salt water, but I still don't need a jacket. The water I'm wading through up to my ankles isn't even cold. Apparently, Fiji doesn't know how to do real winters.

It's only our first dinner since arriving here, and I had to sneak out under the excuse that I'd had too much to drink, which is true, and I needed air, which is also true. But I needed to get out of there because of the stark reminder everyone back there has their life together. I'm older than all of them, and I'm the one who's *lost*.

It's been months since Bryce and I finally called it quits for good, but it still feels a lot like failure hanging over my head.

Just like my contract negotiations. They aren't going well

either. Damon has been in talks with the team since before last season even ended. What they've been offering is good money-wise, but what I want is a no-trade clause. Getting that at thirty-three is like asking for a pet unicorn as part of the contract deal.

There's a very real chance I could lose my boyfriend and my career in the same year.

I kick the water at my feet.

When Bryce took me back after I came out publicly, I thought all our problems were solved.

Turns out we had more than closet problems.

We had *relationship* problems.

They were even worse.

Yet, I stayed with him because I came out for him. *I changed my life for him.* And, apart from one sweaty night with a twinkish rock star three years ago, I'd never thought of having anyone else but him.

I knew the minute we all stepped onto our chartered flight here that I'd made a mistake in accepting Matt and Noah's offer to come with them to Fiji. They do this trip yearly, but this time, they invited all of us to join them.

I'm not in the right headspace to be *on* and sociable, especially when we're supposed to be here for a celebration.

Matt's youngest brother, Wade, is coming to live with Matt and Noah in the fall to attend private school in Chicago. They're calling this vacation their *final play* before they become guardians of a teenager, so they wanted to make it huge.

Everyone is all coupled up, and for the whole flight, they stared at each other lovingly, silently promising two weeks of sun, surf, and sex.

It's disgusting.

And I'm disgustingly jealous.

I sink my feet into the coarse sand, and the water laps at my shins as I move deeper.

The owners of this private island, Joni and his wife, Ema, were gracious enough to rent the whole place to us, so at least while all the guys are distracted with mocking each other and arguing who are the better athletes—baseball players, football players, or hockey players—no one should interrupt my little pity party for one.

And please, like that's an argument anyway. Hockey players, hands down. The end. No need for more discussion.

There's one thing I should remember about this particular group of guys though. Most of them are egotistical athletes with frat-bro syndrome, but they're also perceptive fuckers.

I sense someone's presence and turn to find Ollie ditching his flip-flops at the edge of the water to join me.

"Go back to all the fun," I say.

"Sorry, can't."

Of course, he can't.

Out of everyone here, I'm closest to Ollie. He also plays hockey, and when he found out I'd announced my orientation at a press conference, he stepped up and came out to support me so I didn't have to do it alone. It cemented our friendship.

"How are you doing?" he asks, holding out a bottle of water for me with his tatted-up arm.

I take a sip. I probably need it after how much I've had to drink in the last hour. "Fan-fucking-tastic." Does that sound bitter? Eh. Oh well.

"Was it all the jokes about hiring you a very illegal rent boy?"

I snort. "No. It also wasn't the Canada bashing, offers of threesomes, or… I dunno, whatever you guys moved on to after that. I tuned out after a while."

"It's our poor way of trying to take your mind off everything."

Because it's no secret my life's a mess right now. That makes me feel a whole lot better.

"I'm thankful for it," I say because I really am. It's just not what I need right now. "But maybe I shouldn't have come here."

"Bryce wasn't the right guy for you." Ollie says this as if I didn't already know that. He's not the reason I'm upset.

"It's not so much him. It's hockey, it's my uncertain future, it's ... everything. What if the team doesn't want me anymore?"

"If New Jersey doesn't offer you another contract, then they're assholes, and you'll sign with someone else."

"That's just it. Signing with another team is more daunting than retiring at this point." It was an adjustment for everyone to get used to playing next to the gay guy. Ollie's team appeared to accept him better than mine had accepted me, but what if the next team is worse?

"What's your ultimate goal when it comes to hockey?" Ollie asks, and it's such a loaded question that I don't know how to answer.

"What's yours?"

"The Cup, obviously, but that's every player's dream. If I get to your age—"

"You're not that much younger, asshole."

Ollie smirks. "As I was saying, if I get to your ... level of experience—"

"Better."

"I'd be happy with the type of career you've had. You've won a Selke Trophy."

"I won that *eight* years ago."

"And you were in the Stanley Cup final three years ago. I haven't ever made it to a championship game."

"There's a major difference between us though. You still have time. I feel like mine's running out."

Ollie lets out a loud whistle. "That's dark. No wonder you drank so much at dinner."

Coconuts filled with liquor might be my downfall this trip. I sip more water. "They were good, but they were strong and sickly sweet. Now they're sitting wrong." I rub my stomach.

"Maybe go easy on them if your old body can't handle it."

I kick at the water and splash him all the way up to his shirt. I may be older but that doesn't mean I'm more mature.

"Really? Is that how it's gonna be?"

Before he gets a chance to retaliate, I run for the beach and away from the water so he can't get me. My knees protest, but I tell them to shut the fuck up. Water goes everywhere, and I'm probably as wet as I would have been if I'd just let him splash me.

Ollie catches up as we hit the sand and tries to drag me back toward the water, but we're both laughing so hard we don't get far.

That's when the sound of a helicopter hits our ears and makes us pause. The loud rhythmic thumping of propeller blades becomes louder, and a blinking red light in the sky gets brighter and lower to the ground.

"Paparazzi?" I ask.

"Matt and Noah say next to no one recognizes them in Fiji. It's why they love coming here."

We move back toward everyone else, who are now huddled by the entryway to the food hut, each of them as curious as we are.

"Then who—"

The idea of paparazzi crashes and burns when someone far worse steps out of the helicopter when it lands in the clearing close by.

I blink a few times to make sure I didn't somehow wish him into an illusion.

He's not supposed to be here. Matt said he couldn't get out of his music tour.

There's a reason I refer to Matt's brother as the twinkish rock star, the random guy I had one night with a billion years ago. Because the reality is, he's not some random guy, and it wasn't some random hookup.

He's forbidden fruit. Not only because he's Matt Jackson's *little* brother who's ten years younger than me, but because he's a famous rock star now.

No one knows what happened between us, and unless I want to get beaten up, I have no plans to let anyone here find out. Matt and Noah are overprotective, and the rest of the group all see Jet —sorry, *Jay*—as the little brother they never had.

Now, he's here in front of me.

My heart pounds while memories of our past flash through my head.

His shaggy brown hair is unstyled, his ripped jeans are tight, and the cocky smirk that has haunted me for three years is still the same.

This vacation just became a whole lot more interesting.

As we lock eyes, I realize I'm wrong.

It's awkward. The word I'm looking for is awkward.

CHAPTER TWO

JET

THE HOOKUP

There should've been a tingle in my stomach. Or perhaps an alert in my subconsciousness that I was about to meet someone who'd change my life. There was nothing but the usual buzz of energy under my skin and the thousand thoughts per minute running through my head.

People always wondered why creative people were neurotic and a little batshit. All I had to say to those people was "You try living in my head for a day. You'll understand."

I entered the New Jersey locker room on a mission to invite Caleb "Soren" Sorensen to Fever with the rest of the group who I'd dubbed the gay brigade.

Lennon had given me his press pass after he was swamped by paparazzi. It was official. His and Ollie's relationship was no longer on the down low.

I had tunnel vision going into that locker room. Lost in the mindless beat thrumming through my head to a song I hadn't yet written, I was taken aback when Soren turned to me as I approached.

His wide pecs and sculpted abs made my feet trip over themselves. I was assaulted with a sight my young and naïve eyes couldn't handle.

Pfft, naïve.

I told my conscience to shut up.

Soren cocked his head. "Aren't you …"

I forced my gaze to his face, but that was worse. Honey-colored eyes burned me from head to toe as he took me in. He looked horrified by what he found, but that couldn't be right. I was gorgeous, damn it. And modest about it too.

"You were at the Rainbow Beds benefit," he said.

My ears heard him, but my brain was still stumbling over the look of mortification it had seen not two seconds ago, so it didn't register the actual words.

I managed to get out what I needed to. "Ollie and Lennon are going to Fever. Like … after this. With the rest of the gay brigade. You. Fever. Uhhh …" *Way to make sentences, dude.*

"Gay brigade?"

"Matt. Ollie. Damon. Lennon. You know … gay." *Get it together, Jet, I swear to Kurt Cobain.* I shook my head. "They're all going to Fever, and you're invited."

"Because I'm gay?" Soren asked, his lips curving in amusement.

"And because you lost the Cup and need to drown your sorrows."

His face fell. His team had been one goal away from holding the Stanley Cup over their heads, and I was rubbing it in his face.

My bad.

Then I realized he wasn't the only one who had heard me, and I was surrounded by copious amounts of dick. And not in the fun way. The other players didn't even try to cover up, and being the gay guy in a room full of hot, naked, *straight* manly men, my feet found the momentum to get the hell outta there before I did something stupid like offer myself as some sort of towel boy.

But I'd done my job—I passed on the message for Soren to meet us at the newest gay club to hit the streets of New York. Whether or not he'd turn up was another issue. It would have nothing to do with my babbling if he didn't come. Nope. Not at all. Not my fault, guys.

I caught up with the others outside the arena, and we took two cabs to Fever. When our group entered the bar, everyone turned their heads and checked us out ... well, everyone else out. Being invisible was a side effect of hanging out with these guys—famous athletes who were around six foot or taller. I was average at five ten, but next to these guys, I was the shorty of the group. Because of the invisibility, the bouncer didn't bother carding me when we all came in, so I went straight to the bar for drinks.

I drank. I danced. I got lost in the beat and sweaty bodies around me. And the minute Soren stepped through the doors, the energy in the room shifted. My pulse thrummed stronger in my veins, trying to compete with the loud bass coming from the speakers. Even though there was a sea of men surrounding me at any given moment, my gaze went straight to his.

From that moment on, his gaze burned into me everywhere I went. To the bar to get drinks. On the dance floor with Ollie. Flirting with a cute guy near the hallway to the bathrooms. Everywhere I went, he was watching. Not that I was complaining—I just didn't know *why*.

His bright eyes stood out, even in the dark, and I noticed whenever a guy would say anything to me, a line creased Soren's forehead.

Older guys weren't my thing. In fact, I spent a lot of my time ribbing my brother-in-law about being old, and he was only twenty-seven. This Soren guy was at least that, if not older, and I didn't need a daddy in my life to deal with my daddy issues, fuck-youverymuch, Mom and Dad.

Still, the high it gave me knowing he was watching me made me want to put on a show for him.

I waded my way through the crowded bar and back onto the dance floor. It took less than five seconds for someone to approach and start grinding on me.

Before I moved to New York, I'd had little experience with guys. I couldn't deny I was gay, but the sex was ... awkward. It made me question why people liked it so much. It was possible that I only ever hooked up with other inexperienced closeted guys like me, so neither of us knew what we were doing.

I had faith I'd eventually find the type of love my brother Matt had with his husband, but until then I'd have fun.

And watching Soren squirm was definitely fun.

Only, it seemed he was done with squirming. He left his post at the cocktail table with the rest of the guys and charged toward me. I thought he'd interrupt my dance with Mr. Handsy and maybe try to take his place. But that was not what happened.

His beefy hand wrapped around my upper arm, and then he pushed me off the dance floor.

I was going to make a caveman joke, but it was so loud in the club I could barely hear my own thoughts let alone my voice.

Soren dragged me into the corridor leading to the bathrooms.

Presumptuous much?

Surprising me yet again, he kept dragging me past the bathrooms and toward the emergency exit.

"Are you kidnapping me?" I yelled over the loud noise of the club.

He stared down at me, and his lips twitched, but he didn't answer.

When he pushed me out into the alley behind the bar, I didn't know if I was supposed to be scared. Anyone else, I probably would've been, but my flight instinct was nowhere around. My gut said the others wouldn't have invited Soren if he was dangerous, but there'd already been too many assholes in my life, so I was still wary.

"Want to explain to me what you were doing in there?" Soren's voice was gruff, and it immediately went to my cock.

I hadn't had such a visceral reaction to a guy's voice before, but I pushed that from my mind as I tried to work out what he meant.

"Dancing?" I asked. "Having fun?"

Soren ran a hand through his hair. "The song was complete bullshit then?" He took a deep breath. "I don't think I can handle that."

"What song?" *What the fuck is he talking about?*

"The song you sang at the Rainbow Beds benefit. The original."

Rainbow Beds was my brother-in-law's project, and my band played the benefit to raise money to help launch the charity. But that was months ago.

I stumbled back until I bumped into the wall behind me. "*My* song? You ... you know my song?"

"He's Mine" was everything to me. Benji, my bass player, was convinced it would be our first hit. He was almost right. It was the song that got us signed with a record label, but it wouldn't be our first single. The label said releasing a love song first would limit our stylistic choices in the future.

"*I came out* because of that song," Soren said. "And if you ... if it's not real, I'm going to lose my ever-loving mind. So, please, tell me that song was about your boyfriend and you're as happy as ever and that love conquers all and all that other bullshit because with the way you're throwing yourself at every single—and *taken*—guy in there, I'm starting to think it meant nothing. Isn't Lennon your friend? And you're in there all over Ollie—"

I ignored what was supposed to be an offensive comment because I couldn't get past the first thing he'd said. "You came out. Because of my song. Like, *my* song ..."

"Yes. Your song, your song, your song. If it's not real ..." Soren didn't look upset; he looked *distraught*. "It's gonna be like finding out Bobby Orr was on steroids."

"Who?"

"Jesus Christ," he muttered.

I was stunned. I couldn't believe it. I always hoped my words could get through to people, to touch them and make them feel comforted or brave or whatever they needed to feel. I just thought I'd be famous before that happened.

"You were at the Rainbow Beds benefit ..."

Soren continued to stare at me, disappointment clouding his face with every second I didn't clarify about the damn song.

"That song," I said slowly, "was about my brother and his husband. The song is real. It's just not my story."

I saw the moment it clicked for him.

Hope bloomed in his light eyes. "For real?"

"One hundred percent."

Soren bent at the waist, his hands going to his knees. "Oh, thank fuck."

I couldn't help but find his reaction amusing, but more importantly, I couldn't believe he was that deeply invested in my music.

Me. A poor kid from nowhere Tennessee. No college degree. Hell, barely even a high school diploma. I inspired someone to step outside their comfort zone.

I had to do something to remember this moment. "Seeing as you're technically my first-ever fanboy ... wait, you can't be called any type of boy ... fanman?"

Soren let out a deep laugh.

"Can I please buy you a drink?"

In a few years' time—hopefully—I wouldn't let fame go to my head because I'd remember the six-foot-one mountain of a hockey player having an identity crisis because of one of my songs. I'd remember the bravery it took for Soren to sit in front of a room full of journalists and announce to the world he was gay. He did that because of me. Jethro Jackson. The biggest white trash to ever trash.

I'd hold on to Soren's story to keep me humble.

Soren finally composed himself and stood tall. "Buy me a drink? No way. If anything, I owe you several drinks. You ... you changed my life."

Pride was quickly replaced with the crushing weight of pressure. Ever since signing with Joystar Records, I had a bad feeling the creative side of me was going to get squashed by the label.

They wanted to change the band's name, my name, and our eclectic sound.

Knowing someone out there loved "He's Mine" enough to change their life and come out publicly, I was terrified I'd never write anything that would live up to it. Especially with the record company already trying to put me in a box.

I wanted to savor this moment and turn it into one of those memories I'd think about until the day I died. It was the first time I had a fan tell me my words truly meant something.

We were about to wade our way through the giant crowd again when I stopped short.

"Soren ..." The guys had been calling him that, but it

occurred to me that it might've only been a bro thing to do like athletes did. "Uh ... Caleb?" I tugged on his arm.

He shuddered. "No, Soren's good. Everyone calls me Soren." He must've seen something in my eyes because concern etched into his gorgeous face. "What's wrong?"

I shook my head. "How about we don't drink at all?"

Soren's brow scrunched as if he didn't understand, but that cleared the second I stepped forward and pressed my body against his.

"Wanna get out of here?" I asked.

His hesitance was evident. "You're, like, this rock god, and I'm—"

"A hockey god. We should stick together, no?" The notion I was a god of anything was unrealistically awesome. Even if I acted like I believed it sometimes, hearing it from someone else was surreal.

Soren's tongue darted out and ran along his lips. They were shiny with spit and so tempting, but the hesitance on his face hadn't wavered.

"Want the truth?" I asked and didn't give him time to respond. "I'm a struggling musician who can't even keep cool about someone liking one of my songs."

"*Loving* one of your songs," he corrected. "I tried to find more online but couldn't."

We were still pressed against each other in the seedy corridor between the bathrooms and the noise of the club.

"Take me home?" I asked again.

"Fuck, yes." Soren's voice was croaky, and my body responded just as it had earlier.

Benji had a beautiful voice. He totally could've taken over lead vocals if he wanted to, but he didn't. Yet, his raspy voice never had my cock at full attention or my hands wanting to explore all of him like Soren's did.

"Where do you live?" I asked.

"Jersey."

"Hmm, too far," I murmured. "Bathroom?" My hand ran down his chest as I leaned in and kissed the side of his neck.

Soren moaned. "You're better than a fuck in a bathroom stall."

Hmm, debatable.

"There's a hotel down the block."

I stepped back and pulled him off the wall. "Sold."

We held hands the entire way to the upscale hotel, and I ignored the way it lit a fire in my gut. I didn't know holding someone's hand could turn me on so much.

The lobby was marble-tiled and dimly lit, giving it that elegance only expensive places had. The people behind the desk looked at me as if I were some by-the-hour rent boy, or maybe I was reading into it because that was kinda how I felt.

It wasn't the first time a random guy had taken me home, but it was the first time I'd felt out of place and nervous about it.

Soren wasn't like any of those other guys. Actually, he wasn't my type at all. I didn't do the jock thing.

Yet, there was no denying Soren did it for me.

My expectations were low, though. One disappointing sexual encounter after the next made it hard to get excited about things.

Oh, I'd brag and be a douche about my exploits, but really, they left me hollow inside. I was always putting on a show, being someone else—even to those closest to me.

When Soren took my hand again and led me to the elevators, there was no denying the flare of arousal.

We hadn't even reached our floor when Soren backed me up and pushed me against the side of the elevator.

The quip about liking it rough made it to the tip of my tongue before I swallowed it back down.

Soren's eyes were hypnotic as they roamed over me from my face, down my body, and then back up again.

It wasn't in the way a million other guys had done it before.

This was hot. It made me feel appreciated and worshiped instead of cheap and trashy.

Stuck in his gaze, I was taken off guard when he lowered his head.

His mouth came down on mine, his tongue teasing my lips before forcing its way into my mouth. A loud groan filled the small space of the elevator.

Soren was tall and overpowering. Yet, his feathery-light fingers cupped my face before trailing down my neck.

A shot of want traveled down my spine, and with every second that passed, I moved dangerously closer to the edge. If he was to go anywhere near my dick right now, I'd probably come in my jeans. To get there so fast ...

"How are you ... I mean, what are you ..." I was unable to get my words out. *What is he doing to me?*

The elevator dinged, and Soren backed off as the doors opened.

His smile did things to my insides. When he held out his hand for me, I knew following him was going to break me in the best way possible. Which would also turn out to be the worst way.

I didn't know it yet, but my night with Caleb Sorensen would be one of the only times someone wanted me as *Jet*—some non-famous twenty-year-old who wrote music and craved fame. Everyone else I'd meet would want me because I was *Jay*, the lead singer of Radioactive.

CHAPTER THREE

SOREN

Matt rushes toward the chopper, yelling, "JJ. What are you doing here?" His happy energy at his brother's arrival is palpable, whereas I'm hoping my mixture of dread, excitement, and a touch of want is hidden.

I watch from behind everyone as Matt practically crash-tackles Jet into a hug. Their bond is strong—something I didn't know that night I took him to a hotel and fucked his brains out.

I wince at that description of what happened. It was so much more than that, but I've never allowed myself to think of it as anything more because I can't afford to.

As Matt refuses to let Jet go, I can't help noticing their differences in appearance. Matt's a tight end in the NFL. He's a brick house. His dark hair is cut short, and he looks like a stereotypical jock. Jet's on the thinner side and shorter. He has shaggy and unkempt dark-brown hair the same shade as his brother's. That's the only similarity they have.

It's no wonder I had no idea how Jet fit into the group when I first met them all. I thought he was Lennon and Ollie's friend, not Matt Jackson's brother.

In the few years since Matt came out, he's become a legend in his own right. First out NFL player to play an official NFL game. First out player to win the Super Bowl. And then there's the LGBTQ charity he belongs to. His husband started it, and they help get homeless youth off the street.

He's a great guy, and I fucked his *little* brother.

Jet is an adult, I get that, but again, I have to use thoughts to trick my brain. Twinkish rock star. Little brother. I need to think of him like that and not like the flirty and forward man I took home from that nightclub.

I knew he was young, and when he'd approached me in my locker room that night while I was half undressed, I actually freaked out about lusting after the boy onstage at the benefit. He didn't look young under the stage lights, and he performed in a way that told me he'd been doing it for years. In his non-performance getup, he looked way too young for me.

That should've stopped me from taking him home that night, but my mind was filled with the images of the guy I'd seen onstage, shaking his ass and singing the song that made me reevaluate my life.

And watching him now, I'm torn between seeing him as that guy and the *little brother* image the rest of the group projects on him.

Jet makes his rounds, hugging Noah and then Ollie and Lennon. The others slap him on his back in a brotherly way, and I'm kinda glad he didn't hug them too because then we'd have to do the awkward "well, you hugged everyone else, so I guess you have to hug me" dance. What I get is even less than the others though. When his gaze lands on me, his lips flatten, and he gives me a cursory nod.

A nod without even a smile.

What do I do back? Nothing. Zilch. Nada.

Smooth.

I try to steady my pounding heart as I follow them all back into the dining hut. Joni and Ema have already set another place setting, and as luck or fate would have it, or because the owners know I'm the only single one here, they place Jet next to me.

Eyes burn into me, but when I glance at him to my side, he's shoveling food into his mouth. Looking up, I realize it's everyone else staring at me. Only, it's not me they're interested in.

"We're waiting," Matt says.

Jet lifts his head. "Huh?" His mouth is full of half-chewed food.

"Your tour?" Noah asks. "Concert dates, no time off, no rest for the famous. All your words."

"Fiji must not get the news. Rest of Radioactive's part of the tour has been canceled."

"Why?" Matt asks.

Jet chews and swallows hard. "Well, it's gonna be all over social media soon enough, so you may as well know now. I have nodes. Need to rest my voice."

"What are nodes?" Maddox asks.

"Nodules. Lesions on my vocal cords."

"Ouch," Maddox says.

Something about Jet's words doesn't ring true to me. Or ... completely true. Looking at him more closely, I notice the bags under his eyes, his skin is a little pale, and he has all the telltale signs of exhaustion, but it's something in his brown eyes that tells me there's more to the story. The usual spark in them is missing. There's only one other time I've seen his eyes that lifeless, and it was when I'd serendipitously played a game in Tampa the same night his band was performing a few blocks away from the arena.

For two people who'd met and hooked up in New York, who both traveled for a living and had crazy schedules, I took it as a sign that I needed to go to his concert after the game.

Biggest mistake I've probably ever made.

I try not to think of that night in Tampa. I not only hurt Jet, but the fight that followed brought reality crashing down on us. Our one night in New York was random magic that fate let us temporarily share, but it wasn't real. It was a fantasy. One perfect night with a perfect stranger who changed my life.

I'm brought out of the memory and thrust into a brotherly argument.

"I don't need surgery to fix it," Jet says, his exasperation sounding like that of a teenager's. "I just need rest. I figured a Fijian vacation would be the best place to do that, but not if you're gonna get all parent-y."

Everyone at the table goes silent.

"No need to bite my head off," Matt says. "I was just asking."

Jet runs a hand over his face. "Sorry. I'm wrecked. Is there a room for me, or am I bunking on the floor of one of your rooms?"

Joni steps forward. "Ema is setting up a room for you now, sir."

"You can take my room," I find myself saying. Everyone looks at me weird. "It's ready, and I haven't unpacked yet. I only used the shower after we got in."

Jet gives me a tight smile. "Thanks. I'm kinda dead on my feet."

"No problem. I'll walk you to it and grab my things while I'm there." I go to stand when Joni puts his hand up to stop me.

"We can arrange that. I can walk Mr. Jay to the room."

Nooo. There goes my chance of having a one-on-one conversation with Jet tonight.

As I watch them walk away, though, I realize that even if I had time with Jet alone, I wouldn't have anything to say to him. I'm not sure if *sorry* would cut it. Because, let's face it, I was a total ass to him the last time I saw him.

Out of the corner of my eye, I see Noah throw a bread roll at Maddox's head.

"Dude, what the fuck?" Maddox has his phone in hand, and Damon's reading over his shoulder.

"I thought we were going cell phone free," Noah says.

"Yeah, but then Jet turned up spouting some bullshit about nodes." Maddox goes back to looking at his phone. "'Radioactive will be leaving the Heart tour following health concerns for lead singer Jay,' but then it goes on to say there's a rumored rift between Radioactive and Eleven."

"Eleven?" Damon asks. "That boy band?"

"Radioactive has been opening for them for the past eighteen months," Matt says. "His band was supposed to get their own headlining tour this year, but then they went out on a second tour with Eleven. Didn't make much sense to me, but JJ says that happens."

"Why are they called Eleven when there's only five of them?" Noah asks.

My mouth, for some reason, thinks it's a good idea to let everyone know the answer because it's totally normal for a thirty-three-year-old guy to know random boy band facts. "They used to be 11OZ. As in eleven ounces—the weight of the human heart." My brain finally catches up and forces my mouth shut, but it's too late. I prepare for the inevitable ribbing about knowing the origin of a boy band's name. The reason I know it? They're a part of Jet's life and I'm not. I may or may not have been secretly checking up on him for the past few years.

Everyone blinks at me a few times but must decide to let it go.

Matt turns to Maddox. "You're gonna believe a tabloid? Remember when they claimed I was a manwhoring alcoholic?"

"Good point," Maddox says. "But I dunno. He seemed ... weird, right? Like, that isn't the Jet I know."

"He looked exhausted," Lennon says.

"He's been touring for, what, three years now?" I ask. *As if I don't know how long it's been.*

His band has had a few number ones, and they're on the brink of being the next biggest thing in music. Everyone's probably heard of them but could only name one or two songs of theirs. Me? I could name every single song off both their albums.

The band's rise to stardom started about two years ago with a hit called "Hat Trick Heartbreak."

Matt nods. "He's barely had time off, and we've rarely seen him. I'm glad he's finally taking a break."

Me too, but I call bullshit on his excuse for being here.

Ollie leans in and mutters under his breath. "If you think you're getting away with that boy band knowledge scot-free, you're mistaken."

So close.

The dinner and drinks portion of the night can't end fast enough, and even though I stop drinking, the others keep going. And going. And going.

As soon as Joni presents me with my new room key, I want to leave.

I want to get to Jet's cabin before he crashes, but I don't know how long an unsuspicious amount of time would be in between Jet leaving and me following.

Fuck it, I can't sit here any longer.

I stand. "I think I'm gonna turn in. Night, guys."

There's a chorus of drunken goodnights, and I leave them all glassy-eyed and looking lovingly at each other. And not just toward their partners, but, like, to everyone.

Yay for all that chosen family bond crap.

They're all like brothers in there, and for the most part, I've felt like one of them for the last three years. But then I remember Jet and that one night we had, and I realize I've never belonged to their group when I've been keeping such a big secret from them all this time.

I can still taste the salty skin of Jet's neck from where he'd gotten all sweaty while dancing. I remember him tracing every inch of my body with his tongue. But mostly, I remember the way I felt inside him—the way he responded with needy moans and demands for more. He almost seemed shocked at what I was doing to him. It was probably totally bullshit when he said he'd never been fucked like that before, but the way he came unglued in my hands, I really didn't care.

Now I'm hard at the memory of it, but my body doesn't understand that the path leading to Jet's room isn't a path leading to a repeat.

No matter how much I'd love it to be.

The plan is to clear the air between us once and for all and to call a truce on what's been years of avoidance.

And maybe, he has the same plan because when I round the corner to my old cabin, he's not in bed like he said he'd be. He's sitting on the top step of his deck with his guitar in his hands.

I watch the tattoos on his arm dance as his muscles contract. I remember tracing over the images of the guitar and the vintage microphone with my finger the night we were together. They're surrounded by music notes, and the shading makes his whole arm pop like the images are in 3D.

He strums no real tune—at least, not one I recognize—and hums with that husky and deep voice of his that only comes out when he sings.

Jet stops as soon as he senses my presence. "They've already sent your bags to your new room."

"I know. It's that one right there." I point to the cabin next to his.

"Of course, it is. Sorry you got stuck next to the kid."

"Jet …"

He stands. "My name's Jay, or don't you read the tabloids?"

I never understood why they had to change his name, but between his real name Jethro, his nickname Jet, his brother calling him JJ, and the world knowing him as Jay, I can't help wondering how he keeps track.

"Can we not do this?" I ask.

"Do what?" He gives me nothing but attitude.

I grunt. "For someone who wants to be seen as an adult, you're sure not acting like one."

He opens his mouth to talk back, but I cut him off.

"Look, what happened between us was years ago. We should be able to put it behind us and move on."

"Yeah. You already did that. With *Bryce*. So why don't you go find him? I thought he'd be here."

I swallow hard. "We broke up."

It may be quick, but I see it. The flash of happiness in Jet's eyes. He covers it quickly and clears his throat. "Sorry."

I shrug. "It's for the best. I couldn't see that getting back together with him was a horrible idea until I made the mistakes to prove it. You know, over and over and over again."

Jet looks triumphant. "I tried to warn you. The morning after we …"

I scoff. "Bullshit. You practically pushed me to call him."

"That's not how I remember it."

"Then how do you remember it?"

CHAPTER FOUR

JET

THE MORNING AFTER

Never—like never, ever, ever, ever—had I woken up so sated, so loose, and yet so achy at the same time.

An arm was draped over my middle, the heat of Soren making my back sticky with sweat. I was hard again because, apparently, my body hadn't had enough ravishing from the hockey god. No, *sex* god.

I rolled over to face him, and in the bright light of early morning, I'd never seen someone so beautiful. He had high cheekbones for a guy, and his light-brown hair fell across his forehead. His morning scruff was thicker than I could grow in a week, and his lips were plump, making me want to run my fingers over them.

"Why are you staring at me?" he mumbled, and I laughed. He hadn't yet opened his eyes.

"Wondering if I should wake you up or sneak out of here." I didn't want to pull a disappearing act, but that was the deal with one-night stands.

His large arm pulled me closer. "Waking me up is mean, but I'll take that over you leaving."

"Is it still mean if I wake you up with another round?"

"Mmm, less mean." He finally opened his eyes, and the shine in his honey-colored gaze made my breath catch in my throat.

"You're kinda beautiful," I whispered. It took all my energy not to cringe at how stupid I sounded.

Instead of thinking I'm an idiot, Soren's lips turned up. "I feel objectified."

"Good. Because that's exactly how I meant it."

A firm hand gripped my ass, and Soren rolled over, pulling me on top of him. "You were saying something about another round?"

Even though I was achy all over, my cock didn't care. It wanted more of Soren—as much as it could get.

"What'd you have in mind?"

Soren's hand trailed down my back, and his finger slipped into the crease of my ass. I must've winced or tensed because he pulled back and looked into my eyes. "Are you sore?"

"A little."

"Okay, there goes that idea." He gripped my hips and pulled me up. "Wiggle up here. I'll suck you off."

"Nnghh."

Soren shoved an extra pillow behind his head. "I take it you like that idea?"

"I *love* that idea." I crawled my way up the bed until I was straddling his chest.

He looked up at me with this smile that took my breath away, and I immediately knew this hookup would be hard to forget. Not the sex, but his face, his body ... the way his hands ran up and down my thighs.

Just like last night, this guy did things to me I didn't understand. He brought new sensations that were indescribable. And finally—*finally*—I was finding out firsthand what the huge fuss was over sex.

I inched closer, my cock brushing his lips, until he opened wide and sucked the tip into his mouth.

I wanted more.

My cock disappeared between his lips. His tongue swirled around me, and then his cheeks hollowed as he sucked me deep.

I had to hold on to the bed frame, or I was likely going to hit my head on the wall in front of me.

Through shuddery breaths and grunting, I found a steady pace without choking him. "You look even hotter with my cock in your mouth."

He hummed around me.

My whole body vibrated.

One of his hands remained on my hip while his other began jerking himself. Even though I couldn't see it, the motion of his hand and knowing what he was doing had my dick leaking.

I pulled out to the tip, and precum smeared on Soren's lips and chin. "Can I come in your mouth?"

Soren nodded.

The sight of my cock sliding in and out had my balls drawing up tight. He took me all the way to the root easily, and I was able to move in fast and shallow movements.

His hand stilled, and he moaned around me, shuddering and writhing beneath me. Even through his orgasm, he kept sucking me off.

My breathing ended up syncing with my thrusts until my orgasm hit, and Soren swallowed me down, every last drop.

He was still licking me clean when I managed to climb off and collapse beside him.

Soren reached for the bedside table for tissues to clean himself up.

When he was done, he rolled to face me.

I wanted to pass out again. "I'll be out of your hair in a minute. Gotta catch my breath."

"No rush." His words seemed genuine and made my stomach annoyingly fluttery. "Checkout isn't until ten."

As tempting as it was to ask to stay and order room service, I knew I needed to get out of there before I was too far gone over a guy I wasn't going to see again. I was going on tour. He was a hockey player. Anything past one night was doomed for us the minute our eyes met in his locker room last night.

Once I got my breathing under control again, I climbed out of bed and went in search of my clothes. They had kinda gotten thrown all over the place in the rush to get rid of them.

I found my boxer briefs and jeans but only one sock and no shoes or shirt. Soren watched me search with a lazy smile on his face.

"Can I see you again?" he asked.

"Umm, sure." I should've said no, I knew that, but I couldn't. My mouth, brain, and cock wouldn't let me. I got on my knees and found my shoes under the bed, and when I stood upright again, Soren was staring at me as if he was expecting me to give more information—like when. "My band just got signed to a record label, so we need to fly to L.A. to record the song you love so much and talk albums and tours, but I think I'll be back in a few weeks."

His face lit up. "That's amazing, Jet. Congratulations."

"Thanks."

Soren frowned at my nonchalance. "You don't sound excited. Isn't this every musician's dream?"

Yeah, it was, and I hated I couldn't get excited over it. "Yes and no. We got a contract, but it comes with stipulations."

"Like what?"

Before I could answer, Soren's phone buzzed on his nightstand. He reached for it and clearly wasn't happy about whoever was calling. His finger paused on the answer button, and then he glanced at me.

"Who is it?" I asked.

"It's my ex. We broke up because I wasn't out."

"Ah. And now that you are, he wants you back."

Soren pursed his lips. "Maybe. I've been trying to call him since I came out, but he's been ignoring me."

"Answer it."

His gaze flicked to mine. "What?"

"I mean, if you ask me, going back to an ex is never a good idea because you broke up for a reason, right? But you've been trying to call him, so it's clear you're not done with him."

Soren sighed. "I thought he was my hat trick."

"Hat trick?"

"The perfect package. Everything I want in a partner. Hot, sweet, smart enough to hold a real conversation."

If he was looking for someone with brains, I was shit out of luck.

The phone finally stopped ringing.

"Call him back," I say, my voice soft.

"What about …" He waved a finger in between us.

Did I want more of Soren? Hell yes. But I also knew there was no future here.

I rounded the bed and leaned in. His lips were warm, and I had to force myself to pull back and make our last kiss sweet. "If things don't work out with what's-his-face, then totally call me, but don't let a one-night stand get in the way of reconnecting with your ... hat trick."

Soren's mouth dropped open, but before he could say anything, my phone buzzed.

"My turn. Although I doubt mine is as exciting as an ex calling." Mainly because I didn't have an ex. I slumped at my brother's name on my screen. "Nope. Just Matt wondering where I am."

"Matt?" Soren asked.

"Yeah. My keeper," I joked.

"Your keeper?"

"Matt Jackson's my brother. I thought you knew that?"

From the freaked-out look in Soren's eyes, it was clear he hadn't known. And a second after the revelation, he switched from one-night stand to someone who stared at me the same way Lennon and Ollie and all of Matt's friends did—like I was a fucking kid.

Even if an ex wasn't involved, with that one look, this thing was over.

Defeated, I gave up my hunt for my other sock, grabbed my shirt by my feet, and made my way to the door.

"Thanks for the fun." I left Soren staring after me with his stupid expression.

CHAPTER FIVE

SOREN

The night-time breeze in Fiji picks up and has a cold bite to it now, but it's still not as cold as Jet's glare. Even though I can barely see him because the only light is coming from tiki torches lining the pathways and a light from inside Jet's cabin, I know the stare he's giving me is full of annoyance.

"Why are you even here?"

I run a hand through my hair. "I've been asking myself the same thing. Coming to an all couples retreat as a single kinda sucks."

Jet laughs. "I bet, but I actually meant here. Like, in this spot, dredging up old shit that doesn't need revisiting."

My gaze rakes over him because I don't know how to answer that. He's thinner than the last time I saw him, and even though he looks exhausted, he's still one of the most stunningly attractive men I've ever seen.

"You look good, Jet. I just wanted to say that." *Lamest excuse ever.*

"Liar. I look fucking tired."

"Why are *you* here?" I ask.

"Nodes."

"Liar." I throw his own word back at him.

"Needed a break from touring. Matt and Noah had been bugging me about trying to make it out here, so I made it happen."

There's still something he's holding back. I'm sure of it.

"Can we hang out while we're here?" I find myself asking.

Jet's lips form a thin line. "We will be anyway. No doubt, you motley crew of athletes will be all competitive and grunty with each other and organize some stupid extreme sport to measure dick sizes without having to whip them out."

"Have you met Talon and Miller? They'd whip theirs out for the sake of it. And then sword fight with them."

Jet relents with a small smile. "Yeah, I can see that."

"Besides, most of our contracts forbid us from partaking in dangerous off-season activities, so you won't be subjected to extremism." Although, I'm currently contract-less so I guess that doesn't apply to me.

"Still, I'm sure we'll find times where we're hanging out by default," Jet says.

Meaning, he doesn't want to make time for me on his vacation. I guess I have to respect that.

I nod. "For what it's worth, I'm sorry. For what happened between us."

Jet stands. "That's the problem. I wouldn't take back what happened between us for anything."

Wait, what?

"I would take back leaving you that next day. I'd take back telling you to get back together with your ex-boyfriend who, according to the guys, is a dickface. But most of all, I'd take back the way you looked at me once you found out who I was. And the way you treated me in Tampa. I don't need a babysitter. Thanks."

"That's not what—"

"Goodnight, Caleb."

He first-named me. There's no coming back from that.

The sound of the Pacific Ocean crashing against the shoreline a few feet outside my cabin does nothing to lull me to sleep. I toss and turn all night, smelling nothing but coconut and some fruit I can't place. The whole cabin smells like it, and while it's nice on the nose, I can't help wishing for the overpowering scent of Jet's cologne which is a mix of sweet orange with a hint of cinnamon. Add in the subtle scent of sweat and it could be bottled and called Jet. No, *Jay*.

I hate the name Jay. Especially on him. He deserves a name that's more unique. Jay doesn't suit him.

Sleeplessness means I relive my conversation with Jet over and over, relive the night we hooked up, and then remember the harsh words I left him with the night in Tampa two years ago.

I don't know why I have the need to clear the air between us, and I don't know what else I can say other than what I've already said, but I want ... shit, I don't know what I want. I asked to hang out with him, but I don't know what I meant by it. Do I want to go see the sights with him or have him naked in my bed?

Jet and I can't have a thing. The guys would kill me.

But I know there's no way I can stay away. He's still the guy who changed my life. He's still the one who gave me the courage to face my teammates and say two simple words with a weighted meaning that is so far from simple. "I'm gay."

That's all Jet.

He gave me courage before I'd even met him. I have to spend time with him while I have the chance.

I roll out of bed at the break of dawn and throw on some sweats to walk the hundred feet across the grass to Jet's cabin. Only, when I step out onto my deck, I realize I'm about to go wake up a rock star who no doubt sleeps away most of the morning, and that's not a good idea if I want him to forgive me.

I go back inside and grab my runners instead. A morning run will help get rid of the icky hungover feeling. Even though I stopped drinking last night when Jet turned up, add the few I did have to very little sleep, and I'm left seedy and gross this morning.

Where there was a breeze on the island last night, everything is calm this morning. As I take off running on the paved pathway that weaves in between all the cabins and the main house, my mind clears. For a brief moment in time, I'm at peace.

The path disappears on the other side of the small island and turns into beach. I slow down to a walk because the softness of the sand isn't good for my knees.

Thirty-three isn't old if you're a normal person, but I'm a hockey player. I'm officially nearing the end of my career, and any small injury could mean it's all over in a millisecond.

I don't know if I'm ready for that yet. Part of me—mainly my achy joints—begs for it, but the part that's only known hockey my whole life wants to hold on for as long as possible.

I trudge through the soft sand but stall when a lean figure comes from the opposite direction.

When I left my cabin, I purposefully started my run heading past Jet's. It looked still and quiet, and I assumed he was asleep.

But by the look of him now—skin flushed, sweat dripping down his face, his usually shaggy hair that has a bit of a curl to it—he's been out here a while. He's in a loose pair of basketball shorts and a tank top that shows off his full sleeve tattoo.

"Told you we'd run into each other." He's smiling this morning at least.

I breathe hard, only I don't know if it's because of the workout, seeing Jet, or if I'm just mirroring the rapid rise and fall of his chest. "I expected a rock god like you to still be asleep."

"I'm on artist time."

I cock a brow.

"Push myself until I pass out no matter what time it is."

"How do you not die?"

"Drugs," Jet deadpans.

My face falls.

"Dude, that was a joke. Don't get your panties in a twist again."

Instead of lecturing him on recreational drug use, I try for comedy like him. "I only wear panties on the ice."

It's his turn to lose the smile. "Seriously?"

I burst into laughter. "No. Jockstraps are kinda a necessity."

"Could wear them over the top. I'm picturing red lace."

I ignore the way his eyes scan down to my crotch. "Sure, because that's a great idea in a locker room. Like I don't get enough shit for being the only gay guy on the team."

A moment passes between us where neither of us say any more.

Jet kicks at the sand lazily. "I don't sleep well on the road. I was kinda hoping a vacation would be different, but it's another unfamiliar bed in a random place. Makes trying to sleep pointless because I know it's not gonna happen."

"You don't sleep at all while you're away?"

He shrugs. "The tour doctor thinks I have ADHD, which can affect sleep. Eventually, I'll get so tired I'll pass out for sixteen hours or so, but that usually doesn't happen unless I'm home in

New York or with my brothers in Chicago. I reckon it's more a comfort thing than a hyperactive thing."

"That's no way to live."

"The life of a rock star," Jet says proudly though I think it's forced. "So why are you up at ass o'clock on your vacation?"

"Ass o'clock sounds a whole lot more fun than the crack of dawn."

"Ass crack of dawn then?"

"Better. And, uh, I couldn't sleep. Was thinking about ..." *God, don't tell him what you were thinking about.*

"Thinking about ..."

"Tampa." *Idiot.*

"Oh."

I mentally prepare myself for the apology that's about to come out of my mouth. "I was a dick and completely out of line."

"You weren't a dick."

I pull back, surprised. Until he keeps talking.

"I like dicks, and I certainly didn't like you after that night."

I laugh again. There's something about this guy that makes me lighter without even trying. His music, his personality ... It's everything about him.

"I still stand by a lot of what I said, but I handled it so wrong."

"*So* wrong," Jet agrees.

"Well, I'm sorry." I hesitate to ask him something I don't want to know the answer to. "Did you at least do what I said?"

His eyes flutter as he stares down at the ground. Jet's voice comes out soft, almost ashamed. "Yeah. I did."

And I'm right. I didn't want to hear the answer. "Are you—"

Jet shakes his head. "I'm not doing this with you." He tries to charge past me, but I step in front of him.

"Jet—"

His deep-brown eyes stare right through me. "I'm not doing this."

I let him go. There's nothing I can do as he jogs out of my sight. It's the third time I've watched him walk away from me in the last twelve hours, and each time I want to take it back. I want to tell him to stop being a brat, and I want to forget the last three years even existed.

I don't know why I can't act normal around Jet. Everything is heightened when I'm near him, and it makes me do and say stupid things. The natural thing to do around him is joke and touch him and have fun, but then I overthink it and what it would mean to flirt with Matt's little brother.

Maybe all my mind games trying to get myself to see Jet a certain way are finally catching up to me, and now I have no idea how I'm supposed to see him.

I so haven't had enough sleep to analyze this shit, and all I keep wondering is where it all went wrong.

CHAPTER SIX

JET

TAMPA

Another city, another dingy club, another show. The glamorous life of a rock star that was supposed to be all parties, sex, and luxury? Yeah, that didn't happen if you didn't have any number ones.

Our debut album had tanked. Well, tanked isn't really the correct term. We found minor success. Super minor. We'd done enough to do another album with the label but hadn't hit any charts. We'd gained thousands of followers on social media and our YouTube channel. We had fans turning up to our shows. The small clubs we booked were selling out. The label was impressed enough with us to send us to Australia next month for a Joystar festival, but our stage time for that show was set for three a.m. on one of the side stages. Still, free trip overseas. We couldn't wait, and Benji was excited to go back to his homeland to visit his family.

But we were over the seedy dive bar thing. We'd done that back in New York, and now we were getting the same benefits for more exhaustion. Being on the road was hard. Harder than I thought it would be.

Between band drama like my bass player and drummer being totally in love with each other but both too stubborn to admit it, sleeping in cheap-ass motels every night, not knowing what city I was in, and the encompassing feeling of being lost, I missed New York and the family I'd built.

My brother Matt. His husband, Noah, who I referred to as my brother. Ollie and Lennon. Heck, I even missed Matt's weirdly overprotective friends. They all still treated me like I was a kid, but oddly, I missed it coming from them. I missed all of them.

I loved every minute of touring, but fuck, I was tired. My throat felt raw the majority of the time.

We had to pay our dues, I knew that, but the tour was putting me in a funk. I wondered if maybe I didn't have it in me. Music had been my entire life, but when it became work, the love I had for it wasn't there anymore.

I hadn't written for about six months of the year we'd been away. No time, too tired, and no inspiration.

But as I took to the stage that fateful night in Tampa, the universe sent me a gift. A piece of home. A warm memory. No wait, not warm. Scorching hot.

I had no idea what Soren was doing in Florida—playing hockey I presumed—but even more, I had no idea what he was doing in this bar, waiting for my band to perform.

It was a fluke I picked him out of the crowd at all, and I wasn't sure what gave him away. My eyes found him immediately upon taking my place in the spotlight. While a part of me thought my mind was playing tricks on me or the lighting made me imagine him—maybe it could've simply been a guy who looked a hell of a lot like my Soren wearing a baseball cap—but as soon as he broke out into a grin, I knew it was him.

The guy I'd had one night with almost a year ago and hadn't seen since. Hadn't even spoken to him.

Last I'd heard from everyone back home was Soren had gotten back together with his ex.

I'd like to say I wasn't disappointed by that news, but I was. I wanted to act cool like I did the morning after we'd hooked up. Because I'd meant every word I said back then. I would've loved more of Soren, but it was only one night, and if he was still hung up on his ex, then he should've gone for it.

But after a year on the road, realizing how lonely this life was, how superficial and shallow the music industry could be, I wanted someone who was real. Not a groupie, not a sleazy tour manager, and not a musician—all of which I'd had the pleasure, or *displeasure*, of having this past year, and all of who had left me unsatisfied. Just like the hookups before Soren had.

"What's up, Tampa?" I yelled into my mic.

The crowd went wild, but the object of my attention stayed cool as ever, still smiling at me with that blinding gorgeousness that was Soren.

Weren't hockey players supposed to be roughed up, toothless, and, I dunno, grunty looking?

I wanted to talk to him. Forget the set and run into his arms. Instead, I turned to my bandmates.

"Changing it up, guys. Let's open with 'He's Mine.'"

Benji looked confused for a second, but then he glanced out at the crowd and back to me. "Bloody hell, is the guy here?"

"The guy is here."

Benji knew the whole story. So did Freya. She banged her drumsticks together, starting the count.

My eyes locked on Soren again as the song broke out, and I didn't know it was possible, but his smile widened.

I might not have been able to call him out publicly and point and say, "Hey, everyone, Caleb Sorensen is in the house!" but I could still communicate with him. Well, technically, I could have announced an NHL hunk was here, but I didn't want anyone to approach him. As soon as the gig was over, he was going to be all mine.

For the first time in months, I felt alive onstage. I was performing for Soren and Soren only.

I used my voice to lure him in and promise a wild, hot repeat, and if the way he stared at me with heat in his eyes was any indication, I knew it was working.

The set couldn't have ended soon enough.

As soon as I strummed that last chord on that last song, I was off the stage and in the crappy back room which was one of the nicer "dressing rooms" we'd had on the road, but it was still a shithole.

A couch, a folding table, and a whole lot of stored junk was back there.

Our two-man roadie team was already getting stuck into some blow.

On big gigs or nights like tonight where it was fucking epic to be onstage, I'd partake, but I wasn't going to this time.

I wanted to be levelheaded when I saw Soren. Remember every single detail.

That, and it turned out what they say about the music industry was right. That shit was everywhere. I refrained most times, only dabbling here and there. I refused to become the clichéd rock star addicted to coke before he'd even become famous.

I was going to wait until I could afford rehab to need it.

Hashtag life goals.

And our tour manager said we didn't have any direction.

Benji and Freya caught up and stepped through the door.

"We were on fire," Benji said and immediately took a seat at the table with the coke. He didn't share my views on the rehab thing.

Freya stared at him with concern etched across her face.

I threw my sweaty arm around her. "He's a big boy and can make his own decisions."

"I know."

My lips found the top of her head. "Now, excuse me while I get out of this sweaty-as-fuck shirt and into a clean one before the hockey player runs away."

I tried to whip my shirt off, but my head got stuck, and then the sound of the deep voice made me pause.

"Not gonna run away."

Unable to see, I pointlessly turned toward the voice and then realized how stupid I must've looked with my arms in the air, my shirt on my head, and my abs on full display.

Yep, on cue, there was Soren's chuckle.

Freya helped me get my shirt off, and then there he was. All ten-foot-whatever of him.

His cap now on backward, a beard that wasn't there last year, his killer smile on display, sculpted body, and all-around hotness, Caleb Sorensen was sex personified.

"Your security is shit, by the way," he said. "All I had to do to get back here was say I knew you."

"Well, it is true," I pointed out. "Biblically speaking."

Benji laughed behind me. Freya backhanded my arm.

Soren just smiled wider and met me halfway for a hug.

"I'm all sweaty and gross," I warned.

"You're not gross." He threw his arms around me as if we were lifelong friends instead of what we actually were—a hookup from a year ago. "It's good to see you."

"Umm …" I didn't know what to say to that. Usual me would

say, "Duh, it's always good to see me," but my mouth wasn't working.

The hug was short, a lot shorter than I would've liked, so he probably agreed about the grossness to some degree.

"Your set was awesome."

"Yep." Again, duh.

Still couldn't talk, though.

Apparently, my mouth could only make sounds, not sentences.

Freya laughed beside me. "Can we adopt you? If you've rendered this one speechless"—she nudged me—"I would love to have you around for when he won't shut up."

"She loves me, really," I said.

"Obviously," he replied.

"Yeah. Obvs." *Oh my God, get it together, Jay ... er, Jet.*

With the new identity the label put on me, I was struggling to remember which name to go by. Having someone like Soren in front of me, it mixed me up even more.

"I'm, uh, gonna put on a fresh shirt, and we can get out of here."

"Stay. Party," Benji called out. "Jay, you want a bump?"

Soren stiffened beside me.

"Nah, I'm good. Thanks."

Benji frowned. "You sure?"

"I'm good."

I played it off casual, but I could feel the burn of Soren's stare as I found a washed shirt in one of our bags. I wished it was the heat of lust he was throwing my way, but it wasn't. I wouldn't have felt two feet tall if it were.

"Yo, hockey man. You want?" Benji asked.

Soren's hands balled at his sides.

"He can't," I answered for him and went to his side. "NHL rules."

"Aww, fuck that for a job," Benji said.

"And it's, you know, the law," Soren mumbled so only I could hear.

Benji turned to Freya. "Baby, you want some?"

She immediately went to Benji with a sigh of resignation.

"Have fun, kids," I said, wanting to get away from their toxic behavior.

It had been nothing but drama with them since we signed with the label. I thought it had to do with the small taste of fame we had and the groupies who followed Benji around like flies. Their on-again, off-again routine was already old, and I wasn't even supposed to know about it because they thought it was all secretive and shit.

It was not.

I took Soren's hand to drag him away where I could have him to myself. "Tell Wayne I'm goin' out."

"Dude, he left halfway through the set," Benji said.

Of course, he did.

Our tour manager was the worst. He didn't believe in us, in our music, or that we were good enough for the label.

And he was a sleazebag.

A convincing one.

But I wasn't going to think about that with Soren there.

"Don't wait up," I called on the way out.

"Where are we going?" Soren asked over the house music.

"To get a drink. I can legally buy you one this time."

His body shook as he laughed. "You know, I was under the impression you could legally buy me one last year."

I gave him my best innocent face.

"You're trouble."

"Duh."

Once back in the bar area of the venue, I was approached by

fans all the way to the bar. I said a quick hi to each of them and took selfies. At one point, I lost Soren, but by the time I made it to the bar, he was waiting there for me with two drinks.

I leaned in close to his ear so he could hear me. "I was supposed to buy you a drink."

"I still owed you from last time." Soren slid the glass over to me.

"So, uh ... I—"

A piercing screech echoed in my ear. "Jay! Oh my God, oh my God, oh my God!"

I put on a publicity-ready smile and faced the barely dressed chick. "Hi."

"Can I get a photo?"

I gritted my teeth. I loved my fans, I really did. But I was with Soren. *The Soren.*

"Of course."

She threw her arm around my shoulder and took a selfie. But as soon as she walked away, another person approached.

Then another.

Then a guy came up to us. "You're Roman Josi!"

"Who?" I asked.

"Nice to meet you." Soren held out his hand to shake.

It was the guy's turn to fanboy over the hotness of Soren. "Whoa, this is so cool." Then he spotted me. "Hey, you were onstage!"

"Yup."

"Cool. So cool."

Soren chatted to the guy about hockey, but I was still confused.

The fan got a pen off the bartender and asked Soren to sign his shirt.

Finally, after he left, I leaned in. "Who's Roman Josi?"

Soren grinned. "He plays for Tennessee. We get mixed up all the time because we apparently look alike. I don't see it."

"You just sign someone else's name?"

"Nah, I wrote 'I'm not Roman Josi' and then signed my name and team underneath it."

"Brilliant." I took out my phone. "I so have to Google this." As soon as the image popped up, my eyes widened. "Damn, there's two of you. That's too much for my brain to handle." And my cock, but I didn't say that aloud. "Please tell me he's gay too. No, wait, don't. I'll never get that image out of my head."

"Sorry. Still only Ollie and me on team gay so far in the league."

"Shame."

"Hey." Another guy approached.

This time, I didn't know who he was approaching. Me or Mr. Hockey. It became obvious when he leaned closer to me, pressing his side against mine.

Hello, personal space boundaries.

Although the scowl on Soren's face was a nice consequence.

"I read somewhere you're gay," the guy said.

"I am, but sorry, you're not my type."

He cocked his head.

"I prefer guys who can't read."

He laughed. Any other night, I would've been all over him. He was tall, cute, and scruffy. Definitely my actual type.

But, Soren.

The random guy pressed in closer. "Can I buy you a drink?"

"He's good," Soren growled.

I kinda loved it.

The guy glanced between the two of us and then backed away with his hands up. "Worth a shot."

I threw back the rest of my drink. "Can we go somewhere neither of us could be recognized?"

Soren stood. "Let's go."

We were stopped another handful of times, me more so than Soren, but I wasn't counting ... much.

It was surreal to be next to Soren again. Last time I'd seen him, I was talking about becoming famous, and now I was being recognized by people in a bar.

Finally, after months of being exhausted and thinking about how shitty touring was, I saw the payoff. I could not only see how far I'd come but could *feel* it.

"We should go dancing," I said as we hit the warm Tampa air.

"Or we could go coffeeing."

"Compromise. Dancing then coffee."

Soren groaned.

"Come on, old man. Not up for it?"

"Don't call me *old man*."

"Big Daddy?"

"Fuck no."

"Roman Josi ..."

Soren shoved me, and I laughed. It was easy to find my laugh with him. I was used to playing the goofball card, trying to pull everyone into my madness. The truth was, my outlandish personality was my armor—something I needed to protect the inner broody artist I tried to tame.

Like that night last year in the club, Soren let me breathe easy and just ... be.

I didn't have to think of the quips coming out my mouth. They fell out on their own.

"Okay. Compromise, eh? Dancing and then coffee. You're not getting out of talking about the tour. I want to hear everything."

"What do you want to know?"

"Well, first, does that happen often?" He glanced back in the direction of the club. "Groupies? Drugs?"

I held in my eye roll but barely. "It's the music industry. What do you think?"

"I think I ... uh, your brother wouldn't like it."

"My brother, huh? You gonna tell him?"

"Do I need to?"

"What he doesn't know won't worry him, and I'm not being stupid about it. I barely partake, and when I do, I refrain from getting stupid."

"Oh, well then. As long as you're being smart about doing drugs." There was an edge to Soren's tone, and it made me want to slap him, but I wasn't going to let his stupid big brother act ruin tonight. He had no right to play it with me.

Instead of pushing the issue and bringing down the mood, I deflected. "I am. I'm super smart."

"Pretty sure that's what dumb people say."

"Whatever. We went past a bar with a rainbow flag on our way to the venue earlier today. We should find that."

Tension coiled around us, the spell cast between us last year cracking.

I knew after he found out I was Matt's little brother he'd treat me differently.

We walked the few blocks in silence, and he must've sensed how pissed I was because, before I could cross the threshold to the gay bar, Soren pulled me back.

"Hey, I'm sorry. It wasn't my place, and I overstepped."

"Good. Now let's go have fun. I haven't had real fun in forever." Probably since the last time I was with Soren.

Flying to L.A. and recording for the first time in a real-life studio was amazing. It gave me a high that followed me all the way through our first few months of touring, but I wouldn't call that fun. Awesome, fucking insane, and brilliant, but not fun. The constant threat of not making it and the label dropping us made it not fun.

Perhaps because Soren was my first ever fan or because he was a piece of home or maybe it was a combination of it all, I wanted to make this night last and hold on to it to get me through the next few months. Just like our last night together had.

I led Soren straight to the dance floor and pulled him close. His big body wrapped around me, his arms on my waist, my head on his shoulder.

We moved and danced to the beat, getting lost in some pop song.

Soren's hand trailed over my back as we ground against each other. His thick thigh was between mine, his breath on my skin, and my cock begged for more.

I wanted to touch him everywhere. Kiss him. Take him back to my hotel room and fuck him. But I also wanted to stay in this moment.

My body was eager, and anticipation kept building.

Hot, sweaty men moved around us, bumping us and pushing us closer together.

Soren's normally clean-shaven face was covered with a beard that hadn't yet softened, so it scraped along my skin.

I pulled back and ran my hand over his cheek. Ollie was the same during the playoffs. "You hockey players and your superstitions."

"It's the *playoffs*."

"Mmhmm ... You didn't have that last year."

"Yeah, and we lost the Cup. Not gonna let that happen again." His lips twitched.

Our eyes locked, my hand still stroking his beard.

The air became thick.

"Jet." Soren swallowed.

I took my shot, angling my head. Inch by inch, my mouth moved closer.

I wanted to feel his kiss and the strong way his tongue dominated mine like it had the year before.

The club, the music, and the people around us faded into a haze.

Expectations of his lips meeting mine smashed into a pile on the floor when Soren stepped back.

"Let's go get that coffee."

It took a second for my brain to trip on the rejection.

Soren hightailed it to the exit. I was slower to follow because I had no idea what just happened.

When we hit the street again, I had to scramble to catch up to him. And when I did, he stopped and turned to face me. He looked the same way he did a year ago when he'd thought my song wasn't real.

That's when I realized it wasn't going to happen between us.

Why the fuck did he show up tonight?

He didn't say anything and started walking again, his feet working double-time up the sidewalk.

"What was that?" I yelled after him because there was no way I could keep pace.

He stopped and shook his head. "I shouldn't have come tonight."

"Why did you?"

He threw his arms wide. "I don't know. I thought ... I thought I could go and see you play and not get caught up in it. In you. I thought I could sneak away and you wouldn't even be able to see me under the stage lights, but as soon as you opened with that song, I knew. I knew you'd spotted me. I wasn't going to talk to you or go backstage, but—"

"Why not?"

"I'm ... I have ..." Soren's phone went off, and he dug it out of his pocket. With an apologetic look my way, he turned away from me as he answered. "Hey, babe."

It was like a sucker punch to the nuts.

Soren glanced back at me and lowered his voice, but I still heard his exact words. "My friend's little brother is in town, so we met up, but I'll be going back to the hotel soon."

Friend's little brother. I'd heard enough. I turned on my heel and headed for the venue where Benji and Freya would still be.

"Jet, wait up." Loud footsteps sounded behind me, and I told myself to keep walking, but I didn't.

"What the fuck, Soren?"

"I'm sorry. Let me explain."

I waited for him to continue. He didn't.

Soren took his hat off and rubbed a hand through his thick hair.

"Great explanation." I turned again.

"I'm all wrong for you."

I froze and stared at him over my shoulder. "What?"

His hands gripped my shoulders and spun me to face him. "You're ... you're amazing, Jet. You're inspiring and lively and ... young."

He said *young* like it was the worst thing in the world to be.

"That's your issue? The *age* thing? You're thirty-one." I knew because I'd Googled. Ten years between us. That was nothing. "That's not old."

"You're at the point in your life where you should be doing young and dumb shit—"

"As long as it doesn't include groupies and drugs," I said dryly.

"That groupie only wanted one thing."

"Duh. That's the definition of *groupie*."

"You deserve better."

"Lord, here we go. More big brother shit? Really?"

Soren shook his head. "Sorry. Again, I shouldn't have said that. It's your life. I know how hard you've worked to be where you are. I have no right to butt in."

I folded my arms. "No, you don't."

"For one night, I loved being a part of your world, and since then, I've watched you live your dream. Every performance, every song ... you belong on that stage."

I narrowed my eyes. "Caleb Sorensen, have you been following me on social media?"

He stepped closer. "Every. Fucking. Show. Every interview. Anything I can find online."

Our chests pressed together, Soren breathed hard, and I had no clue which way was up anymore.

"But you have a boyfriend."

"I'm at the point in my life where I'm talking mortgages and settling down. You're partying and touring and living the rock star life. The life you deserve."

He had a point. Boyfriend aside, if he was single and we hooked up tonight, that was all it could be again.

"Go back to your hat trick boyfriend, Caleb."

Soren took hold of my hand. "No, wait, don't leave it like this."

"Like what?"

Soren needed to fuck off back to Jersey with his perfect boyfriend and mortgage.

"I want you to promise me something," he said.

"What?"

"I want you to find someone who will love you for the guy I

know. The one who fanboyed over his first fanboy. Or fanman in your words."

I chuckled.

"That guy deserves someone as awesome as he is. So, go out and do stupid shit, but do it with someone special. Okay?"

Why? Why did he have to come tonight and fuck up my memory of him with logic?

"You're perfect, Jet."

Right. That was why he was rejecting me.

"Yeah. Perfect for someone else. Got it."

CHAPTER SEVEN

SOREN

My feet pound the path around our private Fijian island. Reliving that night in Tampa makes me want to run as fast as possible. Run away from the memory and from my stupidity.

I should've told him as soon as I saw him that night. *Oh, by the way, I'm with Bryce.* But no, I wanted to spend time with him. Plus, who says, "Hey, I haven't seen you in a year, you know, since the last time we fucked, but I'm seeing someone now. I just wanted to get that out of the way."

Still, I should've played that night differently. I shouldn't have danced with him, and I shouldn't have flirted. I definitely shouldn't have acted like a jealous asshole with that guy at the bar. Maybe I should've walked away after his show and not seen him at all.

Because even though it's been two years, he's still mad at me.

Worse than that, when I asked him if he'd done what I'd asked of him, he'd said yes.

He fell in love.

That thought makes me push harder and tell my thirty-three-year-old knees to take the pain and just run.

I should be happy for him. He got to share his last couple of years with someone special, which is what I wanted for him. Only now I can't remember why I wanted that when it makes something go wrong in my chest. I don't like the thought of him with someone else even though it was never an option to be with me.

Hello, selfish asshole.

I was too wrapped up and determined to make it work with Bryce to see how anything with the young, vibrant musician could happen. And nothing has changed in that regard. Jet's still young and vibrant, and we're both still on the road for most of the year.

Making the wrong choice by staying with Bryce back then still doesn't mean hooking up with Jet would've been the right choice.

While Jet was the man who inspired me to come out, I did it for Bryce. I stupidly thought that meant I had to make it work between us. It's why I told myself to forget about the rock star and have avoided him since that night in Tampa.

We can say how much our schedules have clashed which is why we've never seen each other since then, but the truth is, when he's been in New York, I made sure Bryce and I were too busy to catch up with the guys. Then again, most times Jet came home fell while my team was at away games, and I have to wonder if Jet's been avoiding me as much as I have him.

Now he's here, I don't want to avoid him. I don't want to stay away, and I have no reason to anymore, other than the guys will kick my ass. But for Jet, an ass-kicking might be worth it.

Unless …

I stop in my tracks.

Unless he's *still* in love.

Maybe he's the one with the boyfriend now.

Well, isn't that a jagged little pill. It would be karma in its finest form.

I have to know if that's the case. Spinning on my heel, I cut through the unpaved trail instead of following the path any longer.

I need to know if there's hope.

The island is small, only a few miles trek around the whole thing. It only takes me twenty minutes to walk back to our cabins. But as I climb the steps to Jet's, I pause at the sound of his brother's voice.

"We're telling the other guys tonight, but we wanted you to know first."

"A baby? I'm gonna be an uncle? Wait … Noah's going to be a dad? To a baby … like, a baby *and* Wade? I don't know which is scarier, really." Jet's excited energy is palpable from here, and even I know not to intrude on that.

"Ha, ha, sooo funny," Noah says.

Matt and Noah are going to be parents. I knew about Wade, the youngest Jackson brother, but a baby too?

Unwilling to break up their family moment, I trudge back to my cabin and decide I need a shower. A cold one. Because dredging up all this stuff with Jet has our one night together running through my head on a loop.

His eagerness, that smirk under hungry eyes, the way he rode my dick until I couldn't take it anymore and rolled us over so I could take him as hard and fast as I needed to. I can still picture the face he made as he came all over his stomach and chest.

Yep, definitely need a cold shower.

Maybe that'll snap me out of the ridiculous notion that I have any chance at a do-over with him because he's not interested. He doesn't seem to even want to spend time with me as a friend.

After a shower, I dress in board shorts and a T-shirt and head to the dining hut for breakfast.

Talon and Miller are the only ones there.

"Everyone still sleeping?" I ask, knowing full well at least three of the others are up.

"Matt and Noah are spending the day catching up with little bro," Talon says. "Maddox and Damon started their hike early and have already left, and I think your boy and Lennon are still in bed."

I freeze until I realize he's talking about Ollie. Not Jet.

Brain needs coffee.

I pour a large cup and pile my plate high with eggs, bacon, hash browns, and pancakes with a side of maple syrup. And by a side, I mean a gallon of it; I'm Canadian.

"We're heading out wakeboarding in ten if you want to join us," Miller says.

It's either that or wander around aimlessly all day wondering when I'll be able to sneak past Matt and Noah to talk to Jet again. "Yeah, okay, I'll go."

I thought I'd spend this vacation cursing Bryce and wallowing over our failed relationship and my bleak career. Nope. Turns out I'll be spending it pining over a memory I thought I'd already put behind me.

Wakeboarding is fucking killer, but after a day on the water, the sun is setting, the wind and swell are picking up, and Miller's starting to look green around the gills.

He was fine in the small inlet with calm water Joni took us to, but he never got off the boat—only Talon and I ended up wakeboarding. Maybe the whole day sitting on the rocking boat and the rougher water on the way back to our island is too much for Miller to handle.

"Seasick, man?" I ask. "Just look at the horizon."

"The horizon that's all wobbly?"

I laugh. "Yeah. That one."

Talon's on the other side of his boyfriend, but it's taking both of us to hold the giant up.

Thing is, being a hockey player, I'm used to seeing blood. We bleed on the ice. A lot.

Puke? It's one thing I can't handle.

So I pray to the gods of vomitus that Miller's able to keep it all in. He doesn't. By the time we hit land, I'm ready to kiss the sand because I almost join him in vomiting over the side of the boat.

"No more boat trips," Miller croaks.

"Kinda hard when we're on an island," Talon says.

I clap him on the shoulder. "Feel better. I'm gonna hit the shower and then get Ema to bring me dinner in my room so I can pass out. After today, I'm exhausted."

"You forgetting Matt and Noah asked us all to come to dinner tonight because they have something they want to tell us?" Talon asks.

"Shit." I already know what they're going to say after overhearing it this morning, but that doesn't mean I can't show up for it. "Fine. Still gonna get in a shower and maybe a nap beforehand."

Miller complains that the ground is wobbly now too.

Sorry, Talon, you're on your own.

On my way back to my cabin, I hope to see Jet, but I'm outta luck.

So much for a day on the water being a distraction. The

second I'm back on land, I'm back where I was this morning—working out how to make Jet talk to me.

Which is what I'll do instead of nap. But first, I definitely need a shower. I smell of saltwater and have sand in places no one ever should.

And when I look in the mirror in the bathroom, I realize I have sunburn in places no one ever should too. Is it possible for nipples to be sunburned?

I take a cold shower, which feels amazing on my overheated skin, but it's clear by the time I'm clean I might've gotten too much sun. Or maybe I'm still a little green from watching Miller throw up his lunch.

Dizziness hits full force, and I have to reach for the wall to steady myself.

Fuck, maybe I need a nap after all. I shut off the water and dry myself, slipping into bed without bothering to put on any clothes.

Mmm, the sheets are soft, and my head sinks into the pillows.

I'll nap first and then go see Jet before dinner.

My mind conjures an image of Jet's curls around his face falling into his eyes as he climbs on top of me. My hand grips his hair tight, and his tight body moves over mine. A wet, hot mouth trails over my skin.

It's easy to get lost in the fantasy that's more memory than imagination, but it's as if I can feel his hands on me, moving down over my chest and abs and lower again until his fingers brush against my straining cock.

I try to pull him up so he can kiss me, but he refuses and kisses along my burning skin.

Down.

Down.

"You need a minute with your hand or what?"

My eyes fly open at a voice that is definitely not the voice of the guy I'm thinking about.

Ollie stands at the door to my darkened cabin. "Maybe the guys do need to get you a rent boy if you're this hard up."

I stare down at the tenting sheet. "You mind?"

"Normally, I'd let you get back to it, but everyone's waiting for you."

I squint and look around, catching sight of the old, cheap clock radio on the bedside table.

"It feels like I only just put my head on the pillow." Apparently, that was two hours ago, and apparently, I've been dreaming of Jet that whole time.

I throw my legs off the side of the bed and go to stand when my hand hesitates on the sheet. "You can run back to them and tell them I'm on my way."

"I was told not to go back without you."

"At least turn around."

He faces the water. "You know, I've seen a million hockey players naked before."

Yeah, but I bet none of them have been this hard in a locker room.

I pull on some khaki shorts and a gray T-shirt, not bothering with underwear or shoes. "Okay, I'm ready."

Ollie looks at me over his shoulder. "You sure about that? Might wanna ..." He points to my hair.

Ugh. I went to sleep with wet hair, and now it's dried at all different angles. I reach for my trusty old hat and put it on backward to tame the mess.

"So much better," Ollie says sarcastically.

I shove him out the door.

The meals are already served when we find our seats. Matt's at the head of the table tonight, Noah next to him. Then Lennon,

Ollie, Jet ... and, of course, there's the spare meal for me, right next to that.

Everyone looks at me expectantly.

"Sorry. I fell asleep."

"None of you three ever hear of sunblock?" Damon asks.

My gaze goes to Talon, natural-born blond, and he resembles something like a cooked lobster.

Miller's naturally olive-skinned, but even he looks a little burned.

"We didn't realize it'd take three hours to get back to the island," Talon says. "Probably should've reapplied."

Jet snorts. "No shit. Soren's practically glowing."

Here we go.

"Aww, maybe he's pregnant," Noah says.

Maddox cuts in. "Now, we know that's impossible, guys. Come on, don't be silly ..." I'm about to thank him, when he continues. "You have to have sex to get pregnant."

Hosers. All of them.

"Unless his hand counts," Ollie says. "Which, by the way, if Soren's ever late again, dibs not being the one to go get him. I'm scarred for life."

I feel Jet's burning gaze on me. Or maybe that's the sunburn, I don't know.

"Why'd I get out of bed for this again?" I complain.

"Because we have something to tell you." Matt reaches for Noah's hand on top of the table.

"Yeah," Noah says. "Speaking of babies ..."

"You are one," Damon says. "Not at all an announcement."

Noah flips him off.

"There's a pregnant girl in Indiana who chose us to adopt her baby," Matt says.

The room falls deathly silent as if they announced one of them has terminal cancer.

"Wait, what about your brother?" Miller asks.

"Uh, I'm sitting right here." Jet raises his hand.

Miller waves him off. "Not you, the little one."

Noah laughs. "Little? Wade is taller than everyone in this room. And he's still coming to live with us too. He's got three years before college, and after that, he'll be at Harvard or Yale or any other Ivy League. The kid is super smart." There's pride shining in Noah's words already.

Damon's expression sobers. "Hold up. Let me get this straight. We're living in a world where not one but two people have granted Noah custody of a child." He feigns real concern until Noah rolls his eyes at him.

"Okay, okay, fine, serious time. Congratulations. You two are going to make great dads." Damon stands and lifts a drink for a toast, when we all freeze at what's on his ring finger.

"What the fuck is that?" Noah asks.

Damon glances at Maddox with wide eyes. "Shit."

Maddox stands too. "We have an announcement as well."

Whoa, they're getting married?

"We're *not* getting married!" they say together.

We all open our mouths to say congrats, but then we must register what their words. They're both smiling, they have their arms around each other, but ... did I hear it right?

"You're *not* getting married?" I ask.

"Maddox proposed," Damon says. "I said no."

"But you're still together?" My head hurts.

"I told Damon I wanted to marry him, had a full-on romantic proposal planned out, and then ..."

"Then I found the ring and said no." Damon smiles lovingly at his boyfriend. "He only wants to get married because I thought it was important. Turns out, it's not a big deal to me. I'm just happy I get to wake up next to him every day, and I don't need a piece of paper to remind me of that. I have the most important thing right here." He pulls Maddox close and kisses him softly, and my chest lurches while longing fills my veins.

Not for marriage, not for kids, but for *that*—a loving relationship that's so emotionally secure that nothing, not a piece of paper, not what anyone else thinks, not anything, can create doubt. Not even a rejected marriage proposal.

"Wait, why are you wearing the ring then?" I ask.

Damon shrugs. "He's every bit my husband already but without the title."

"So, no wedding, but you're going to live like husbands?" Miller seems as confused as I am.

Damon looks as if he's wondering why we're not getting it. "Exactly."

Miller turns to Talon. "Maybe we should do that."

"No wedding?" Talon exclaims. "No way. We're doing it and selling the pics for a shit ton of money."

"Like we need more money."

"Fine. Then we'll do it to inspire all those scared queer kids out there and reassure them that the world is changing."

A light bulb practically goes off above Miller's head when he realizes what his fiancé's up to. "You just want a bachelor party, don't you?"

"Duh. Is that so much to ask?"

Miller laughs. "Fine. We'll do it your way, but just so you know, the kid thing was the swaying factor, not the bachelor party."

Jet remains unusually quiet beside me.

Noah says some smartass comment to Ollie and Lennon, but I tune out and shovel food into my mouth. It's the only thing I can do to try not to think about being here alone. Chasing Jet for twenty-four hours has distracted me from everything I'm here to forget, but even my pull toward him isn't enough to drown out the happy couples surrounding me.

It's not that I'm not happy for them. I love these guys ... maybe not like brothers like everyone else sees the group, but definitely cousins of sorts. Wait, if Matt was my cousin, that would mean Jet would be too, and that's not cool. Then again, if I saw these guys as brothers, that would be even worse.

My gaze lands on Jet, and I notice he's as overjoyed about it as I am.

Maybe the answer to my burning question for him lies in his downcast eyes and the small pout of his lips.

He might've fallen in love with someone else, but I know that look. I've worn that look before.

Jet's not here because of nodes.

He's here because he's heartbroken.

CHAPTER EIGHT

JET

All the love in the air is making me choke. I can deep throat like a champ, but love and romance? That I gag on.

I thought I was over it. I really thought I was.

Harley and I ended things months ago, and even though that hasn't kept him out of my bed, it has kept me from pining.

Then he had to go and ruin it all by announcing his engagement.

To a woman.

If he was moving on, it'd be one thing, but no. My ex-boyfriend, fan favorite in the most popular boy band in the world, is gayer than RuPaul's wig collection. Yet, because of his contract, he's marrying a woman to save face.

He's the real reason I'm here in Fiji. Not nodes. Not exhaustion like I claimed to Noah and Matt when they grilled me this morning.

It was the pure need to get away from the tour where I had to see Harley every day.

When the rumors started on tabloid sites about Harley being gay, his management team worked overtime to cover it up, which

HAT TRICK

included banning him from "risky behavior" like hooking up with the lead singer from their opening act. Yet, there he was, every week or so, still sneaking into my hotel room. If he was feeling particularly strong, he'd last a month before he'd cave and come crawling back.

Touring is lonely, and pretty boys make me weak.

And Harley is really fuckin' pretty. Boy next door but with piercing eyes that promise a hint of rebellion. He's the good boy who looks like he wants to go bad.

Women and gay men everywhere salivate over him, and for a little while, he was mine.

I thought he'd eventually do the big grand gesture thing. Tell his label to get fucked, come out to the world, and then I'd have the epic love I've always wanted. I'm starting to think that doesn't exist.

I can't tour with Harley anymore. I just can't.

Same as I can't sit at this table with all this love, marriage, to have and to hold forever and ever bullshit.

My chest hurts.

I need to get out of here.

Before I can stand and make an excuse, Soren beats me to it.

"Congrats again, guys. To all of you. I'd love to stay and drink but—"

The guys break out into rounds of "Come on" and "We have to celebrate!"

"Have at it," Soren says, "but I'm going back to bed. I think I'm burning up."

He is looking a little red. If you can call crimson *a little red*.

I watch as he walks out of the hut, both jealous that he gets to leave and fighting my urge to chase him.

Ever since I landed on this stupid island, I've been telling myself to run away from the tempting hockey player who broke my heart two years ago.

Melodramatic, sure, because I've spent a total of one night with him, but Tampa crushed the idealistic image I had of him in my head.

Yet, he still has the ability to make my heart race and dreamer Jet come out. The Jet who had stars in his eyes and fame in his heart.

I assumed Soren would be here, but I also assumed he'd be here with Bryce and would avoid me. The guys didn't tell me they'd broken up, but at the same time, I've made it a habit not to ask about him or his precious hat trick. There's no reason for the gay brigade to tell me either because as far as they know, Soren and I only know each other in passing.

The only knowledge I've gathered over time about the ex-boyfriend is that he wasn't a hockey fan and was kinda high maintenance.

But they've broken up now.

It's over.

Much like my relationship with Harley. Even if Harley's having a hard time getting that through his head.

The closet thing, I understood. It's legitimately a clause in his contract that he cannot discuss his sexuality publicly. This fake marriage to a woman with me being his side piece, yeah, that I'm not okay with.

Boy bands rely on the fans of twelve-to-seventeen-year-old girls who believe they have a chance at falling in love with one of them. He couldn't even say if he had a girlfriend or not. Which he never did anyway for obvious reasons.

Until now.

Where suddenly being unavailable because he's married is

more appealing and acceptable to the outside world than him liking dudes.

And people think the entertainment industry is so progressive.

I've learned over the last few years that Hollywood types can be as bad as the sports industry, and because of my brother, I've seen how shitty that can be.

I'm happy for the guys. I am. They're paving the way so real change can be made.

But right now? I want to wallow and drink and ...

I stare in the direction where Soren went, and I have to fight the urge to go after him. I won't know which Soren I'd get. Perfect night Soren or Tampa Soren. The guy who wants me or the guy who's overprotective and says things like I'm perfect ... for someone else.

I thought if I ever saw Soren again, I'd be over him. I thought my Harley relationship might've tempered those feelings toward the hockey player.

Nope. Despite our encounter in Tampa ending dramatically, when I saw Soren last night for the first time in two years, all I could see was *my* Soren. The Soren who begged me to tell him love exists and is true—as if my songs held the answers to the entire universe.

I want that guy again.

"Hey, guys?" I stand. "I'm out too."

"What's the matter, junior?" Miller asks. "Where's this rock star stamina of yours?"

Everyone at the table snickers, but I can't bring myself to care.

"Y'all can mock me about stamina after you've performed a stadium tour. One hundred twenty-three shows in eight months."

My brother smiles at me. "Rest up, bro."

"I'll help celebrate tomorrow. I promise. Should be over the jet lag by then. And before anyone cracks a joke about Jet being jet-lagged, don't bother."

Lennon, my ex-roommate, frowns. "Are you okay?" he mouths.

I fake a smile and hope I can pull off an "I'm fine" expression.

Which I am.

I'm fine.

Or I will be.

How long is this thing called heartbreak supposed to last?

The plan is to go back to my hut, maybe troll some tabloid sites to torture myself, and then try to sleep.

But as my feet hit the cool grass to cut across the property, they stall completely at the sight of Caleb Sorensen sitting on his deck. His legs hang off the edge as he stares out at the ocean, and I wish I wasn't drawn to him.

I wish my feet wouldn't head in his direction.

His gaze meets mine, and damn, those eyes. Normally, light and warm, they're now dark and distant but still hypnotic.

"You needed to get away from the love-fest too?"

Irrational as it is, I don't want to get into the reasons why I needed out of there tonight. Not with Soren. In my messed-up mind, I want to partially blame him for this mood I'm in. He's the one who told me to go out and fall in love. Look where it got me.

"I'm just exhausted." I approach and take a seat next to him because apparently, my draw to him is stronger than my willpower.

My hand grips the edge of the deck precariously close to his. That shouldn't spark something inside me, but it does.

I want to be over this ridiculous hold he has over me. I thought I was, and all it took to come back was laying eyes on him again.

"Just exhausted? Are we lying to each other now? Nice."

I cock my head. "If either of us is a liar, it might be the guy who forgot to mention he was in a serious relationship while he flirted with me."

"I did not flirt."

I give him my best *I call bullshit* face.

"I didn't *intentionally* flirt," he amends.

"I'm not in the habit of trying to kiss guys who *don't* flirt with me."

Soren purses his lips. "No. I don't suppose you'd need to."

"What's *that* supposed to mean?"

"Calm down. I meant you'd have a million guys lining up to flirt with you. You wouldn't have to waste time with someone who wasn't putting in any effort."

"Well, that is true."

"You going to tell me about the guy?"

My brow furrows. "What guy?"

He leans in, bumping me with his shoulder. "The one you're running away from."

I want to lie and keep up the exhaustion excuse, but trying to keep up with that is more exhausting than dealing with my unresolved feelings for Harley. "I met him on tour."

"Bad breakup?"

"How do you know we're not just fighting?"

"I don't know anyone who'd fly halfway around the world to escape a fight."

"You underestimate overdramatic musicians."

"Ah, so he's a musician too."

Shit. I've probably already violated a term in the NDA I signed.

"Yeah. He's, uh, part of the Eleven backup band," I lie.

"I'm guessing none of the guys know."

"They'd turn all big brother on me and coddle me and ... yeah, I'm good, thanks. I'm dealing."

"Did you want to ... maybe ... if you need an ear—"

"You look about as willing as a hooker facing a fifteen-inch cock."

Soren's forehead scrunches. "I don't know what that means. Would a hooker like that or not?"

"That's way too big."

"Oh. Then yeah, true. Because I don't exactly want to hear about you with other guys, but if you need to talk, I'm here."

"Why don't you want to hear about it? This is what you wanted for me. To *fall in love*. Though I don't know why because it fucking sucks."

Soren huffs. "I didn't want you to get hurt. I wanted you to find someone you could be happy with."

I'm convinced true happiness might not exist. "Were *you* happy? With Bryce?"

"I thought I was. For a long time, I figured all relationships have issues like we did. You never hear a married person say, 'We love each other so darn much and it's so easy!' I expected coming out would fix us, but it just brought other problems forward."

"But you were with him for, like, three years. Something had to have been right."

"I *wanted* it to be right, so I forced something to fit when it didn't. He's not a bad guy. He's particular and likes to have things his way, which is why the guys didn't get along with him, but he's not inherently bad. I wish I could say there was a certain thing that drove a wedge between us so I could have something to blame or a reason for why we didn't work out, but the truth is ... I think I made the wrong choice three years ago."

"What do you mean?"

"Even though this hot rock star I met turned out to be Matt Jackson's little brother, and even though he was leaving to go on tour ... I should've fought to see him again instead of trying to make something work that had already failed once."

"Oh." I hate what that does to my insides—turns them into lovey mush. Eww. "It's probably for the better. The first year of the tour for me was sucky. Having someone back home would've made it impossible. I was close to quitting as it was."

Soren pulls back in surprise. "Really? You were born to have that life though. It's obvious in the way you perform."

I thought that once upon a time too. And I do love it. But ever since leaving New York, I've had the constant fear of not being good enough and not wanting it hard enough to hack it. "It's not as easy as everyone makes it out to be. It's hard work and exhausting, and if you're doing it alone ..."

"Why don't you quit?"

"It got better after that first year. Enough to keep pushing forward anyway. It's still not easy, but I can handle it a lot better now."

"What changed to make it better?" Soren asks.

"We fired Wayne. Our manager."

"The guy who didn't even watch your show in Tampa?"

"You remember that?"

"I remember a lot of things I shouldn't when it comes to you." The heat in Soren's gaze thaws some of the coldness I still hold toward him but not enough to ask him to tell me every single thing he remembers about me.

"Well, yeah, him. He was ... a shit manager. Actually, he was a shit person in general. Aside from treating the band horribly, he was an asshole who thought it was his right to help himself." I gesture to myself and shudder.

Soren's jaw hardens. "Wait, he—"

I hold up my hand to stop him from jumping to the wrong conclusions. "It was consensual but only because I was lonely, naïve, and wanted someone. *Anyone*. But that made him believe he could have it whenever he wanted. And to add insult to injury, it wasn't until after Luce took us on that I found out Wayne was married to a woman and had kids."

"Luce?"

"He's our new manager ... well, I guess he's not new. We hired him after that Australia trip we went on not long after Tampa. We met him there. He kinda took me under his wing and taught me all the stuff I should've already known about the industry—like how common it is for situations like Wayne and me to happen. Here I was thinking Wayne was an out, gay man. Nope."

"But why ..."

I know what he's asking. I was shocked too when I found out. "You'd be surprised how bigoted the entertainment industry is. We all like to think Hollywood is liberal and progressive, but seriously, it's not."

"And I thought being gay in sports was bad," Soren mutters.

"I guess I was lucky I was never in the closet, so to speak. The label might've made me change my name and the band's name, but at least they didn't make me hide my sexuality."

Small mercies.

"With a song like 'He's Mine,' it was probably too hard to hide anyway," Soren says.

I laugh. "I reckon it had more to do with them trying to replicate Panic! At the Disco's brand until Luce came along and took us in the Eleven direction. We went from kind of emo rock slash grunge to pop rock, and it made us more marketable."

"Rock star politics, eh?"

"You don't know the half of it."

Soren's hand covers mine, and it throws me. I want to pull away, I want to turn my hand over and hold on for dear life, but most of all, I want to be strong enough not to climb into Soren's lap and feel the heat of him against me again.

"I'd like to know more about it. About your life," he says. "I never stopped following you online and watching your videos. It reminds me of how you made me brave enough to face the scariest part of my life and say, 'fuck it.'"

Damn him. He knows exactly what to say to make me forget all the mistakes he made two years ago. I mean, I know realistically he was only a little bit of a dick, and technically did nothing wrong, but it's been easier to forget about him by painting him as an asshole than remembering that he truly gets me.

He takes his hand back. "If you don't want to get into it with me, I understand. We can talk about the guy, if you want. He got a name?"

"Why do we have to talk at all?" I can think of a million things I'd rather do with Soren.

He stares out at the water. "Guess we don't. I just figure this is the most you've said to me since you landed on the island. I'm scared if we stop you'll run away again."

I hesitate only for a second because if I'm honest, I might run away again, but I don't want to. If I had a logical side, it'd yell at me to run, but lucky for Soren, I never did have that part of the brain stopping me from doing stupid shit.

"It's Harry," I blurt. Technically not lying. Harley's real name is Harry, but just like I had to change my name because of some Nickelodeon character from the nineties named Jett Jackson, Harley had to change his because of Harry from One Direction. It happens a lot in the industry. We couldn't record as Fallout because it was too close to *Fallout Boy*. So that's why we became Radioactive.

"How over is it between you two?"

"He's getting married, and after Wayne, I promised myself I wouldn't go there with a married person again. Not that I knew about Wayne. He didn't wear a ring and basically barked instructions at us, so it's not like we talked much for him to say, 'Oh, by the way, my wife and daughters say hi.'"

"What about the new manager?"

"Luce? He's one hundred percent in a committed relationship with his assistant, but even if he wasn't, he's the most professional guy I know. We lucked out with him finding us. He only did because Marty—that's his partner—was a huge fan of ours." I can pinpoint the exact moment my career turned around, and it started with Luce knocking on my hotel door in Australia.

I was a mess. It was a month after the night in Tampa with Soren, and everything was going to shit. We got booed off the stage at the festival because their roadies sucked and got wires mixed up. Our mics weren't working properly. My guitar wasn't tuned right. Massive mess.

I thought Luce was there to drop us from the label. Instead, he promised to make my life ten times easier. Not only that, but we hit our first number one, thanks to him. He fought to take us in a new direction, and while we're not Eleven famous yet, thanks to Luce, we're halfway there.

"I'm glad you've got someone in your corner to look out for you."

I'm about to say, "me too" because I owe everything to Marty and Luce, but Soren beats me to talking.

"And I don't mean that to say you can't look after yourself or you need a babysitter. I purely mean it because being alone sucks, and even the strongest people need support sometimes."

He makes a point. I know Luce would support me in anything, and so would Benji and Freya. But at the end of the day, Luce goes home to Marty, Benji and Freya are too busy fighting to see when I'm struggling, and I'm constantly surrounded by people who see me but don't know me.

Even when I was with Harley, he'd always leave. We weren't allowed to be together, and some would say that's some romantic Romeo and *Julien* bullshit, but everyone seems to forget how that story ends when they claim it to be so fucking romantic.

Not being able to be with the person you love is not romantic.

It's painful.

It's why I can't do it to myself anymore.

I stand before I do something stupid like ask Soren to share a bed with me so I can fill the emptiness in my chest for a little while. "I'm gonna go to bed."

"Jet."

I step off his deck and freeze at my name. Jet sounds like a foreign name to me now, but when Soren says it, it feels like three years ago. I close my eyes, trying to hold on to it.

"You're not running away again, are you? I thought we were getting somewhere."

Staring at him over my shoulder, I force a smile. "Not running. Super tired."

I try to stay strong in case he's thinking the same thing as me.

We're both hurting. We're both trying to move on from bad breakups. It makes sense to seek comfort in each other.

But I don't know if I'll survive it. Not with Soren.

The night I met him, there was a spark I haven't experienced since. There was potential for more and that fluttery feeling of us possibly having epic love. Reality crushed that. An ex-boyfriend, a music tour, and conflicting schedules don't mix.

Then when he turned up at my show in Tampa, I thought … *stupidly* thought it meant something.

I went into the music industry with fewer expectations than the ones I put on Soren that night. I'm not usually a naïve kid, but when it comes to him, I'm ridiculously and hopelessly idealistic.

The last thing I want is for him to see me that way.

"Try to get some actual sleep tonight," Soren says with genuine care in his voice.

Caleb Sorensen caring about me is the last thing I need right now because the stupid kid with love hearts in his eyes is fighting to make an appearance again.

CHAPTER NINE

SOREN

Fiji is officially the land of the best dreams ever. What's even better is not being woken by someone interrupting the wicked things Jet was doing to me in my sleep.

I don't know if I sleep until lunchtime because I needed to catch up from the previous night or if I didn't want to leave the dream, but when I do finally climb out of bed, shower, and head out, I can't find anyone anywhere.

You'd think that would be statistically impossible.

The pool's empty, the beach is deserted, and unless they all went for a walk to the top of the headland, I'm thinking there was an alien invasion and the only ones left are the people who slept through it. It's the only logical explanation.

That is, until I find Ema in the main house.

"Hungry?" she asks. "You slept through breakfast."

"Starving. Thank you. Where is everyone?"

"Joni took the other hockey player, his partner, and the musician to the mainland to do some sightseeing. Mr. Jackson and Mr. Huntington should be on the private beach outside their suite. The football players are resting up and preparing for tonight, and the other two ... I don't know where they are."

I smile.

"Sorry. I'm terrible with names. Great with faces. Names, not so much." She gestures for me to sit on a stool at the kitchen counter and slides a cup of coffee in front of me.

"No problem. Why are the football players preparing for tonight?"

The door to the front entrance opens, and Damon steps through.

"You're all going to Rua Daulomani Island," Ema says.

"We are? What's that?"

Damon claps my shoulder and joins me. "It's a gay island."

"The whole island is gay?" I quip.

Ema gives Damon a cup of coffee too. "Homosexuality is still frowned upon in Fiji. There are no gay bars, no same-sex marriage, and not many rights at all. Rua Daulomani is owned by friends of ours. They wanted to create that safe space for those who need it."

"Oh, wow. I knew it wasn't exactly liberal here, but I didn't know it was still that bad."

"Our boy is gay, but he recently moved to Australia with his partner so they could get married and have kids."

There's an ugly truth no one really thinks about anymore. Some people still need to move countries to be with the person they love.

"It's why we advertise as gay-friendly accommodation. We don't care who people love."

"That's very cool of you," I say.

"Here is nothing like Rua Daulomani though. This is more a vacation spot where you can relax and sunbake. The island is more ... uh ... like a party? That's probably the tame way of saying it."

"Is everyone going?" I ask Damon and hope I'm not being obvious.

He nods. "After dinner."

"Wait, why're Talon and Miller getting ready now?"

Damon laughs. "Miller's trying to convince himself to get on another boat. I think Talon's helping."

Sure. *Helping*.

I wish I had someone to *help* when I needed it.

"While I've got you," Damon says, "Carly called."

His assistant. The person doing his job while he's away.

I swallow hard. "And?"

"They finally caved on the no-trade clause."

"Yes!"

"Calm down. It's only a one-year contract."

Fuck.

"There's still the three-year deal without the no-trade clause on the table."

"Option for an extension on the one-year?"

"Yes. Want me to counter for two with no trade? They'll probably lowball you for it, though."

The one year will take me to thirty-four. It's not a bad age to retire if I can't get an extension, but it's not ideal because if I have a bad season, then I'm done. I need to think of my priorities though, and right now, my priority is a no-trade clause.

"I'll sign the one-year and hope to extend it."

"Are you sure?" Damon asks.

"It's done then and signed, and I won't have to stress about them dumping me completely."

"I'll have the papers sent to Joni and Ema's office, and you can sign today. Then that's all the shop talk I'm allowed. I'm supposed to be on vacation."

"So ... a gay island, eh?" I ask.

Tonight should be interesting.

⨯

The whole boat rocks violently as we climb in to go to Rua Daulomani, and there are just enough seats for all of us if we squish together. Jet takes the last seat on the other side at the front near his brother, and the only one left for me is at the back next to Miller.

"Wait ... are you going to puke again? Anyone wanna swap places?" *Preferably Matt.*

"It'll be fine," Joni says. "Water's not rough tonight, and it's not far. He should be fine."

While we wait for Joni to get the boat ready, I kick Ollie's foot as he is sitting opposite me. "What'd you guys get up to today?"

Ollie smiles. "Just went to the mainland to look around. I was gonna wake you to see if you wanted to join us today but thought better of it after last night."

"What happened last night?" Jet asks. "Were you really jerking it when Ollie walked in?"

"No," I say at the same time Ollie says, "Yes."

Asswipe.

Everyone laughs.

"I might have been in the middle of a hot memory, but my hands were nowhere near my dick."

"Memory of who? A puck bunny?" Ollie jokes.

"Nah. Cute twink."

Jet chokes on God knows what, coughing until Matt reaches over to pat his back.

"Wrong pipe," he rasps.

He's in tight red skinny jeans, a black shirt, and rainbow Converse. His silky hair is all curly and wild and falling in his face. The bags under his eyes are gone, and it's the first time since he got here that he looks like the Jet I remember. Lively and charismatic.

When we take off, the boat speeds across the water in the pitch-black night, the only light bouncing off the navigation system next to the steering wheel. The whole boat ride, I can't take my eyes off Jet's silhouette. Ever since he stepped off that helicopter, I haven't been able to do anything but think about him.

Bright, rainbow lights appear on the horizon, and as we get closer, the entire island is lit up in pride colors.

Joni slows the boat down on approach and turns to us. "Word of warning. This might be a safe space, but if the owners see anything that might constitute payment for sex, the authorities will be called." He gives me a pointed look.

I blame the guys and all their rent boy jokes when we first got to the island. Joni probably thinks I have a prostitute habit or something.

"A few years ago, this island wasn't even allowed to exist because anything that resembled gay behavior in public could have you arrested. Remember that while you're here, but go and have fun."

"Well, with that depressing pep talk, how could we not?" Jet says, and the guys snicker.

Joni pulls the boat up to the dock where we're welcomed by island staff in blue button-down shirts and khaki pants.

It goes to show the difference in cultural expectations. I hear gay island and think of half-naked men and everything you might see at a pride parade back home. A gay island in Fiji means a safe place where you can hold another man's hand without being persecuted.

It takes some time for us to file out of the boat and climb the ladder from the pontoon to the wharf.

"This is gonna be fun getting back down later," Talon says.

I guess we can't get too drunk tonight then.

Even though I was first off the boat, somehow I end up at the back of the pack, walking next to Jet. It wasn't done on purpose at all. Not even a little bit.

Jet has his hands in his pockets, his head down, his shaggy dark hair in his face. I have to fight the urge to reach over and brush it away with my hand.

We're led up a pathway through some trees and come to a large terracotta building with open wooden doors and live music, bright lights, and rowdy noise spilling out.

We turn heads as we enter. It always happens when we're out. It's the jock effect. Tall, athletic guys in a group.

The bar is packed and seems to have a mix of locals and tourists—if the loud group of drunk white guys in the back is anything to go by.

I try to be sly about sitting near Jet, but as we take up a corner spot reserved for us, Jet goes to sit on the very end, which means I have to take the other side of the L-shape we're in ... next to his brother.

Taking a deep breath, I act casual and slide in next to Matt.

I haven't been this awkward around him since I first found out who he was to Jet. For the first six months of our friendship, I walked on eggshells around Matt, not knowing whether or not he was aware of what I'd done with his little brother.

A waiter comes and gets our drink order so we don't have to go to the bar, and the guys order pitchers of beer to go around.

A few guys walk by, eyeing each and every one of us. I suddenly know how lobsters in tanks at restaurants feel.

Maddox leans forward a few seats over to get my attention. "Hey, Canada, looks like you and Jet have ample chance of getting some tonight."

My eyes widen. "W-what?"

He waves in the general vicinity of a table of guys across the room. "Lots of potential."

Oh, right. A chance of getting some from *other* people. Not each other.

My gaze catches on Jet whose eyes are locked on me, but he quickly looks back at Lennon beside him and nods as if he's listening to whatever Lennon's saying.

Matt and Noah start talking about Wade and the baby with Maddox and Damon, but I tune them out.

The busy dance floor catches my attention. The live band on stage sings some song I don't recognize, but it's happy and bouncy.

Drinks arrive, and as I pour myself a glass, a tall, buff-looking guy inches closer to our table. When I turn to look at him, he spins on his heel and goes the other way. He looks over his shoulder and pauses but then keeps walking.

I've seen this happen before. This isn't *build up the courage to go hit on someone* hesitance. It's someone wanting to ask for an autograph. But with three of us in the NFL and two in the NHL, there's no way to tell who he wants.

Matt leans in close to me. "What or who are we laughing at?"

I tilt my head in the direction of the guy. "I think one of us has been recognized. Guy at my four o'clock. Muscle shirt, tight pants."

Matt checks him out and grins before turning to the others. "All right. Let's place our bets, boys. There's a guy trying to build up the courage to come over here. Which one of us is he gonna ask for an autograph? I'm going with Soren seeing as they've already locked eyes."

"I'll take Matt," Maddox says.

"Talon and or Miller," Damon says, "because they come as a package."

"You want to do what with my package?" Talon yells.

Miller rolls his eyes. "We'll take Ollie then, I guess."

Lennon laughs. "Egotistical athletes. The logical choice here is *Jet*."

Like a pack of dogs being told we're going for a walk, we all cock our heads.

The guy doesn't give me a chance to put my bet in because, apparently, he has built the confidence to go for it.

And, shit. Lennon is right.

He bypasses all of us and goes straight to Jet. "You're from Radioactive, yeah?" He's Australian.

Jet smiles and nods.

"I thought it was you but couldn't be sure, and ..."

It's not as endearing to see a two-hundred-pound muscle-type fanboying as I thought it would be.

"Can I buy you a drink?" the guy asks.

Jet holds up his beer. "Got one, thanks."

"A dance?"

He's persistent, isn't he?

Jet seems uncomfortable as he glances around the table, looking at everyone but me. Then he downs the rest of his glass and stands, and all I can do is watch as he takes to the dance floor with the Aussie guy. He's handsy, and I try to read anything in Jet's expression that tells me he doesn't like it, but his smile doesn't appear fake, and his hands are all over the guy's chest.

I keep drinking my beer and try not to act like a jealous

asshole while they dance for two entire songs. At three and a half minutes a song, that's seven minutes. Six minutes too long for my liking.

Word of Jet's presence must've spread, because when the third song kicks in, the opening riff is one I'd recognize instantly.

It's our song.

Not "He's Mine," the one that started my whole obsession with Jet, but "Hat Trick Heartbreak." It's the song he wrote about me, about us, and the last time we saw each other.

The lead singer of the band speaks into the mic. "We have the one and only Jay from Radioactive in the house!"

The small crowd on the dance floor cheers, but Jet's gaze meets mine. Just like nearly every time we've locked eyes, he quickly averts his as if he was never looking in the first place.

He waves politely to the adoring fans now swarming him on the dance floor.

"This one's for you, boy," the lead singer says and starts belting out Jet's words.

"Hey, it's our song." Ollie wraps his arm around Lennon.

Sure. *His and Lennon's song.*

It's the logical connection. Jet wrote a song about Matt and Noah. Ollie plays hockey. "Hat Trick Heartbreak." It makes sense. I'm not supposed to know Jet the way I do.

I watch Jet dancing to our song with that other guy.

I want to close the distance between us. I want that Aussie guy to stop trying to find every excuse to touch him. But most of all, I want to take back the night that made this song.

I can't help wondering where we'd be tonight had I not gone to his show two years ago. This would be my first time seeing him since we slept together.

We could've started fresh.

The end of the verse catches my attention, highlighting why that might be impossible now:

You fit perfection
The ultimate hat trick
But you slipped and then you flaked
Now you're nothing but my hat trick heartbreak.

"Yeah, there might not be any coming back from that," I mumble.

"What?" Matt says beside me.

"Uh, nothing. Isn't it weird hearing your brother's songs?"

"It's fucking awesome." He leans in closer to me. "Jet deserves the world."

Is that a lump the size of a puck in my throat? He can't mean anything by that other than what he said. He thinks Jet deserves everything. That doesn't mean he suspects ...

I side-eye him, too scared to make proper eye contact, but he's not looking at me. He's focused on the band.

The song ends, and Jet tries to pry himself away to come back to us, but the lead singer and the ever-growing group of fans encourage him onto the stage instead.

He does the coy thing where he tries to refuse, but this is him in his element. There's no way he'll be able to resist, and I'm dying to hear him live again. Twice isn't enough. I'd listen to him sing the alphabet on repeat.

After speaking with the band for a minute, as predicted, he takes the mic.

"Hey, Fiji!"

Everyone in the bar goes crazy but no one more than the group of guys I'm with.

Jet eyes us from the stage and lifts his chin with a giant smile.

"I, uh, feel weird singing one of my songs without the rest of my band here, but I don't mind hanging out for a bit."

The guy he was dancing with sticks his fingers in his mouth and lets out a loud whistle.

Jet opens with Queen's "I Want to Break Free" and like every gay bar that breaks into an LGBT anthem, everyone joins in. But Jet is louder.

Turns out, he doesn't even have to be singing his own songs for me to get lost in his voice.

The rasp. The need in his tone. The soulful way in which he makes me experience every single word.

I feel it in my chest. In my heart.

When the song comes to a close, Jet thanks the crowd and hedges to get off the stage, but everyone loves him. Of course, they do. They scream for more, chanting his name ... well, *Jay* anyway.

His eyes lock on mine, and his lips form into a thin line. I'm frozen in his gaze until he spins on his heel and says something to the band.

They look at him with arched brows and weird expressions, but Jet says something that looks like "Trust me" though I can't tell for sure from back here.

Jet's handed an acoustic guitar, and after he strums it a couple of times, he approaches the mic again. "This is one y'all should recognize."

The opening riffs make me question that statement because I can't place the song.

Jet stares down at his hands as he plays the guitar effortlessly. When he starts singing, it's soft and he still doesn't raise his head.

It takes a couple of lines to realize it's a slower version of that pop song "Someone Else's Perfect" by Eleven.

The song completely transforms coming out of Jet's mouth.

It's no longer a teenybopper love song, but one of heartbreak and angst. I guess I've never listened to the lyrics before.

Under your spell,
Living in hell,
You say I'm perfect,
Too good to be someone's reject,
But that's what you did when you walked away,
You left me to find myself

Something niggles at me. Whether it's the way he's singing it or that we both relate to it, I don't know. It's like he's singing it to me. About me.

Then he finally raises his head and holds my gaze just as he sings a telling line.

You said I was perfect ...
Perfect for someone else.

Holy. Shit.

That phrase is in the song repeatedly, and every time he sings it, more pain comes through in his voice. It gets to the point where I'm sure this isn't an Eleven song. It can't be. While Jet has the ability to turn any song into his own, just like he did with Queen, this is different. It not only comes across as genuine, but the heartache and rejection make me feel guilty—as if I did something wrong.

He finishes the song and leaves the stage before people can beg him for another encore.

Only, he doesn't come back to our table. He beelines it for outside, leaving the rest of us staring at each other wondering what happened. His friend on the dance floor is confused too.

I'm the only one who knows for sure.

Matt stands to go after him, but I push him back down.

"I'll go."

"What would you know about anything?"

How am I supposed to answer that? "He ... uh ... I ..." I fluster under Matt's gaze, and now Noah's watching too.

Lennon appears in front of us. "Jet doesn't want to tell you guys, but he was dating someone on tour, and it all went to shit." He turns to me. "Go. You're the only one who won't big brother him."

Either Lennon's the most intuitive guy ever or he knows more than I thought he did, but right now I don't care. I want to get to Jet.

I follow where he went but reach outside and have no idea which way he's gone. Following the path down to the wharf, I check to see if he's sitting on the dock, but it's empty. It's on my way back that I see movement against the side of the main building.

Jet paces back and forth, running a hand through his hair and muttering words I can't make out, but as I get closer, I hear "Get it together, Jay. Hold it to-fucking-gether."

I step through the row of palm trees lining the path. "Jet."

He freezes. "Of course, it's you." He goes back to pacing.

"That song ..."

Jet stares but doesn't stop moving.

"You wrote it."

This makes him pause again. "I ... I—"

"About me."

He composes himself. "Conceited much? You think you get more than one song?"

"I *knew* 'Hat Trick Heartbreak' was about me and not Ollie

and Lennon." I take a step forward. "But tell me I'm wrong about this one."

Jet's mouth opens and then closes.

I step closer again. "Jet."

"Why do you keep saying my name like that?"

"To remind you that I know the real you. Not Jay. I still know you as the aspiring musician reveling over his first fan."

"The naïve kid, you mean." Bitterness doesn't suit the bubbly guy I know. Or ... knew, I guess.

I keep moving closer. He steps back. We keep going until his back is against the wall and my hand is above his head, boxing him in.

"I've never seen you as a kid. Never."

"Bullshit."

"I've tried to get myself to think of you that way, and when you're not in my presence, it's easy to write you off as Matt Jackson's little brother. But I can't when we're in the same room sharing the same air. I can't when you're two feet in front of me, and all I want to do is reach for you. Touch you. Kiss you."

"Then what was all the overprotective shit you pulled that night in Tampa with all the drugs and groupie bullshit?"

"That wasn't me trying to protect you. That was me wanting to *claim* you."

Jet breathes hard. "Oh, holy mother of gay Jesus."

"I had no right to act or feel that way about you back then."

Our eyes lock on each other, and for a moment in time, we're both frozen.

"I'm sorry I wrote two emo songs about you," Jet says quietly.

I laugh. "So, I am right."

"You're the only one who's ever picked up on that. Everyone thinks Harley wrote that song."

"Maybe because I experienced it with you ..."

Jet shakes his head. "No, it's *you*. You understand me more than anyone ever has. More than any groupie who's tried to explain my songs to me. You came out because you knew 'He's Mine' wasn't just a stupid love song." He reaches for me, his fingertips trailing down my cheek. "It's you."

"Was singing that song in there some sort of test?" I ask.

He doesn't answer.

Jet's thumb moves slowly across my bottom lip, and that's invitation enough for me.

I close the small gap between us, our mouths coming together, hungry and hot. His other hand joins the first, holding me to him as his tongue seeks out mine.

Urgency and need have me pulling him closer.

Jet moans, and I can't help replying with my own desperate sound.

I want more.

Jet evidently doesn't feel the same way. He pushes me off him, and I stumble back.

"Damn it. I shouldn't have come here."

"Outside?" I stupidly ask.

"Fiji. I thought anything would be better than touring with Har—" He clears his throat. "This is worse than dealing with him. I was hoping you and Bryce hadn't come on this stupid trip."

"Well you got half your wish. Bryce isn't here."

"Caleb—"

"You always call me Caleb when you're mad. Is it because of what I said and did in Tampa?"

"No. It's because I ..."

I wait for him to finish, but he doesn't. "You what?"

"I'm not over *him*. And you ... I don't know what it is about you, but every time I see you or I'm near you, I just ..."

I can't help feeling sympathetic because I know exactly what he means. "When I'm near you, I don't even know what I saw in Bryce."

"What are we supposed to do with that?"

"I'm guessing sex is not the right thing to say here."

Jet bursts into laughter. "You wish."

"I really do." I step closer again, dipping my head so we're mere centimeters away. "I don't know what we're supposed to do. I know what I *want* to do and what I *should* do, but I don't think either is the right solution."

"What are you supposed to do?"

That's easy. "Walk away."

"What do you want to do?"

Less easy. I swallow hard as I say the words I know I shouldn't. "Never stop touching you."

"What are you gonna do?" Jet whispers.

"I don't know."

"Soren?"

"Yeah?"

"The correct answer to that was kiss me again."

CHAPTER TEN

JET

Soren's mouth ravishes mine again, strong and demanding, leading me to only one conclusion.

I'm screwed. I'm so screwed.

Twenty-year-old me with love hearts in his eyes takes over twenty-three-year-old me like some sci-fi body snatchers movie.

Soren kisses me as if he thinks he'll never get the chance again.

I'd like to say I'm strong enough to make that happen, but I'm not.

Soren makes me weak and greedy.

His knee goes between my thighs, and it takes all my effort not to rub against him like an animal in heat.

Fuck it. I need it.

But before I can take it, Soren pulls back.

"Shit," he hisses. "We better stop before we get arrested."

I push away the disappointment and go for the joke. "Pretty sure you just said I look like a hooker …"

Soren rests his forehead against mine. "Jet. Sweet, sarcastic Jet. What are we doing?"

"You tell me."

"What do you want this to be? This can be a moment of weakness, or it could be a promise of things we both know won't happen."

"Ain't there a happy medium?"

"Like what?"

"Drowning our sorrows in each other?" Fuck, what am I saying?

"Will that work?"

No. "Maybe?"

All I know is I want to keep kissing him. Now that I've started, I'm not sure I can stop. Bottom line is, Soren might be the one person on this planet who could make me forget about Harley. I just have to remind myself that naïve Jet can't get in over his head.

I'm going to be smart about this. "So, we have fun on vacation and that's it."

Worst. Idea. Ever.

"Fun ..." Soren says. "Just fun." He purses his lips. "I don't know if I could ever only have fun with you, but if that's all you can give me—"

"It is." Well, it's not all I *can* give. It's all I'm willing to give.

"What exactly does fun entail? Are we talking, like, hanging out or sex or ..."

"You want boundaries, you mean?"

"Right. Like, am I allowed to flirt with you?"

"Do you have the balls to in front of my brother?" I challenge.

Soren doesn't say anything.

"Okay, how's this for keeping it simple. We can only talk about things you'd be willing to say in front of Matt." That should keep the flirting to a minimum. "Fun doesn't have to mean sex stuff, though that's definitely on the table. Hmm, sex on a table

…" I shake my thoughts free. "We can hang out and go sightseeing together. I want to stop wallowing and have *fun*. Real fun. *Every type* of fun."

"Have meaningless fun and fuck the consequences? I don't think I've heard a more typical Jet saying."

"What would you know? From what the gay brigade has told you? You don't actually know me, Soren."

"Then maybe that's what we should be doing the next two weeks. Getting to know the real people behind the memories. Because when I think of you, I confuse you with the guy I know and the guy everyone else says you are."

If I'm honest with myself, I do the same thing. It's as if I'm a different person when I'm performing than I am backstage, and then when I'm with Matt and Noah, I'm someone else again.

I'm desperate to do as Soren says—be the real me for once. But it's not that easy. I'm all my personas and none of them at the same time.

"I'm telling ya," a loud Ollie says, "I don't think they came out this way."

Soren steps back from me, and I try to compose myself before the guys find us.

They sound like a herd of elephants with their big-ass athlete feet.

"We're here," Soren says, taking another step away but turning his back on the guys to adjust himself.

All of them have come looking for us because they're, well, *them*. They converge through the palm trees like a zombie pack.

"You okay?" Matt asks.

"I'm fine. My throat was hurting. That's all."

Lennon avoids my gaze. "I told them. About the guy."

Motherfucking Lennon. I love him, but I should've thought twice before telling him about Harley … well, "Harry." He and

Ollie asked what was really up with canceling the tour while we were on the mainland today, and I thought they'd back off if I told them a smidgen of what happened. They know about as much as Soren.

Tour love gone bad.

"Okay, so I'm out here wallowing. I'm allowed to do that in private, ain't I?"

"Aww, our baby boy's first heartbreak," Noah, the smartass, says. He holds his hand over his heart.

"This is why I didn't tell you guys and why Lennon should've kept his mouth shut."

Lennon eyes me as if in challenge, and I have no idea why he's looking at me like that. He should've kept it to himself, and he and I are gonna have words.

"What, you don't think we would've been supportive?" Matt asks.

"The opposite. Too supportive. And y'all gonna try to make me feel better, and I'm fine."

"Operation *Get Jet So Drunk He Can't Remember His Name* is underway already," Noah says. "Can't stop it now."

Yep. I was afraid of that. "Great plan … Wait, until I can't remember the guy's name or my own name?"

Noah looks pensive. "Both."

I laugh. "Cool. Can you guys start executing it while I hang out here and execute Lennon first? Thanks."

Lennon hangs his head.

"Five minutes," Noah says. "Then you're ours."

Great. How to get out of this one? I've seen what self-medicating does on the road, and I still have no desire to join that club even if I can afford my own rehab now.

Having gambling addicts for parents makes addiction a touchy subject for me and something I have no desire to develop.

The guys make their way back through the trees, but Ollie and Soren stay back with Lennon.

"You need me to stay for protection?" Ollie asks.

"I'm not really going to kill him," I say.

Ollie scoffs. "I was actually talking to *you* because Lennon did you a favor back there."

"A favor? How is telling my brothers I'm going through a breakup a favor?"

"Because it's better than telling them you and Soren have been making eyes at each other all night," Ollie says.

Soren stiffens. "Oh, shit."

Lennon looks smug. "You guys are playing with fire."

"Yeah, well, I light fires to feel joy." I try to not let it show how them knowing about us affects me.

"Tell us the truth," Ollie says. "You guys hooked up years ago, didn't you?"

My façade drops. "H-how …"

"How did you know?" Soren asks.

"Boom." Ollie turns to Lennon. "Someone owes me twenty bucks."

Lennon grumbles.

"It was the night you lost the Stanley Cup, wasn't it?" Ollie is way too enthusiastic about this. "You guys were doing the exact same thing you've been doing tonight."

Soren and I meet each other's gaze, our faces stoic. At least, he looks stoic.

I must be doing the heart eyes thing again because Ollie adds, "Yes. Exactly what you're doing now." His face falls. "Wait. That means 'Hat Trick Heartbreak' isn't about me and Lennon?"

"Do you really want it to be?" I ask. "It's about being treated like shit."

Lennon runs his hand down Ollie's arm. "Can you take Soren and get your dance on while I talk with Jet?"

Uh-oh.

"Yes. I need to dance." Ollie grabs Soren's arm.

"You need to dance with me?" Soren asks.

"Lennon still refuses to. I love him, but he's ridiculously uncoordinated on a dance floor."

"Trust me. I do it for your benefit more than mine," Lennon calls after them as they make their way back inside. Then he turns on me. "What's going on?"

"What do you mean?"

"Why are you and Soren being all ... you and Soren again? It's been like ..."

"Three years." Shit. I slam my mouth shut. "But I still have no idea what you're talking about. And even if I did, why would I tell you when you'll run and tell Matt and Noah everything?"

He gestures toward the building. "I did that for you. It was either that or have them wondering why Soren was chasing after you."

"He wasn't chasing ... okay, he was, but it's none of their goddamn business."

"What happened between you two?"

"What, you want the intimate details? Perv."

Lennon's unamused at my attempt at deflection. "No. I mean, what *happened*?"

"He didn't know I was Matt's brother until the morning after. That was a fun conversation. He looked like he was going to vomit."

Lennon laughs.

"Then I went on tour, he got back together with Bryce, and that was it. It was nothing. There was no big drama or breakup or anything like that. And we've only seen each other once since then. Now he's here, we're both single—no, we're both *hurting*. It makes sense we'd gravitate toward each other."

"That's all it is?"

"Last night was the first time since I broke up with Harry that I didn't go to bed thinking about how lonely I am."

Instead, I couldn't get Soren out of my head and that he's here. In Fiji. Eight thousand miles away from where we first met. What does that say about my relationship with Harley if the minute I'm away from him, I'm thinking about another guy? A guy from my past, sure, but I don't know if that makes a difference.

Lennon's arm wraps around me. "Aww, Jet. I didn't know."

It's funny to me when the guys call Lennon small because he's not. He's tall and lean. It's that he hangs around guys who do weight training for a living and are all over six foot. He looks small compared to them.

I fit against him, and it feels nice to be held by a friend—someone who doesn't want anything from me.

"I figured you need a hug. I can let go if you want me to."

"Not yet," I mumble. "You're right. I needed this."

"You should've told me."

"It's not like you could have done anything about it if you knew."

"I could've come to see you or you could've called. We may have only lived together for a few months, but I consider you one of my closest friends. I'd do anything for you."

I lay my head on his shoulder. "I know. I … I dunno. I don't want to burden you. Or Matt and Noah."

"You're never a burden. Especially for your brothers."

"Knowing that doesn't take the crappy feeling away though."

"No, I guess not. What are you and Soren going to do now?"

"Have fun? It's not like we can do much else. If I didn't piss the label off too much by pulling a disappearing act, I'll be back on tour soon. He'll be playing hockey. It's not like there's a future here."

"Do you want a future?" Lennon asks.

"I barely know the guy."

But something Soren said last night has me thinking about it—what our lives would've looked like had we aimed for something more. He said he shouldn't have picked Bryce, and I can't help wondering what would've happened had he pursued me instead.

I have no doubt he made the right decision and didn't waste the last three years. Logically, I probably would've cheated on him or something during that first year I was on tour. I was so lonely. Lonely enough to sleep with my forty-five-year-old dick of a manager and countless groupies.

Being surrounded by people who want you is intoxicating. And for a while, it was a thrill.

The only other person I've had an actual connection with is Harley. He understood me because he's been through it all. We started out as friends—him teaching me how to deal with rising fame and how to stay levelheaded. Well, relatively levelheaded. It is me I'm talking about.

I thought Harley was straight for about four months. Tabloids always had him with the latest actress or pop star. It wasn't until our hundredth time hanging out I realized he spent all his spare time with me.

I asked if he was trying to hit on me, and he laughed and said, "Fucking finally."

Insert a whirlwind, forbidden romance that didn't fool any of the crew, a forcible separation by his management team, enforced by my own, and then the nail that finally sealed the coffin—his engagement to a beard.

I don't care if the marriage is fake, they're still going to be fucking married. And from what I understand, she's not in on the whole *fake* part. Worse yet? It's a fan his management team picked out for him. It'll give all the other girls out there even more reason to believe they could bag one of the Eleven boys.

That's not cool.

And I refuse to be involved.

But maybe … just maybe … if Soren had picked me all those years ago, maybe I wouldn't be in pieces now.

"Oh, Jethro!" Noah's singing voice comes from near the trees.

"Ah, fuck. Time's up." I pull away from Lennon, but he grabs hold of my hand.

"Be careful with Soren."

Ha, right. Be careful with *Soren*. Because he's the one who's risking heartache here.

Sure.

CHAPTER ELEVEN

SOREN

I'm still dancing with Ollie when Jet and Lennon are dragged back into the bar by Noah. The tray of shots the guys ordered still sits untouched at our table. They're waiting for Jet so he can drown his sorrows.

I had a better way for him to do that, but no. Apparently drinking is the key.

Jet takes a shot reluctantly and swallows it down and then slams the glass on the table as if to say, "There. I drank your stupid drink."

But then they put another in front of him. He rolls his eyes but takes it.

They all join him on this one.

Ollie's body presses in closer to me. "You want to go over there, don't you?"

Yes. "Don't know what you're talking about."

"For what it's worth, I think you should go for it with the kid."

"He's not a kid."

Ollie bursts into laughter. "That's what you've been calling him for years. I knew it was too emphatic."

"You're having way too much fun with this."

"You're two of my best friends. It'd be cool. I mean, I will miss you when Matt and Noah hire a hitman to take you out, but until then, it'll be good for both of you."

"How much did Jet tell you about his ex?" I ask.

"Not a lot. Just that he was a guy on tour with the Eleven crew."

Yeah, that's what he told me too. "I think there's more to the story he's not telling us."

"He probably doesn't want to be seen as weak. Jet can put on a convincing front."

I don't want him to put on a front with me.

"Go," Ollie says. "We should take some of those shots so Jet doesn't end up in a Fijian hospital with alcohol poisoning."

Good point.

We make our way back to the table, and I drink down a shot while I hand one to Ollie. Then we take another. That should help.

Jet's surrounded by the others, so I can't get close, but when I catch his gaze, I mouth, "You okay?"

He replies by taking another shot and then lifting the empty glass in the air.

Big brother logic: they're overprotective as fuck when it comes to Jet, but they can handfeed him a shit ton of alcohol.

Confusing much?

Bitter much? a voice says in the back of my head.

It's no secret I'd rather have Jet outside, pinned against that wall.

But clearly, that's not going to happen again tonight. And if he keeps drinking the way he is, I have no hope of it happening later when we get back to our island.

Drinks flow to the point the music thrums in my veins and my head feels the right amount of fuzzy.

When Matt and Noah drunkenly stumble toward the bathrooms, I assume they're going to hook up in there, so I have some time.

I slide into the seat next to Jet and lean in close to his ear. "How are you holding up? I think I've seen you drink a gallon of tequila."

Jet inches closer and looks up at me with glassy eyes. "I'm a rock star. I could drink any of you under the table."

"You're looking kinda drunk."

"Eh. Tispy."

"Tispy?" I laugh. "Not tipsy?"

"Yeah. That. But s'all good. I drink a lot on tour. Mainly when we have good nights. I've always found drinking to escape is like a huge rabbit hole I don't want to go down, you know?"

"That ship has sailed tonight, my friend."

Jet grins. "Friend. That's cool. We can be friends. Friends who have fun."

"That's the plan … or so I've been told."

"It's a good plan."

At least we're on the same page.

I have the sudden urge to lean in and kiss his cute button nose, but I refrain.

I catch movement out of the corner of my eye, and I lift my head to see Matt and Noah on their way back. "Guess I better move."

Jet pouts. "Guess so."

"We'll catch up later back on our island. You should hang with your brothers."

He lets me go, and I make my way over to Ollie to ask him to dance some more. He has a partner who won't dance, and I have someone I can't dance with without drawing attention.

Still, song after song, my gaze can't help finding Jet's again and again.

I don't know his exact intentions with this whole 'let's have fun' thing, but at this point, I'm willing to accept whatever he'll give me.

X

In the history of the longest nights ever, this might go down as one of my top three. The first was a game in the playoffs that went into five overtime periods. The second was that night three years ago with Jet. I'd lost the Cup, I'd found a stranger who already meant more to me than my love of hockey before I even knew his name, and then we spent an incredible night together.

I remember every touch. Every word. I held on to everything he was saying because, in my eyes, he was this perfect symbol of life. And change. And fighting to be yourself in a world that rejected you.

Still, tonight is a close third.

Because all I want to do is be back there again.

When the others finally call it, I'm more than ready to get back so I can hang out with Jet.

Only, it becomes obvious he'll be in no shape to do anything. Matt and Noah hold him up, each taking one of his arms, and we're lucky we picked a time to leave while it's high tide because the ladder to the pontoon is several inches shorter than it was when we arrived.

Jet keeps insisting he's fine, but he sways on his feet. He's not the only one who's in bad shape.

Miller, the biggest guy in the group, stumbles down the few

steps and practically falls into the boat and lies across the seats. Talon climbs in after him, lifting Miller's feet to put in his lap.

It was a tight fit on the way here, and now Miller's taking up two spots. I get on next and take the seat farthest from them. If Miller can puke on a boat while sober, I don't want to be anywhere near him while he's drunk.

The other guys fill up the rest of the spots, and Jet's the last one to get on with the help of Noah who holds him, while Matt climbs in and lifts Jet into the boat.

But as soon as Matt puts his brother down, it's game on, and both he and Noah vie for the last spots. They easily beat Jet who's too slow, too sloppy, and looks confused as to what they're doing.

Realizing there are no more seats, Jet rubs his chin. "Standing room only, huh?"

I'm about to stand to offer him my seat but hesitate. That wouldn't be suspicious, would it? I mean, it's a nice thing to do, but will the others read into it?

I hate that my mind goes there because I don't want the guys on my mind when it comes to Jet.

It confuses me and makes me doubt things.

Before I can make a choice, he takes it out of my hands. His ass lands on my lap.

"Uh ..."

"It was either your lap or my brother's, and I haven't sat on Matt's lap since I was, like, two."

"Aww, baby bro, you can come sit here." Matt pats his knee.

The group snickers.

Jet shudders on top of me. "That's kinda creepy now we're adults. Besides ... this is kinda comfy." Jet stares down at me.

I expect some sort of reaction from the guys, but as I quickly glance at each of their faces, all I see is them waiting for what I'm going to do.

Now's as good a chance as any to test this out. I mean, sure, they might decide I'm not allowed to touch their precious younger brother figure and shove me off the boat halfway back to the island, but Jet is worth the risk.

And he did say I'm allowed to do anything I'm comfortable doing in front of Matt, so …

I put my hands on Jet's waist, and I think I even shock the hell out of him.

"Hey, I'm certainly not complaining." I hold my breath and wait.

"Ooh, looks like Jet's after a Daddy," Maddox says.

Yes, a joke. I can handle that.

Jet shifts on my lap. "Hmm, Big Daddy does have a ring to it."

Oh, I'm going to kill him. Jet's brown doe eyes stare at me while a smirk ghosts his lips.

"JJ," Matt growls.

Jet flips him off without taking his gaze off mine. "Calm your tits. I'm just having *fun* with *old* Soren."

"I'm not old."

"Soren and Jet hooking up makes total sense, though," Ollie says out of nowhere. I know he's excited about the possibility of Jet and me, but does he have to spell it out for everyone?

Lennon elbows his boyfriend hard.

"What was that for?" Ollie rubs his arm. "They do make sense. Soren's all heartbroken. Jet's a—"

"A what?" Matt asks. His tone suggests he doesn't actually want to know the answer.

Jet glares at Ollie. "I'm pretty sure manwhore, slut, or any variation was about to come out his mouth, but what would you know, *Oliver*?"

He glances between Lennon and Jet. "I, uh, read things."

Ollie's head quickly snaps in Lennon's direction. "And don't make a joke about my ability to even do that."

"Let me guess," Jet says. "You heard about the orgy with Adam Lambert, Brendon Urie, and Sam Smith?"

"Holy shit," I exclaim. "Did that really happen?"

"No." Jet slaps my shoulder. "And their people were not so happy with me for making a joke about it. It got printed as if I was being serious."

Ollie laughs. "I told you your mouth was going to get you into trouble one day."

"I told him that too," Lennon adds.

"Me too," everyone else says in unison. Well, apart from Miller who's now snoring.

"Damn straight," Jet says. "My mouth has serious problems with authority, nosy paps, and with people telling me what to do." He stares pointedly at his brother.

Matt shrugs him off. "Whatever. Like you ever listen to me anyway."

"I might have to move to Chicago so Wade learns how to get his way with you two."

Noah shakes his head. "Nah, he doesn't have the innocent look you do that's impossible to say no to."

Jet's mouth opens to argue, but we're ready to go, so Joni unhooks the boat from the dock and moves to the captain's chair. The engine roars to life, effectively cutting off a potential brotherly argument.

I don't understand the way Matt and Noah see Jet. Yeah, he has that innocent look, but he's far from innocent. And he's not that much younger than Matt, yet they treat him like he's fifteen.

I wonder if it's his age, his stature, or his carefree attitude that could easily be seen as irresponsibility that Matt and Noah play off.

Sometimes, I think all Jet wants is to be taken seriously, and when he's not, it makes him act out more—like what he's doing right now.

As much as I'd like this little show to be about me, I get the impression it's got everything to do with his older brother's attitude.

We hit the open water, the boat flying over the swell and making for a bumpy ride.

Every time Jet's ass brushes against my cock, I begin to wish we weren't on a boat in front of an entire group of guys. While I'm at it, I wish we were naked too.

The trip back to our island is short, which is good, because if Jet rubs against me any more, there's a good chance I'll come, and there'll be no hiding that.

Then again, it won't be easy to hide a giant hard-on either.

When we pull up to our private hideaway and the boat slows, Jet shifts on my lap again.

My hand, which has stayed on his hip the whole way, tightens. "Are you trying to drive me crazy?" I ask low in his ear.

"You totally started it by pinning me against a wall earlier and kissing me."

"Payback, eh? Are you sure you want to play that game?"

Jet taps his chin, pretending to think about it. "Oh, I'm sure."

"You know how this game ends though, right?"

"How?" Damn Jet and that innocent pout.

"With—" My gaze flies to Matt as if sensing his eyes on me. Yep, Jet's big brother is for sure plotting my murder.

"With …" Jet prompts.

I open my mouth, but Joni cuts me off.

"All set, boys."

"Guess you'll never find out now," I taunt as Jet climbs off my lap. I stand and lean in close to his ear. "But let's just say it involved minimal clothing."

Matt takes Jet's arm and helps him off the boat, throwing me a "Thanks, I've got him from here."

Yep. That sounds about right.

CHAPTER TWELVE

JET

In the light of a sober morning, I might be questioning my not so brilliant plan to have fun with Soren on this vacation. I knew it was a bad idea last night, and I know it's a bad idea now, but I'd be lying if I said knocking on the door to his hut wasn't the first thing I wanted to do when Matt woke me up to get ready for a day on the water.

Miller is too hungover to join us, so Talon's staying back with him, but the rest of us are taking the jet skis out for a spin.

I almost said no to going so I could hang out with Soren alone, but I'm not sure I can trust myself around him on my own yet. I need to know we can hang out as friends without stupid shit like feelings getting in the way. Then, maybe, I'll be able to handle the sexy type of fun I promised last night.

I climb his deck and go to knock, when my hand pauses midair.

He's almost ready to go, but his hands are moving all over his chest, rubbing in a white substance I assume is sunblock, but I'm imagining something else. His hockey-player muscled chest and tight abs ... His skin is less pink today, leaving a tanned glow. It's kinda annoying he tans easily, but just the sight of him has my brain short-circuiting.

He turns to me, a smile present, along with his trademark backward baseball cap. "Gonna knock or ..."

"Gonna move your hand lower or ..."

Damn the warm sound of his chuckle.

Soren slides open the screen door. "No. Because then you'll tell the guys I was jerking off when you came to get me, and then that'll become a running joke."

"Oh, bless your heart. That's already a running joke."

"I know. And I don't want you making it worse."

I pretend to think about that for a bit. "I might tell 'em anyway. This vacation's all about having fun after all."

"Yeah, but that's fun for *you*."

"Pretty sure if you were jerking off it'd also be fun for you."

"I wasn't jerking off," he exclaims.

"Real shame."

"Are you going to be like this the whole time?"

"Is it a problem if I am?"

"Nope. I wanted to clarify so I know what I'm in for."

"Oh, you're in for a ride, *my friend.* A roller coaster."

Soren's lips twitch. "I have no doubt about that."

"Ready to go?"

"Almost." Soren shoves a towel into a backpack. "Want me to take your towel too?"

"Thanks." I unwrap the towel from around my neck and throw it at him.

"I'm guessing you don't have a bottle of water on you." He eyes me from head to toe. "If you do, I don't want to know where it is."

"No, I don't have water."

He goes to his mini fridge and puts two bottles in his backpack. "Okay, now, we can go."

"Aww, look at you making sure I stay hydrated." I gesture for him to leave first. "After you."

"You just want to check out my ass."

"Duh. And now I don't even need to be subtle about it."

Soren puts a little more hip into his walk as he passes me, making his ass shake.

"Mmm, that's what I'm talking about."

I catch up to him and walk by his side, fighting the urge to reach for him.

"You know, if we weren't about to meet up with your brother, I might've held your hand."

What, is he a mind reader now?

"You don't know where my hand has been, so I'd rethink that." *Charming, Jet. Really charming.*

"See, now that makes me want to ask what you've been doing with it."

We round the corner to head to the beach, but my flirty retort is cut off by Matt and Noah coming from their side of the island.

"Maybe we should've stayed in today," Soren mutters so only I can hear.

"Nah, jet skiing is totally fun. Or so I've heard. I like ... riding things."

Of course, Noah overhears that last part. "Too much information, bro."

"We're talking about jet skis. Duh."

Matt glances between me and Soren but doesn't say anything.

Four jet skis. Eight people. That's the kind of math I like. All the couples pair up, leaving Soren and me to one jet ski.

Such a shame.

Soren does up his life jacket. "You want in front or behind?" His question is so serious I can't help but answer seriously. So … seriously.

"Hmm, I could go either way. I'm super versatile … on a jet ski."

"I'd prefer to be behind you, but I'm good with either too. You pick."

I put on my own jacket. "We could always flip. Take it in turns."

"Now, that sounds promising. You drive first."

Soren lifts the steering column and shuts his backpack in the storage compartment. Then he pushes the jet ski into the shallow part of the water and holds it for me to get on. He slides in behind me, his chest plastering to my back. He's so much wider than me, and with the life jackets, it feels like he's surrounding me. His legs cage me in, as well as his arms, and I have to fight the urge to lean back so I'm his completely.

Joni comes around to each of us, showing us how to work the jet skis before sending us off.

We're last, and I barely hear anything Joni says because I can feel a not-so-mysterious hardness pressing against my lower back.

But I manage to hear enough to get the thing started and to move us forward.

With everyone ahead of us creating their own mini waves, we get a bumpy ride. It reminds me of the boat trip last night.

The sun is warm as it beats down on us, but it's the heat between our bodies that's burning me up.

My cock is harder than granite, and my ass wants nothing more than to shuffle back until I'm in Soren's lap.

I tell my body to calm down and catch up to the other guys.

Damon and Maddox who are in front slow down to a stop, and the others stop beside them.

I go past them and spin, whipping us around to face them all.

"Where are we going?" I ask.

"Joni says there's a deserted island to the northwest, if we're up for it," Damon says. "Or we can stay close to shore here."

Lennon leans forward on his jet ski. "As long as this doesn't turn into an 'if you were stranded on a deserted island with your friends, who would you eat first?' kinda thing."

"Well, Miller would be the obvious choice if he were here," Maddox says. "More to go around."

"Guess it's Ollie or Matt then," I add.

"You'd kill your own brother?" Matt yells.

"Hmm, tough call."

Damon cuts in. "As much as I'd love to see how this *Lord of the Flies* reenactment would work out, the island's not that far, and we have GPS." He holds up a small, bright yellow device attached to the jet ski. "There should be no need to resort to cannibalism."

"Lord of the what?" I ask.

Damon groans. "I take it back. I vote we kill off anyone who doesn't understand that reference."

Everyone agrees.

"What happened to no need to resort to cannibalism?" I exclaim.

"Dire straits," Damon says.

I break out into Dire Straits "Sultans of Swing." Everyone looks at me weird. "Oh, sure, I'm uncultured for not knowing *Lord of the Flies*, but I sing a song that came out before all y'all were born, and I get a blank stare."

"Last ones there are buying drinks tonight," Maddox says.

Before I can point out drinks are included in the astronomical price Matt and Noah already paid for booking Joni and Ema's entire island, the others take off, leaving Soren and me in their waves.

"Competitive motherfuckers," I grumble.

"Eh, let them win," Soren says behind me. "I was thinking of having our own fun along the way." His hand sneaks under my life jacket, and his fingers bite into my skin.

"Yeah? What kind of fun?"

"Start driving and find out." His voice rumbles in my ear.

I take off, going slow.

Soren's warm breath hits my neck. "If we lag too far behind, someone's going to come back for us. Go faster."

I pull on the throttle harder and lean back against Soren even more.

His hand on my stomach moves lower and unties the knot in my board shorts. I startle and accelerate by accident, jolting us, and Soren has to reach with his free hand to hold the other side of the steering column.

"Unless you want your brother to see my hand in your shorts, you might want to slow down."

"Go faster. Slow down. Make up your mind."

"Go fast enough they can still see us coming, but don't catch up to them."

"What are you doing?"

Soren's hand dips into my trunks and wraps around my cock. "I was thinking about getting you off. You know, to help fill our fun quota. Because I cannot take another bumpy ride without touching you, and this is technically in front of your brother … so it doesn't break the rules."

Damn him and his genius logic.

"If we get flung off this thing and die, it's your fault."

He laughs. "You can say no."

"Who the fuck says no to getting off?"

"So, don't crash."

Salty air whips by us, the jet ski speeding across the flat water. Occasionally we hit a small bump, but the guys are far enough away now that we don't have to deal with their wake.

I try to concentrate on where we're going and keep an eye out for the others or any other people on boats, but the water's deserted, and we have a clear path to follow.

Soren strokes my cock teasingly from tip to root and then swipes his thumb over the head.

I shudder and bite back a smartass remark about him being a good stick handler.

With him pressed against my back and his hand on my cock, it's so easy for me to give myself to Soren, wholly and completely, and that should scare me. With one touch, I'm under his spell again, just like I was last night when he kissed me.

Just like I was three years ago—the last time he touched me like this.

As he gets a steady rhythm, there's nothing more I want to do but surrender to him, but I'm too busy trying to focus on his strokes and not crashing this damn jet ski.

Extreme sex sports. It should be a thing.

Soren's hard cock digs into my lower back, and his hips move behind me. My eyes fall shut, enjoying every overwhelming sensation his body does to me.

"I see land," Soren says.

Oh. Right. Need eyes to see so I don't kill us.

"You're running out of time," he says in my ear and then nips at my earlobe.

He jerks me harder, faster, his grip so tight it's almost painful, but it sends me higher and higher. Heat pools in my gut. It's too much.

I teeter on the edge, waiting to fall.

"Come, baby." Soren's rumble pushes me over.

I can no longer see straight, my hand slips on the throttle, and we slow right down while I moan through my release.

We come to a complete stop in the middle of nowhere.

Soren's strong arms surround me, and I relax into them. My head falls back on his shoulder, and using his hand that's not stroking me through my orgasm, he lifts my chin and brings his mouth down on mine.

So much for me not falling into the sex stuff right away. In my defense, he's *Soren.*

Just his name is enough to get me hard, and I knew the second I suggested it last night that it wouldn't take long to happen.

I reach behind me, my hand going to the back of his head and gripping his short hair.

My tongue barely has time to get in on the action when Soren pulls back. "Wha—" I ask, but I'm unable to form any more sounds.

Soren pulls his hand out of my shorts and leans over to wash my cum off in the water. "Incoming. Might want to fix yourself up."

"Huh?" I lower my head, and that's when I see a jet ski heading straight for us.

I scramble to put my cock away and abandon the idea of being able to tie my shorts back up, but at least I'm covered even if there's a very obvious wet patch against the light-yellow fabric.

Soren casually reaches for the key on the jet ski and pulls it out, killing the engine completely.

As the other jet ski approaches, Soren and I both relax when we see it's Ollie and Lennon. They kinda already know about us anyway.

"Everything okay?" Ollie asks.

"Engine stalled," Soren says casually.

Lennon doesn't buy it, probably because he's searching my heated face for the lie in Soren's words. Then he glances down. "You must've pulled your key out."

I lift the bit of plastic attached to my life jacket. "Oh. Yeah. Must've. Dunno how that happened." I put it back in and hit the button to turn the jet ski back on.

"Look at that. It works again," Soren says.

Ollie's lips twitch up in amusement. "Word of advice, if you guys don't want anyone to know there's something between you two, you might want to learn to lie better."

They take off, and we follow, reaching the island where everyone else is already on shore.

I stop short though. "I need to go for a swim. For obvious reasons."

Soren laughs and takes over the controls while I bring my legs over to one side and jump into the water. I swim around awhile as if that was my plan the whole time, not a necessity to hide the evidence of what Soren and I just did.

We explore the small island which has absolutely nothing on it except a few palm trees, thick forest we can't get through, and a giant hill we can't climb.

I'd complain about a wasted trip, but no way was anything about the ride here wasted.

When we decide to head back and Soren takes over the front seat, I settle behind him.

My hands skim up his thighs. "Maybe I can return the favor on the way home."

Soren smiles at me over his shoulder.

But as we take off, that plan goes to shit when Matt and Noah hang back.

"We'll trail you guys in case your jet ski craps out again," Matt says.

Yaaay.

Motherfucking big brothers.

CHAPTER THIRTEEN

SOREN

Either we weren't as subtle on that jet ski as I thought we were, I'm being paranoid, or Matt is suspicious. Maybe all of the above.

Since our trip out to the island, Matt hasn't left Jet's side.

When we get back, Matt whisks Jet away under the proviso they haven't had a real chance to hang out and have bro time yet.

He squeezes his way in between us at dinner.

And for some reason, he keeps bringing up Bryce as often as he can.

So, when Jet says he's beat not long after dessert, I'm surprised Matt doesn't follow him.

That was twenty minutes ago.

Waiting for enough time to pass to make a break for it goes on for way too long, and I realize I need to take matters into my own hands.

I approach Lennon and Ollie. "Hey, I think you guys are super tired and want to go to bed."

"Someone's eager to sneak into Jet's hut," Ollie says.

"Nah, I'm looking after you guys. You're my friends, and we had a big day on the water today."

They both look at me with stupid confused expressions.

"Of course, I want to sneak into Jet's cabin. If I leave first, it'll look suspicious."

They leave while telling me I owe them.

One couple down. Three more to go.

The others will be harder because I can't flat out tell them why I need them to disappear.

I approach Talon and Miller next and take the seat across from them at the table. "How did your day go?"

They both smile.

"Okay, okay, enough said." I hold up my hand before they can answer with words. "You must be tired now. Like, really tired." I yawn, hoping it's contagious.

"Nah, we napped in between," Miller says.

"Oh, so you're all recharged and ready to go again."

They look at me like I'm crazy, but in their defense, I'm basically telling them to go and have sex.

They glance at each other and then back at me.

"Are you ... like ... you know ... trying to ..." Talon starts.

I realize what he's trying to get out. "No, wait—"

"Because we weren't lying when we said we're not into threeways anymore," Miller says.

"What? No. I, uh, you know ... you guys have sex on tap, and I don't, so I'm telling you to go make the most of it. Geez. Not interested in you ... like that. Either of you."

"Good," Talon says. "And no offense, but if we were looking for a threesome, we'd go for someone with boobs."

Miller sighs. "I miss boobs."

"Really?" Talon asks.

"Well, I mean, not enough to want to go back to that, but maybe we should go watch lesbian porn or something."

Talon stands. "We have to go! Goodnight!"

Two couples down. Two left. I should be able to reasonably leave now without having to explain myself.

I stand. "I might as well head off too. Goodnight."

Matt and Noah stare at me as I leave, and I tell myself not to read into it.

They so know, the paranoid voice in the back of my mind says, but I shake it off. I'm going to get Jet all to myself when he's not mad at me for the first time in years.

I contemplate going straight to his cabin, but I have supplies in my room thanks to Joni and Ema thinking of everything.

The pessimist in me said I wouldn't need condoms on this vacation, only lube for my lonely, lonely hand.

The light in Jet's cabin is off when I walk by, so maybe he's asleep.

Maybe I shouldn't bother him.

I hate those cockblocking sons of assholes who took forever to go to bed.

I grumble my way up the stairs to my cabin and slide open the door, only to find the best thing I could've possibly walked in on.

Miles of bare skin greet me in my bed, and the sight is one I don't think I could ever get used to.

Flashbacks from the night Jet and I shared run through my mind like a porno montage.

Jet's here, in my bed, naked.

Or at least shirtless. I can't see under the sheet.

He rests up on one elbow. "Took you long enough."

"I didn't want to be the first to leave." I can't get rid of my shirt or pull my shorts off fast enough.

"Eager, are we?"

"You have no idea. I've only been thinking about doing this again for three years."

"Mmm, then I guess we have some time to make up for." Jet pulls the sheet off his naked body, torturously revealing inch by small inch of skin.

Now that he's laid bare for me and waiting, I hesitate.

"Stage fright?" Jet taunts. "It's not like we haven't done this before."

No, but it's different this time. I don't know how, but it is.

The one night I had with Jet was hot and needy. I can still remember the way he responded to me and every sexy sound that left his mouth.

"Soren?" Jet asks more seriously.

I shake my memories free. "Sorry. Got lost in a hot memory again. Seems to happen around you."

Jet's eyes rake over me and down to my cock which is hard as nails and pointing right at him as if to say *him—I pick him!*

"Must've been super-hot," Jet rasps.

"The hottest."

"Then what are you waiting for?"

What *am* I waiting for?

"Supplies," I croak.

Jet turns his head toward the bedside table. "Brought some over from my hut."

There sits the same brand of condoms and lube as in my bathroom. Joni and Ema really are the best.

"You're still standing there," Jet says.

"Maybe I like standing here. Maybe I like, no, *love*, the way you look in my bed." Lean limbs, pale skin against dark tats. My gaze travels all over him. "Maybe I want to watch you prep yourself." I move to the side of the cabin where there's a desk and lean against it.

"Oh, you think you're gonna have this ass, do you?"

"Yup."

Jet's lips press into a flat line. "I can't tell if that's bossiness or confidence."

"Both." It's neither, actually, because all I'm doing is stalling for time so when I do eventually touch him, I don't embarrass myself by coming within thirty seconds.

This feels like a momentous thing where it has to go a certain way. I want to drag it out, make it last, and I want it to be as epic as the first time we were together.

That adds pressure to what's already a confusing situation.

Jet is only willing to offer me fun, but I want to show him I have the potential to be so much more than that.

"What, you want me to beg?" Jet's pouty lip makes him look so irresistible it's not fair.

"I think we've established you don't need to beg for anything or anyone, Jet."

"You just want me to."

My cock aches. I reach for it and watch as Jet tracks my hand with only his eyes. "I want you desperate for me."

"That can definitely be arranged." Jet bites his bottom lip as he watches me stroke my cock slowly.

It's supposed to give me relief, but with the way his eyes are on me, it only makes my cock want more.

"Get the lube," I order. I'm testing him to see if he'll do as I say. I want him to trust me again like he did before I fucked things up between us.

Jet doesn't hesitate to do it, but I can't tell if it's all for show.

He's always *on*, always pretending to be someone else, but I know I got glimpses of the real Jet that first night and again in Tampa.

I want to bring that guy out.

"And?" Jet asks, one brow cocked.

"Oh, you going to pretend you don't know what to do?"

"Well, with the way some people treat me, you'd think I was some innocent and inexperienced kid."

"Smartass. Slick your cock and then cover your fingers."

He does as I say, shuddering as he applies lube to his overeager dick. I want so badly to approach and lick the precum dribbling out of his tip, but I don't.

I keep my feet planted on the floor and my ass stuck on the desk.

"Now what?" He breathes heavily.

"Roll over and face that ass toward me. I want to see you work yourself open with your fingers."

Jet lets out a muttered curse as he turns so I can see every inch of his pert, round ass. He has his cheek to the mattress, and I can see every expressive emotion on his insanely good-looking face.

One of his hands holds his ass cheek, while the other sneaks through his legs.

His middle finger circles his hole.

As he presses in, I say, "I want you to remember what it was like when it was me doing that to you. When I was the one inside you, turning you out until you couldn't talk. You couldn't breathe."

Jet writhes on the bed. His eyes squeeze shut, and his mouth hangs open.

He fingers himself, adding a second one when he's ready, and I have to grip the base of my cock to stop from coming.

Jet's the hottest thing I've ever seen—and that's fully clothed. Naked and spread open for me, he's so beautiful I can't stand it.

"You're so hot," I say.

"Fucking duh." Jet's response is all gurgled.

"You almost ready for me? I don't think you're quite desperate enough yet." I'm lying. Totally lying.

Jet grunts, deep and guttural.

This is exactly how I wanted him. He's on the brink of losing it, thinking of me, and in a minute, he's going to remember how I rocked his world three years ago.

I move toward the bedside table as quietly as possible and open a condom. I'm sheathed, lubed, and ready to go by the time I get what I want from Jet.

"Soren, please ..."

"I've got you, baby." I grip his wrist and gently pull his hand away. My knees hit the mattress behind him, and slowly, I push inside.

His ass tenses around me, but his shoulders relax and sag as if he's just been released from torture. "Go. Fuck me."

"If you insist." I put my hand on his back between his shoulder blades and hold him down.

I move all the way inside him, loving how his body gives way for me and accepts me easily.

He buries his head so he's facedown and mumbles something that sounds like "harder."

I move in and out of him, gradually increasing my pace.

I remember it being phenomenal and heated between us, but nothing—*nothing*—has ever been this good.

"Fuuuck. Oh fuck. Fuck, fuck, fuck." Jet's words would be laughable if I weren't saying the same thing in my head.

"So hot," I say again. And then again.

The muscles in his back contract with every thrust, and his skin shines with perspiration.

My hair is wet from my own sweat.

"I'm ... I'm—"

"Not yet." I pull out of him and flip him over. "I want to see your face when you come."

He lifts his knees without me having to ask, and I dive right back in.

I'm hovering above him now, staring into a pair of eyes I got lost in all those years ago, and I can't wait for it to happen again.

And again, and again, and again.

I'm not going to take what he's giving me for granted, because for all I know, he'll turn around tomorrow and say he's changed his mind.

I'm going to take my time and make blazing-hot new memories to go with the old ones.

Jet's hand goes between us, and he jerks himself off while I pound his tight ass.

When his skin flushes bright red, and his eyes roll back, I take what I've wanted this whole time—what I've wanted since the moment he arrived on the island.

The kisses Jet and I have shared here in Fiji, while as hot as I remember with him, they've been short and interrupted.

Right now, there's no one else but him and me, and as I lean down to take his mouth and taste him, I feel warm spurts of cum on my stomach.

I don't slow down for his orgasm or stop kissing him. I let him ride out his pleasure while taking my own.

Jet relaxes under me, and when he finally comes down from his high, he pulls his head back, breaking our kiss, and gives me his eyes.

Those deep-brown eyes ...

That's all it takes.

I still inside him until my orgasm passes, and even then, it takes all my strength not to collapse on top of him.

Only when I pull out of him, dump the condom, and land beside him does he make eye contact with me again.

"Guess you've still got it."

I laugh. "Guess so."

⨯

It's totally not creepy to watch Jet sleep, right?

I mean, he did say he doesn't sleep well when he's away from home, so I'm checking to make sure he's doing it right. Sleeping, that is. Because, you know, after twenty-three years, he might not know how.

Okay, I'm being creepy.

I roll onto my back and sigh happily. Jet's back in my arms, and for the first time in a long time, the world feels *right*.

His smaller body moves against me, and he moans. I don't know if he's waking up or dreaming, but it makes me smile.

That is, until there's movement outside.

It's the bright white polo shirt I see first through the small gap in the curtain covering the door. I make out the dark hair and beard next.

Fuck, fuck, fucking fuck.

It's Matt.

"Jet." I nudge his shoulder.

He grumbles and rolls over onto his other side.

My heart pounds erratically. "It's your *brother*."

Jet abruptly sits up, his head swiveling side to side as if he's looking for Matt in the room.

"He's coming up the path," I say.

He squints at me. "Maybe he's going for a walk—"

We hear Matt's feet hitting the wooden steps leading to the deck.

"Shit," Jet hisses and rolls out of bed. He frantically looks around the room before settling for crawling under the thin gap between the bed and the floor.

The blanket pooled on the ground at the foot of the bed will hide him. The heat between Jet and me being tangled in each other last night was enough to keep us warm.

My heart doesn't calm down at all as Matt raises his hand to knock. Then he sees me through the glass and waves.

I gesture for him to come in, but being naked, I don't get up.

He slides open the door and pushes the curtain aside. "Hey."

"What's up?" I try to casually run a hand over my hair as if I'm not full of adrenaline right now.

"I wanted to talk to you."

Uh-oh. "About?"

"I think you know."

Double uh-oh. "I ... umm ... well—"

"I mean, you're not blind. You have to know Jet has a crush on you."

"A ... a crush ..." What, like he's in high school?

"He hasn't told us too much about the guy on tour who broke his heart, but he's kinda fragile. I know it's not my place, and he'd kill me if he knew I was here, but I was hoping ... well, I wanted to ask ..."

Please give me permission to fuck Jet.

"That you let him down gently."

My hope sinks. Guess that was a bit of a long shot. *My brother is depressed. Please use your dick to make him feel better. Thanks for taking one for the team.*

"Let him down?"

"If he makes a move."

"Umm ... okaaay." I'm confused. "And are you assuming I

wouldn't be into Jet, or are you asking me not to be?" I hold my breath.

Matt cocks his head. "Are you into Jet? You're ... like ... *old.*"

"First, fuck you. And second, fuck you."

"I just ... I guess I don't see it. You and him. And I don't know how I'd feel if you used each other to rebound from your last relationships. That's only gonna end badly."

It's so not like that with Jet, but I can see his point. That's probably all it can be even if Jet and I don't mean it to be that way.

"I'll take your concerns under advisement." *I'll take your concerns under advisement? What kind of response is that?* "But I would like to say that Jet is an adult. He can look after himself. He's been doing it for three years."

"I know, but ... he's my kid brother, you know? I practically raised him until I left for college. I don't want to see him hurt."

For the first time since I met Jet, I see Matt's overprotectiveness as something more than an annoyance. Matt is Jet's support system.

"I won't hurt him."

Matt's eyebrows shoot up.

"If he does make a move." Ugh. So close to getting out of this without lying. Well, if hiding Jet under my bed isn't classed as lying to begin with.

"Thanks," Matt says. "What have you got planned for today? Noah and I were going to go to the mainland and do a tour or something. Apparently, there are these old cannibal caves. We keep saying we're gonna check them out every year, but, uh, we never make it." A smile crosses his face.

With Matt and Noah off our island, Jet and I could have the whole day without worrying about being caught by them.

"I think I'm going to spend the day in bed. Maybe go for a swim later."

"Cool. We'll see you tonight then when we get back."

He moves toward the door, and I give a tiny salute as he leaves.

Only when he's gone am I able to breathe properly again.

I get up and close the curtain. "Jet?"

"Yeah?" His adorably muffled voice comes from under the bed.

"He's gone."

CHAPTER FOURTEEN

JET

Jet has a crush.
A crush.
Like I'm fourteen years old.

I'd argue something about maturity, but hey, I'm crawling out from underneath the bed of the guy I'm fucking without my big brother knowing.

Soren's grinning at me when I finally pull myself up.

"Oh, fuck you." I climb back into bed, and he joins me, pulling me close to the warm body I spent all night pressed up against.

Nothing beats the awkward morning after quite like needing to hide, but if his face is any indication, I'm glad we're going the teasing route.

"You have a *crush*. On me." The arrogance all hockey players possess shines through.

"You're too old for anyone to have a crush on."

"Just because my joints think I'm an old man doesn't mean I'm not irresistible. I can still pull a guy in his early twenties. That makes me super-hot."

I can't argue with that. "Well, you are the hottest guy I've ever met in real life. Which is amazing because, you know, I've met *real* celebrities."

Soren looks at me incredulously. "I'm sorry, what? I can't have heard that correctly. I swear you said I'm not a real celebrity."

"Who's been recognized since we've been here?"

"We're in Fiji. Once we're home, you'll see how much I'm recognized."

"Okay, Roman Josi."

"Hey, I'm not Roman in New Jersey."

"Ooh, New Jersey. *Score*."

Soren frowns. "You sound like Maddox. Do you know how much he disses New Jersey? You should've been there the day he found out I was Canadian too. It was murder."

Oh, I need to hear that story. "How did he find out?"

"I said something about taking his toque off indoors."

"Rookie move."

"It was me, Bryce, Damon, and Maddox, and we went out for dinner. As soon as that word came out of my mouth, the whole table went silent. Like so silent I thought someone was stroking out. Maddox turned to me and said, 'Is there anything you'd like to share with the group? Like where you're originally from?'"

I laugh so hard I have to hold on to my stomach. "I can totally see Maddox doing that."

"Damon slumped and said, 'I've kept it from him for as long as I could. I'm sorry. He's irrational when it comes to Canada and New Jersey.' And that was all it took. Cue endless mocking."

"That's hilarious."

"Bryce wasn't too impressed. I understood it was all in good fun, but, uh, yeah, he claimed all my friends were immature frat boys. He'd said the same when we went out with Ollie and Lennon, and Lennon is the smartest of us all."

"Well, he is smart, but he's not very mature."

Soren laughs. "True."

"Bryce was dating a hockey player. What did he expect? Intellectual conversations about foreign politics?"

"Pretty much."

"Why did you date him again? Oh, wait, that's right. He was your 'hat trick.'"

He nudges me. "Shut up."

"There's the intellect talking again."

Soren cracks a smile and lifts his arm to pull me close. When his hand comes around my shoulder and I lay my head on his chest, the playfulness disappears. Like he's trying to change the subject without asking for it. But I want to know more about his ex. About why he was with him for so long and what it was that finally made them break up.

"Did you leave Bryce, or did Bryce leave you?"

Soren stiffens but covers it by shifting onto his side so he can face me. "Does it matter?"

"No, but I'm curious."

"He technically left me, but he said I hadn't been in the relationship for a lot longer, which is true."

"Were you caught off guard, or did you see it coming?"

"If we're going to have the ex talk, I need to go question for question."

I hesitate. "Okay. But you have to understand that I have an NDA in place, so there are things I can't tell you."

He purses his lips. "Like who he really is? Some backstage crew member wouldn't have you sign an NDA. Is he one of the guys from Eleven?"

"I can't—"

"It's Harley."

Oh, shit. "What the—how did you—"

"His real name is Harry."

"How ... and ..."

Soren chuckles. "I still watch your shows and read all your interviews online. I probably know more about your band and Eleven than even you guys do."

"Not all the stuff online is true."

"This is, though, isn't it?"

I shake my head even though it is true. "I can't ... I ..."

"I was surprised when Bryce first left but not after," Soren says. It takes a second for me to realize he's answering my original question. "I hadn't been present in our relationship for a long time. I thought I had to make it work because I came out for him. Coming out would be a waste if it didn't work."

"But you said you came out because of my song. Not for him ... or were you lying about that?" I don't think I could handle it if that first night was based on a lie.

I gaze into Soren's eyes, trying to find signs of deception—whatever the fuck they look like—but all I see is softness.

"Your song gave me the courage to come out, but I thought I had to do it so I wouldn't lose Bryce. In retrospect, the idea that I thought I needed to come out for someone else should've been a red flag."

I want to ask him something, but I'm scared of what his answer will be. I'm even more scared he'll see right through it and know what I truly mean. I sit up and wrap my arms around my legs as I bring them up to my chest. "Do you still love him even though you know you shouldn't?" I don't know if I want him to answer a yes or no here.

I still love Harley ... I think. I don't know. It's been over for months, but there was a part of me that always had hope. Especially when, even though we were technically broken up, we were still sneaking nights together.

Soren makes the heartache lighter. He makes me think a life without Harley is easy and possible. Whereas when Harley—or more specifically, the label and his manager—ripped out my heart, all I could think was I'd never recover.

"I don't love Bryce. I don't think I have for a while," Soren says softly.

I stare at Soren over my shoulder and wonder if this is unfair to him. Me being here. In his bed.

Soren sits up too, and his warm, large arms wrap around me from behind. "But it's perfectly okay if you still have feelings for Harley. And it's understandable. First loves are always hard to get over, and I'm not under any delusion that I could make you move on so fast."

"That's just it. I don't think Harley was my first love ..." Fuck, that did not just come out of my mouth.

"W-what do you mean?"

I turn in his arms.

Soren's expression is guarded, and I don't know if he's reading into what I said or if he's genuinely confused.

"Don't freak out," I blurt. So not the right way to start this. "You were the first guy to show me what love could be."

Soren groans. "God, don't tell me that after I treated you like shit."

"You didn't treat me like shit. At all. Yeah, you should've told me you still had a boyfriend when we met up in Tampa, but hey, you were able to pull back when you needed to. The asshole thing to do would've been to fuck me again and then tell me about Bryce. Definitely wouldn't be the first time someone's done that to me."

He goes to open his mouth again, but I cut him off.

"Hear me out, okay? I wasn't in love with you. We'd had one night together, and I'm not some delusional, naïve kid who thought that meant anything more than it was. But it was the first time I'd been with anyone where I said to myself, *This* ... this is what it's supposed to feel like. I'd hooked up with guys before, had pseudo-relationships with closeted guys back in Tennessee, but it all felt empty. That night with you showed me what an actual connection was like, so when I met Harley and experienced something similar, I always thought it was you who taught me how to love that way. Even if what we had was only a taste of the possibility."

Soren's hand cups my face. "Jet—"

"I don't mean anything else other than what I've said." I can't look him in the eye. "I just ... Even though we will walk away from here and go our separate ways, I thought you should know that."

"Thank you for telling me," he whispers.

"And that doesn't have to change this. What we're doing here. This"—I run my hand over his taut shoulder—"is fun in Fiji—"

"Title of our sex tape."

I laugh. "Oh God, no. No sex tape." Luce would kill me. The NHL wouldn't be happy with Soren either.

"Okay, no sex tape, but I want to say something."

My gaze flicks up to meet his.

"With Bryce and me, I tried to make it work for so long, but looking back, I think I know the moment it was doomed to fail."

"When?" My throat feels like sandpaper.

"The morning after Tampa. I felt it too. Everything you did. I thought we could be so much more than what we had. You know what I told myself three years ago when you walked out of that hotel room in New York after you'd told me to call Bryce?"

I shake my head.

"That even though I'd rather be calling you, I was making the right choice. You were about to chase your dream. You were young, and I didn't want to stand in your way. For that whole year, I watched your band and following grow, and I knew I'd done the right thing. But then in Tampa ... I realized watching you play and hanging out with you was more fun than anything I'd done with Bryce in the previous twelve months. I wanted you when I shouldn't have, which made me run away. And then I stayed with Bryce out of guilt. He knew it too. Guilt over coming out for him, guilt over screwing him around, but worst of all, guilt over leading you on."

"As much as it pains me to admit, you didn't lead me on. I jumped to all the wrong conclusions when you turned up to my gig."

"I figured I couldn't live with hurting you for no reason, so I tried to make Bryce a good enough reason. I fought my draw to you, but you've always been there at the back of my mind and in my internet searches."

"Oh, honey, if your search history is all me, we're gonna need to hook you up with some good porn sites."

Jokes are good. Comedy dims the seriousness of our admissions.

Whatever this connection I have with Soren is, it's too strong to fight. It's too much to handle, and I'm still terrified of walking away from this with a double broken heart.

How many times can it break until I'm completely ruined?

Soft lips land on my shoulder and trail up to my neck. "I have an idea."

"If it involves more of your lips on me, I have to say I'm on board." Even if I shouldn't be.

There's no point trying to hold back. The pull I have toward Soren is insurmountable.

"It does include my lips on you. And certain other body parts. Maybe your cock in certain parts of me." More kissing my neck. More soft caresses.

Yeah, there's no fighting what I have with Soren.

"Hmm, my cock in your mouth?" I ask.

"We could do that, but I was thinking of something else."

"What could you possibly mean?" I feign innocence.

Soren grunts. "You want to fuck me or not?"

I tackle him, pushing him onto his back and climbing on top of him. "That would be a *hell yes*. In case this wasn't obvious." I gesture between our bodies and drag my hard cock along his.

The way Soren's body feels against mine is almost lyrical. He's always been a muse for me—a tap for my heartache and insecurity but with that touch of hope and optimism.

We kiss and drag it out, starting slow and taking the time to enjoy each other.

By the time I move down his body to get him ready, we're both panting.

Soren reaches for the lube on the bedside table and throws me a condom. "I don't need much prep."

"That's what they all say. Then they complain when they get an ass full of this." I grab my dick.

Soren laughs. "I do need prep, but I ... I just want to feel you."

I kiss the head of his cock. "You will."

Guess now that I'm giving in to this, I'm gonna go all out.

I suck his cock into my mouth while I stretch his hole.

I know he said his preference is to top, but he's a pro at letting my fingers inside. His ass contracts around them as if wanting me deeper.

My lips release him and then trail over his thigh to his sac.

"Jet, fuck." His whole body tightens, and for a second, I reckon he's about to come.

When I look up into his eyes, he breathes deep.

"I'm good, but that was close. I need your cock."

Ngh. The words he says.

Rolling the condom on, I give him a chance to come back down from the edge.

Yet, even though he says he needs me, when my tip pushes past his tight ring, he winces.

"You good?"

"Keep going. You know what they say, the burning is good."

"That's not what my doctor says."

Soren winces again. "Can you maybe not make me laugh while you're inside me? Thanks."

"Are you sure you're all good?"

"Yes. I need … more. Give me more."

The pressure surrounding my dick could kill me if I keep going, but I do as he says. I just go really, really slow.

That brings other problems though. Like focusing on Soren's face as he takes more of me. The heat in his gaze. The want in his flushed cheeks. The adoration in his half-smile.

Nope, nope, nope.

Love hearts are trying to fill my eyes again. I can feel them trying to blind me to what the truth of this is—something with no future.

We both know this.

"I have an idea." I pull out of him and fall to the bed. "Face the wall."

Soren rolls onto his side and bends his top leg.

I enter him again, pushing in the tightest hole known to man, but now with him facing the other way, I can pretend for a moment it's not Soren. My Soren.

And that works for a while.

I'm able to imagine the brown hair in front of me belongs to some random fan and prepare myself for the inevitable emptiness that will come once we've both gotten off.

I've never, ever, been the type of person to equate sex with love. For me, in my world, the two don't correlate. But when I'm with Soren, even that first night, it's hard to separate the two.

It's easy to confuse this consuming lust with something deeper when it's not.

It *can't* be.

Yet, when Soren calls out my name and lifts his arm to reach behind him and wrap it around my neck, it's even easier to put that confusion aside and let go.

I get lost in him.

Drowning in his body.

In everything Soren.

Which is why what we're doing is so dangerous.

CHAPTER FIFTEEN

SOREN

Jet and I pull ourselves out of bed midafternoon, and that's only because our stomachs rumble with hunger.

After almost an entire day in bed with Jet, walking around the island without touching stings a little.

"Hey, do you think Joni and Ema gave the other guys condoms too?" Jet asks. "We're gonna run out. We should sneak into their rooms and steal them."

"That won't be suspicious if they go missing."

"They probably don't even know they're there. They wouldn't have looked. They're all committed and lovey and crap and most likely go bareback."

I have to smother a moan because the word *bareback* coming out of Jet's mouth should be illegal. "Are you proposing we *Mission Impossible* them out of there? You know what we could do?"

"What?"

"Ask Joni and Ema if they have any more."

"Well, that sounds a lot less fun, but okay."

The island is quiet again, and I wonder if everyone went to the mainland with Matt and Noah or if they're all in their rooms having an afternoon nap.

We enter the main house, and Ema immediately comes down from upstairs. I wonder if they have some sort of sensor when someone's approaching or if Joni and Ema have ninja senses.

"I thought you boys might have gone to the mainland seeing as you've been absent all day." She says this with a warm smile, but I can hear the inquisitiveness too. *Where have you been?*

"We've been hanging out," Jet says. "Our appetites brought us out of hiding."

"What would you like to eat?"

"Anything," I say. "I could eat a horse."

"Leave it to me," Ema says and goes into the kitchen.

Jet leans in. "I have something you could eat that's as big as a horse's."

I snort. "I need actual food."

"Hey, cum is totally full of protein."

A loud crashing sound comes from the kitchen.

"I reckon she heard me," Jet says.

"You know, your brother didn't seem entirely opposed to the idea of us. And clearly, Ema knows something's going on. Ollie and Lennon know. Maybe we should tell the other guys?"

If Jet's face is anything to go by, he doesn't like that idea. "Is there really any point? You don't think when we go back to our normal lives they won't give us sympathetic stares and do the whole 'How are you doing since the big breakup?' And no matter how many times we tell them it wasn't a breakup because you need to be in an actual relationship to break up, that they won't still look at you like 'Aww, poor baby is heartbroken.'"

"That's an oddly specific scenario."

"I just don't see the point."

"Uh, so that when they do find out, I don't get my ass kicked by the entire offensive line of the Chicago Warriors?"

Jet makes a "pfft" noise. "Three guys is hardly the entire offensive line."

"Oh, sure, because three NFL players aren't scary on their own. Plus, Noah. Plus, maybe Maddox. Damon would have to stay neutral because Matt and I are both his clients. If we're up front about it, there'll be a lot less backlash than if they find out another way."

Jet hesitates, and I wish he'd tell me why he's so reluctant. I should be the reluctant one. It's my ass that's going to get kicked.

"I'll think about it," he says.

I guess that's all I can ask for.

After lunch, we go our separate ways to get changed into our swim trunks and casually meet at the pool at separate times in case anyone is there.

They're not.

"Mmm, got the whole pool to ourselves." Jet waggles his eyebrows.

"Hey, you're the one who doesn't want anyone finding out about us, so you need to keep your hands to yourself. Any of them could come by at any minute."

"Fine. If that's the way you're gonna play." Jet drops his towel on a pool chair.

I expect him to jump right in, but instead, he stares at me with a gleam in his eye. He unties his board shorts and shimmies them down his thighs, revealing teeny, tiny Andrew Christian pride bikini bottoms.

"You did that on purpose."

"Did what?" With a practiced innocent look, Jet bends over to pick up the bottle of sunblock he brought with him.

"You're a fucking tease," I growl.

"You love it."

I do, but that's not the point. "I love it when I can do something about it, not—" I stare down at my hard cock.

Jet laughs as I rearrange myself, and he applies sunblock. That makes my predicament even worse.

"You know, I totally thought you'd be out of steam after last night and today, Big Daddy."

I point at him. "No. That is not catching on, and it's not a thing."

"No problem, Big D."

Another protest almost passes my lips, but then I really think about it. "Hmm, actually I can live with that."

"Of course, you'd like that one."

"Naturally."

Jet's still laughing when Ollie and Lennon appear out of nowhere.

"Did you guys get Matt's message?" Ollie asks.

I cock my head. "Message? I thought we weren't allowed phones."

Ollie hands his over. "Turned off all social media. But apparently, it's time to put our money where our mouths are."

There's a photo of all the others outside an ice-skating rink. They've captioned it "May the best athletes win."

"They're in Suva, and they found an ice-skating rink, so they've rented the whole place out for us tomorrow."

"They're seriously challenging us to a game of hockey? For real?"

"I'm assuming there's stipulations, but yup."

"Oh, I am so there." I give Ollie his phone back, and he raises his other hand for a fist bump.

"What are you guys up to?" Lennon asks.

"We just had some lunch. Now we're going swimming." How Jet manages to make that sound dirty, I have no idea.

"You guys were going to fuck in the pool, weren't you?" Ollie asks.

"Eww. I refuse to swim in jizz," Lennon says.

Jet squeezes his eyes shut and mutters to himself. "It's too easy a shot. Do not take it."

Lennon throws his towel at Jet, smacking him in the face. "No fucking in the pool."

"Do handjobs count in that?" Jet asks.

"Yes," Ollie and Lennon say at the same time.

I climb into the pool, using the steps off to the side. "You guys are no fun."

"Jet's a bad influence on you," Ollie says.

"Why do people think you're all humble and innocent?" Jet asks. "The things you've done to me—"

Lennon blocks his ears. Ollie looks horrified.

I laugh. "I take it back. You guys *are* fun."

Jet runs and jumps into the pool, cannonballing right next to me.

I flick the water from my hair and glare at Jet. "You're asking for it."

"What if I am?"

I pounce, but I'll give him one thing—the rock star is fast. He manages to evade me but not for long. Wrapping my legs around his waist, I pull him under with me.

Bad idea. Skin on skin, his tiny swimsuit taunting me, and visions of the last twelve hours of being in bed with him, my body thinks it's time for another round.

"Is this all you two are gonna do all day?" Ollie asks when Jet and I come up for air.

Jet wraps himself around me. "Nah. Seeing as we're not allowed to fuck in here, I reckon we'll be leaving soon."

"Really soon," I agree.

Ollie smiles this time.

"What?" I ask him.

"Nothing, man. You look happy."

Jet and I share a glance, and his lips pull tight. He turns to Ollie. "Well, duh. Sex makes you happy."

I'm a little offended he thinks him making me happy has only got to do with sex.

I grab Jet's hand and pull him toward the steps of the pool. Turning to Ollie and Lennon, I ask, "Can you guys cover for us tonight at dinner? We're not going to make it."

Jet's in obvious agreement because he walks right past his things and heads in the direction of our cabins.

Yeah, he makes me happy. Even if he's not ready to accept that.

As soon as we enter the ice rink the following morning, I take a deep breath.

Ah, there's the smell of home ... with a touch of coconut. Seriously, how does everything smell like that here?

I'm used to smelling the ice with a side of man sweat that no one should ever have to endure.

We're fitted with shitty skates, and there's a bucket of old hockey pads and equipment for us to use.

We leave the pads for now because Ollie and I can't get out there fast enough. By the end of the season, I need a break from everything hockey, but a month later, I crave flying across freshly resurfaced ice again.

I chase Ollie around the rink, and we both skate around the others who try to get their bearings.

"Sorry, who are the ultimate athletes again?" I taunt Damon. "Baseball players, right? I think that's what you said."

Ollie approaches and uses a hockey stop to shave ice all over us. Maddox flinches as if he expects Ollie not to stop in time.

"We never said we had to be good at your sport," Damon says. "Just that we could manage to do it."

I skate backward while Damon and Maddox push forward, holding on to each other for dear life. "Is this you managing it?"

I'm beginning to wonder if most of this group's communication is expressed through our middle fingers because two are pointed my way.

"You don't have to worry about us, but those two seem to have it handled." Damon nods in Lennon and Noah's direction. Matt's holding on to the side, too scared to push off.

Lennon's surprisingly coordinated for someone who can't even dance. He puts his arms wide and pulls himself into a spin.

Who knew that nerd could be so graceful?

As I think that, he loses his balance and almost falls.

I turn back to Damon and deadpan. "I'm scared."

Distracted by the thrill of being back on the ice, I don't notice Jet still off to the side. He's in the stands, biting his bottom lip.

I skate over to him. "Never skated before?"

He shakes his head.

"Didn't you used to work as a game DJ for Ollie's team?"

"I know I sucked at that job, but I didn't realize I was so shit that I was supposed to do it on the ice and not in the booth."

"Smartass. I mean you had to be around the rink a lot. You never skated?"

"Didn't know how to."

I hold out my hand. "Come on. I'll take you around."

"If I break an arm, my label will be pissed."

"If you break an arm, *I'll* be pissed. I kinda like your arms."

Jet grimaces. "That's a weird thing to say."

"You're a weird thing to say."

He's holding back laughter, I can tell. "Who's supposed to be the mature one here?"

"Age has nothing to do with maturity. Look at those two." I point to Talon and Miller who are skating around competently, Miller behind Talon and holding his waist while Talon holds his arms out screaming, "I'm king of the world!"

"Point taken." Jet takes a hesitant step toward the ice. "You won't let me fall?"

My fingers intertwine with his. "Never."

He doesn't need to know I mean in general.

The first step onto the ice is shaky, and he tries to overcompensate by leaning forward, which makes him fall into me.

My free arm goes around his back. "See. I've got you."

And what I've realized is this is a total loophole in the whole "no touching Jet in front of his brothers" rule.

As much as I'd love to have the ice to ourselves, this is the next best thing—holding his hand under the excuse of not letting him fall.

I pull back and trail my hand down Jet's arm, joining our fingers on that hand too.

Skating backward, I pull Jet along with me.

His eyes are wide and terrified, and he keeps glancing between me and his feet.

"Look at me," I say.

He does.

"Trust me."

"How can I when you're going backward and not even looking?"

"I do this for a living. Plus, we're skating at a snail's pace. If I hit anything, we're not going to fall."

Jet lets me pull him along for a lap or two, but whenever I suggest he push with his feet, he says, "I'm good with this."

He's got good balance, only wobbling on occasion. He could easily pick up the basics, but while he's touching me and staring into my eyes, I'm good with just doing this too.

After a few more laps, Jet stops alternating looking between me and the ground and glances at the others who have all picked up a little more skill thanks to Ollie. Whether he's showing them how to skate or taunting them so their egos and competitive natures come out to make them focus harder, I'm not sure.

"Okay, I want to skate now," Jet says.

I grin. "You are skating."

"I want to learn to skate on my own."

"What you want to do is put weight on your right foot and push backward. Bring it back to center. Then do the same with the left."

He takes instruction well, and as suspected, he picks it up easily, but he's still overcompensating and almost falling at times.

If I was anything like my father while he was teaching me to skate, I'd tell Jet falling is a part of hockey, so he should do it and get it out of the way.

If it weren't for my Canadian pride coursing through my veins, I'm sure I would've grown up terrified of the ice after the way my dad coached me.

He was the typical tough love kind of dad. Huge hockey fan. Would've gone pro himself if he had the talent, which he liked to complain about all the time. He had skills, and he was a great coach, but the NHL wasn't his fate.

He coached my high school team, and after I made it to the

NHL, he took the chance at private coaching, using my rep to gain clients.

He's retired now, he and mom living the relaxed life of a retired couple, traveling the world.

"What are you smiling at?" Jet asks.

I'm smiling? "I'm thinking how lucky you are that I take after my mom. If I was like my dad, I'd leave you in the middle of the ice and tell you to get yourself back to the gate."

Jet wobbles again. "But you won't, right?"

I pull him closer to me so fast that he doesn't have time to freak out or register that he might fall. My arm goes around his back, and I hold him to me. "I promised I wouldn't, and I don't make empty promises."

His brown eyes stare up at me.

Our breaths mingle.

Our chests rise and fall in sync.

I want nothing more than to lean forward and kiss him, but doing that and finding a way to explain how that'll teach Jet to skate will take some thought.

A loud whistle echoes through the empty rink.

Jet's skate slams into mine as he turns toward the noise.

I hold on to him tighter.

"We doing this or what?" Ollie asks from the other side of the rink.

"Yeah, I'm definitely going to sit this one out," Jet says.

"Figured." I pull him to the gate so he can go sit in the stands and watch.

Matt decides to sit out too.

"What, they don't have ice skating in Tennessee?" Ollie taunts.

Jet and Matt share a look that screams childhood issues. I know of some of them from what Matt has said, but to say the least, their parents weren't the "let's take the kids skating" type of parents.

We put on the pads, which are half falling apart, and take the hockey sticks, which are light and flimsy. But beggars can't be choosers, and I'm just happy to be back on the ice again.

"How are we doing this?" I ask.

"All of us against you and Ollie," Damon says.

I count. "Six on two?"

"I've seen that porno," Talon says.

"You've probably *lived* that porno," Noah points out.

Talon and Miller smile.

They huddle in a group, but all the planning in the world won't help them.

They're not bad on skates, but chasing a puck? It's laugh-worthy. Ollie and I basically don't even have to try.

We could sit in the stands and watch these guys fall over themselves on their own.

Instead, we skate circles around them.

"Ready to admit defeat?" Ollie asks.

"Never," Talon yells and then trips over his skates and hits the ice hard.

"Okay, yeah," Damon says. "Before you guys break any of my players."

"Hey, we didn't even touch you," I argue.

"We didn't have to." Ollie skates up to me and throws his arm around my shoulder. Then he starts singing "We Are the Champions" at the top of his lungs. Badly.

"All right," Damon says. "How about you two play against each other?"

Fun fact: give an athlete an opportunity to kick ass, it's impossible to turn down.

I nudge Ollie. "Oh, it's on."

The sun is setting, reflecting off the water on the boat ride home, the cool breeze is kicking in again, but the mocking and gloating don't stop.

"Tomorrow, you two fuckers have to play football," Talon says and rubs his shoulder where he fell.

Ollie doesn't miss a beat before saying, "Bring it."

"Why are you so smug?" Jet asks. "You got beat by an old man."

"Hey," I protest. "He got beaten by the *better player*, thank you very much."

"Sure thing, Big Daddy," Maddox says.

"No. That is not becoming a thing."

"Would you rather still be called Canada?" Maddox asks.

Jet gasps. "Canadian Big Daddy."

I can't even be mad. He's too adorable as he blinks at me and pulls that innocent face I can't resist.

If only I could put my arm around his shoulders and pull him close to me.

"I have a question," Maddox says. "When you're talking, how do you decide if you finish the sentence with an *eh* or an *ohhh!*"

"First, your Canadian and New Jersey accents are still appalling. Two, SNL isn't an accurate depiction of how we talk in New Jersey. And three, the answer is always eh ... *eh*?"

Maddox laughs hard, but he's the only one. Hey, it's entertaining to him, so he can have at it. If I can't laugh at myself with him, then I'm taking life too seriously.

Joni pulls the boat up to the dock back at our island. "Come on, Canadian Big Daddy."

"You guys have even got Joni saying it now? I hate you all."

But I'm lying. Outside of being with Jet, today's been the best time I've had on this vacation so far.

Walking up the small pontoon and beach, I'm too busy looking back at Maddox who's still talking shit that I don't see Jet stopped in front of me.

I run into the back of him, and his body is stiff.

The rest of the guys notice and pull up short.

Standing on the pathway up ahead, there's a tall guy in a business shirt and pants. Shades on, hands in his pockets, intimidating posture. Graying hair glints in the fading sun.

"Who's—" I go to ask but am cut off by Matt.

"Is that the ex-boyfriend?"

Jet sighs. "Worse. It's my manager, Luce."

CHAPTER SIXTEEN

JET

"You're a long way from home." I feign my usual Jet-ness in front of everyone.

I have no idea why Luce is here, but I know it can't be good. He knows everything about me and Harley and orchestrated canceling our part of the tour. If he's here, it can only mean one thing.

Something's happened.

Luce's usual casual but firm toughness is missing and is replaced by fury. "You had one job, Jay. Lay low and stay out of the spotlight. Now there's video of you in a gay bar, singing an *Eleven* song, for crying out loud—"

"Hey, that's *my* song," I correct. "And, wait, there's video?"

I knew I shouldn't have joined that band on stage the other night.

"It's *everywhere*," Luce says. "I'm surprised you haven't seen it."

"My brother made us turn off social media."

I feel the shift in the group around us, but I ignore it. Whether it's over the fact "Someone Else's Perfect" is my song or because my manager is here and I'm in trouble, I don't know.

"I don't get what the problem is. I wrote that song, and if Harley is trying to pull some copyright bullshit—"

"He's trying to pull you back on tour and back into the unhealthy grasp he has on you," Luce yells.

"Dude!"

Luce knows about my NDA.

"Jay, you and Harley are about the worst-kept secret in Hollywood right now," Luce says. "Hope your vacation was long enough because he's making you come back."

"Who died and made Harley the fucking pope?"

"Since when does Jet follow what the pope says?" Noah mumbles.

I ignore him. This can't be happening.

Harley cannot do this to me.

"The label wanted us apart. They got their wish. There's no way they want me to come back."

"Harley is throwing a full-on diva tantrum about it. Says you've got to get your ass back or he's walking. He'll refuse to go onstage."

"Oh, so he can threaten the label when it comes to having me as his side piece but not when it has to do with him coming out?"

"I can't believe you were fucking one of the guys from Eleven," Maddox says.

Shiiit. I turn to the guys. "You guys can't say anything. It'll be both our asses if it gets out to the public."

The whole group looks at me as if I've offended them in some way.

Talon gestures between them all. "Kid, you think we don't know how to keep a secret, thank you very much?"

Oh. Right. All have been closeted athletes at some point. "Sorry. I just—"

"I'm sorry for overstepping, but I assumed you told your big brother figures." Luce turns to them. "Hi, I'm Luce. I'm the one who keeps him in line while he's away from you guys." He assesses each of them. "You have to be Matt." He shakes my brother's hand. "I've seen photos."

Meanwhile, I'm seething. "This is bullshit."

Luce turns his attention back to me. "This is serious, Jay. They're talking breach of contract."

"Because he sang two whole songs in a bar?" Soren asks beside me, seemingly as pissed off as I am.

"No. Because there are photos of him partying, drinking, singing, and doing everything he wouldn't be doing if he had serious nodes. I gave you an out, and now we both have to go groveling to the label and Eleven. Not to mention Benji and Freya have both called me asking me what's going on."

My bandmates know about Harley, just like I know they're on and off together, but we don't talk about it. I feel bad for running away without an explanation, but I needed out. I needed away from that environment where Harley kept coming to me and I kept taking him back.

As much as I didn't want to continue after he decided to marry a woman for show, I was scared that I didn't have the strength to say no if I stayed.

"I can't ... I can't go back." Tears pool, threatening to fall, and fuck that guy for making my eyes leak. "I'll pay to get out of that contract."

Luce scoffs. "You can't afford it. Even with 'Someone Else's Perfect' royalties."

Matt steps forward. "Then we'll pay."

"No," I snap.

Noah grips my shoulder. "Don't let your pride get in the way here. If you don't want to go back on tour, we can make that happen."

He's right that it's my pride not letting them bail me out. I've never wanted to take advantage when the rest of our family does it to Matt so often. But it's not just the money. I also don't want Harley to know I had to get my big brother to protect me from him.

"It's my mess," I say. "I'll … I … I need a minute to think." I walk away from all of them without so much as a backward glance.

Of all the footsteps to follow me, there's only one person I could see right now without losing it, and I hate to say it, but Soren's not him. It's Luce.

I'll never admit it to my manager, but he knows how to handle me.

It's a relief when it's Luce's voice behind me. "Jay …"

"Come on. You can lecture me all you want. I just need to get away from them."

"Aren't they all like family?"

"Exactly."

Luce laughs. "Ah. Gotcha."

We enter my hut, and I close the screen door behind us.

My chest is heavy, my brain foggy, and every inch of me vibrates in frustration. "What are we gonna do?"

"Well, first, how about a proper hello?" He holds out his arms for a hug, and I go willingly.

Luce is more than the guy who keeps us in line. He's also my friend. His partner is too.

"How mad is Marty?" I ask after I step back.

"He understands. Though I was pissed our sudden vacation lasted all of five days."

"Fucking Harley."

"About that." Luce puts his hands in his pockets and looks down at his feet.

"What is it now?"

"I found something out. About his fiancée."

"What?"

"She's in on it. We thought ... well, I thought he'd picked some random fan and decided to play this whole charade without clueing her in, but it turns out, she knows. Like you, she has a full-on NDA in place, and she knows he's gay. It's completely fake."

"Is that supposed to make me feel better? Is it supposed to make me go running back into his arms only to watch him in public with *her*? No. I'm not gonna do it."

Luce leans his large frame against the desk in the corner of the hut. "I'm not suggesting you do. But I thought it might be easier to see him knowing he's as miserable as you are because of something out of your control."

This is when I get mixed feelings about the whole thing. It's not Harley's choice to stay closeted. The label threatens his career, convinces him he won't make it as a *gay* solo artist, and then they go with the threat that brings nearly every artist to their knees—breach of contract.

It's enough to pull anyone in line.

I love music, and I love having fans, but I've yet to meet a musician who's one hundred percent happy with their label. Although, that could be because most of the artists I meet are with Joystar too.

They're a big fat corporation who only looks at the bottom line—how we can fill their pockets with millions of dollars.

"I don't get it," I say, exasperated. "There's five of them. Why can't Harley come out? There are four other guys in Eleven that girls can be obsessed with. Let the gay kids have someone. *Please.*"

"Oh, wow, you really have had Harley goggles on. You think he's the only queer one of those boys?"

My immediate response is to protest that, but what am I basing my opinion on? The endless tabloids of each of the boys, putting them with the latest *it* girl. I've hung with all of them, and they've all played the part. Well, except for Ryder, but that's because he has his baby on tour with him most of the time, so whenever he's not on stage, he's with her.

"My gaydar is on the fritz. I used to be able to pick out a straight gay guy with one look. Even in a strip club with tits in his face."

"Why would you be in a girly bar?"

"Tennessee."

"Oh, enough said. Well, yeah, the entertainment industry skews anyone's gaydar. The obviously gay ones are straight and the straight ones are gay, and don't get me started on the ones that swing every which way. We need to come up with some sort of codeword like back in the day where they'd ask if you're a friend of Dorothy's."

"Like when you were a teenager?"

Luce ignores my jab. He's really good at that. It's why he manages the band so well. "My point is, we both know Harley's the most popular. He writes some of their songs and is the main focus in their videos, so out of all the boys, he's the one they least want to come out because he'll make them money long after Eleven splits. Which we know is inevitable."

"The only reason Harley is the most popular is because he's an attention whore. He wants to be the Justin Timberlake. The

Robbie Williams. I'm surprised Harley and I even worked as a couple. Two egos as big as ours shouldn't even be in the same room let alone share a life together."

"I know when you're using humor as a defense mechanism, hon."

See, Luce gets me. Where Matt and all his friends are like big brothers to me, Luce is more like the father figure I never had, even if he's only eleven years older than me.

"Damn you."

"You love me."

"I love Marty more."

"Oh, you're lucky he couldn't come here to drag your ass back to the States. You know how blunt he can be."

It's true. He's unapologetically blunt. Though, unlike me, most of the time, Marty doesn't mean to be.

"I'm sorry I almost gave you a vacation and then took it away from you."

"We still had a good break. Went home. Saw family. It was more than what we were supposed to get, so ..." He shrugs. "But we do have to go back."

"I know we do, but how's this for an option? We don't."

"Hmm, decent idea, but I think I have a better one. We do."

"But we could not."

"Jay ... you know what will happen if we don't. We'll be sued, your career will be over, and all that money you've earned these last few years? Bam, tied up in lawyer bullshit."

"I don't want to leave Fiji. I don't want to leave ..." I almost say Soren.

He makes me forget. He distracts me. Takes care of me. Doesn't take my attitude.

"Don't want to leave what? Or is it a who?" Luce asks.

The sound of someone coming up the steps of the hut has me lighting up. I already know it's him without looking.

I turn, and he's standing there, all tall and Soren-like. Soft features and strong body. Stubble because he hasn't shaved since we got here.

"Hey," he says through the screen door. "I'll leave you to business, but I wanted to make sure you're okay."

See—he takes care of me. Actually cares if I'm upset.

I try to hide the stress Luce showing up has caused. "I'm fine. Thank you. We, uh, you and I ... we'll have to talk and stuff—"

Soren puts up his hand. "It's all good. Take your time."

"I ..." I glance at Luce and then back at Soren, and that must tip Luce off because he moves in behind me and whistles.

"Whoa. Yeah, I can see why you don't want to leave."

I elbow Luce in the gut. "Ignore Luce. He drinks."

Both Luce and Soren laugh. They know I'm lying.

"I'll swing by your hut in a bit."

Soren nods and leaves.

"Damn, his ass is even better than his face," Luce says, and I elbow him again, while I hear Soren chuckle on his way next door. "Quit it." Luce rubs his stomach.

"You have a man. Leave that one alone."

"Can I point out you've been mocking me for my age? That dude can't be far off ..."

"He's still younger than you, gramps." Even if it's only by one year. I don't say that though.

"Who is he?" Luce asks.

"Who is he? Who do you think he is?"

Luce's eyes widen. "He's 'Someone Else's Perfect' and 'Hat Trick Heartbreak'?"

"Yup."

"I'm screwed here. There's no way you're gonna come back on tour with that kind of baggage hanging around."

"That kind of baggage is nothing. We're just having fun. It's not serious." And maybe if I keep saying it out loud, the twenty-year-old romantic inside me will quit telling me it could be so much more.

"You wrote two songs about the guy. Two highly emotional songs. You haven't written any about Harley."

"That you know of."

"Have you?"

"Well, no, but not for lack of inspiration. More like because I know the label will never go for 'Romeo and Julien, locked in a cage. Ripped apart by fucking labels, watching me drown on stage.'"

"Okay, yeah, they'll never go for that."

"Exactly."

We both stare at each other with the same question in our eyes. How am I going to handle seeing Harley again?

"Do you want to hire a bodyguard to babysit you so you don't fall into Harley's trap and keep letting him back into your bed?"

"I'm not that weak." But even my protest sounds weak. I'd like to think now that everything has changed—Harley getting married, me and Soren … being me and Soren—that I wouldn't fall into old patterns, but I know from experience how easy it is to fall when it comes to Harley.

"Jay …"

"Luce," I mimic.

"All I'm saying is if the asshole is forcing you to go back, the least you can do is make sure he doesn't get to use you anymore."

"I know that's what it looks like to you, but Harley and me … we're not like that. What we had was real."

"Yeah, really toxic. You couldn't be together, but you still wouldn't leave each other alone. You both need to move on."

"That's why I'm here. I want to move on, but how can I when he keeps dragging me back in?"

I can't believe this is happening.

I'm going back.

I have to face Harley again.

CHAPTER SEVENTEEN

SOREN

Jet's leaving already.

Just when I thought this vacation had turned around, it's cut short by the only light in it walking away.

I know he has to. It's his job.

If a hockey player is traded, we have no choice in moving or not. It's in our contracts, and work always comes first.

I stare at the ceiling of my cabin, my hands under my head, and try not to think about it. Which means I only think about it more.

He'll go back on tour where he'll see Harley every day. He'll be near him, with him ... most likely, he'll go back to him because I know he's not over him.

After a few days together, I have no right to Jet, but I was hoping we'd get more time to figure this out.

Bryce said I wasn't in our relationship—not completely—and I think it's because I've always had a what-if floating around my head.

What if I'd chased after Jet three years ago?

There's a knock at my door. It's not locked, but I get out of bed anyway because I'm only in boxers, and I might be playing dirty. If he leaves me here, he'll miss my abs. I know he will.

And yep, as soon as I slide open the door, Jet's brown eyes are on my naked torso, taking me in from my neck to the V leading to something else that's very happy to see him.

"Good news," he says.

"You don't have to go?" I sound way too excited about that.

His face falls. "Oh, no. Sorry." Jet reaches into his pocket. "Ema came by while we were out and restocked." He holds up two condoms.

"But you're still leaving."

"Yeah," he says quietly. "I wish I could stay, but we have tonight, maybe tomorrow too, so …" Jet waves the condoms in the air.

"We could do that. Or we could talk about how you have to see Harley again."

"You don't want to talk about that."

"Well, no, but I want to know where your head's at."

"My head is at Harley being a giant dickweed, and I'm pissed he's making me do this."

I pull him in for a hug because as much as I'd love to undress him and make him forget, he needs support right now, not someone mauling him. Sex will make him feel good temporarily, but his problem will still remain.

His hands trail down to my ass.

"Jet," I warn.

"Please? Please don't make me face it yet."

I worry this is some defining moment and that if I do the wrong thing here, it will cement our future. If I give in and take away his pain by momentarily distracting him, that's all I'll ever be to him—*temporary*.

I need to be more than that in Jet's life.

I kiss him softly but keep it controlled, taking it slow and letting my tongue move against his.

When his hand makes its way between us and rubs over my aching cock, I know I need to pull back.

"That's all you're getting from me."

His eyes crack open. "What?"

"I'm serious. We need to talk this out."

"Why? We're not about feelings and all that bullshit. You're supposed to be making me forget love and all the crap that goes with it."

Good to know where he's at. "Since when?"

He waves a hand around. "I don't know. Since there's too much going on in my head right now, and I don't need any more man trouble."

"I want to be the opposite of trouble for you. I want to be there for you. I want you to talk to me." I lead him over to the bed to sit.

Jet stays standing, and I pull him between my legs. My hands make quick work of his jeans, but before he steps out of them, he stares down at me with a smug expression.

"I didn't realize pants weren't a requirement for talking."

"I want you to stay in here with me tonight. We'll get Ema to bring us some food, eat in bed, and chill. But we are going to be talking."

Jet doesn't fight it anymore and reaches back to pull his shirt over his head.

I run my lips along his stomach, leaving light kisses as I go.

"Again, if you wanna talk, you might want to stop doing that."

"Just because this isn't leading to sex, that doesn't mean I can't show you what I want. I want to kiss you, and touch you, and worship the goddamn ground you walk on. I don't want to be your distraction, Jet."

"What do you want to be then?" he croaks.

Your everything.

I can't say that to him, though. Not when he's this edgy. I don't want to push him too far either way. Begging him to be with me will either make him run away or choose me out of guilt or feeling pressured.

"I want to be the guy you can turn to. Whenever you need me."

"Unless it's hockey season," he says dryly.

"We can still video chat, call, and text."

"What do you mean *still*? We've never done that."

"Then we should. Three years ago, we walked away from each other because we knew it would be too hard to stay connected."

"It'll still be hard."

"But it'll be worth it."

"Maybe." Jet sighs. "I'm tired."

I pull on his arm. "Come on. Lie down."

He climbs into bed next to me, and we slip under the sheet. Jet's lean body curls into my side.

"I was going to stay in here anyway," he says. "Luce is taking my bed."

"I'm thankful you've got someone looking out for you on the road."

"Me too. I just wish I hadn't fucked up the other night by singing with that band. Then I could stay."

"You didn't know you were being filmed. And even if you didn't sing, you were drinking. According to Luce, you weren't supposed to be doing that either. Either way, you would've been outed … err so to speak."

"I didn't think. I should've kept up with the nodes lie to get out of it, but—"

"But you belong on that stage and it's hard to turn it off."

"Exactly."

I rub my hand down his arm and back up. "This isn't your fault. It's Harley who shouldn't have demanded you fly halfway around the world again to go back to him. Do …" I bite my lip trying to pluck up the courage to ask what I really want to. "Do you think you'll get back together with him?"

"No."

Emphatic answer. That's good.

"I don't want to. And I don't know what he's playing at. It's like he wants to torture us both."

"Maybe he misses you and wants to be near you?"

"Well, he'll be surprised when I only turn up for my stage time and then bug outta there."

"Are you allowed to do that?" I ask.

"Yep. Luce generally likes us to hang around until after the concert and meet backstage fans, but they're there for Eleven, not us."

"You have fans. I've seen how rabid they can be on social media."

"They're great, but we're still building a brand. We weren't an overnight success like Eleven. We've had to work and put our blood, sweat, and tears into getting where we are."

"Blood?"

Jet laughs. "Totally. One day, Benji and I were roughhousing during a creative session, and we were bored because the inspiration wasn't there. He's this big Aussie guy, you know?"

"I remember from that night in Tampa."

"Yeah, so there's me, all five ten wispy me, trying to overpower him. He was barely using any strength, and I was going all out. We were wrestling on the floor, and somehow, I still don't even know how, I threw him off me, and he rolled and smashed his nose on the end of the coffee table. Blood everywhere."

The reminder that Jet's had this whole amazing life since that night we met makes the regret so much worse. Maybe breaking his bandmate's nose isn't amazing, but it's a great anecdote.

I've never been the type of guy to have the fear of missing out. I've done what I wanted, gone where I wanted, and haven't worried about what I missed. When Bryce would go to gallery openings and art exhibitions and all those other places where his friends would make me feel like a dumb jock, I never got upset when he told me I could stay home or if I had a game and couldn't go. I didn't get jealous when he'd come home and tell me what happened.

But right now, as stupid as it sounds, I wish I'd been there for Jet and Benji hanging out.

Jet's still laughing when I blurt out, "I'm jealous."

"Jealous?" he asks incredulously. "I mean, we could wrestle, and I can accidentally break your nose too if you want."

I shake my head. "Not of that. I'm jealous of the life you have and the people who get to be around you all the time."

"I can tell you now, there's nothing to be jealous of. I have some close friends, and it's amazing I get to experience that life with them, but ... until Harley ... it was miserable being on tour with no one real to share it with."

Share it with me, I want to say, but we both know that can't happen. Preseason training starts in eight weeks. His tour still has three months left.

Jet stares at the same ceiling I was staring at not ten minutes ago with the same contemplative gaze. "I've always dreamed of someone who's mine waiting for me offstage. He'd give me a kiss as soon as I'd finish my set even if I'm sweaty and gross. He'd be there for me. Not for the fame. Not for the public exposure of being with Jay from Radioactive ... He'd be there just for me."

The words tumble out of my mouth without proper thought. "I want to be that guy."

Jet's response is expected. "You can't be. Hockey."

"I can be for a little while." My breathing stalls, and my heart beats erratically. "Take me with you. I'll be that guy for you until I have to report back to New Jersey."

He's hesitant, but I can see he's truly contemplating it.

"I don't mean to put you on the spot, and you can say no. I just ... I don't want this to end yet. I'm not ready to let you go, and you know I love seeing you on stage."

"You'd ... do that? You don't have, like, LGBTQ sports stuff you have to do? And commitments?"

"I may technically be the first out NHL player, but Ollie's story became bigger than mine because he was dating a sports reporter. When I decided to come out, I did it so I could live a normal life without worry. I didn't want to be some gay icon. I knew that came with the territory, but Ollie saved me from becoming that guy. And I'm not a player with a huge amount of endorsement deals, and that's the way I like it too."

"I dunno ... I'm not sure putting you and Harley in the same vicinity is a good idea. I've always felt connected to you, and I was trying to convince myself this means nothing. That I could have fun and not get attached. But that's the problem I'm facing, Caleb."

"Uh-oh. You first-named me."

Jet doesn't even crack a smile. "What if you walk away from the tour in two months and I'm even more heartbroken and lonely than I am now?"

"Aww, baby." I caress Jet's skin along his back and pull him closer.

I'll never say it out loud because he'd want to kick my ass for suggesting it, but underneath Jet's sarcastic confidence is a precious boy wanting to be loved.

I've known loneliness. I've lived it. Being on the road for up to eight months of the year is hard enough. Doing it as a closeted athlete is even worse.

I lived with the constant fear my entire world would reject me. Surrounded by an entire hockey team, plus coaches, and all the staff that work for the NHL, you wouldn't think I could get lonely, but the thing about having a giant secret hanging over your head is you're never truly *with* people. You co-exist alongside them and that's about it.

It's the loneliest existence I've known.

"I understand," I say. "More than you'll ever know. Take me with you."

Jet pauses but I feel the moment the fight leaves him. He sinks into my arms. "Guess we're gonna have to tell my brothers."

Ah. Yeah. That.

Even though I've wanted Jet to tell them, knowing it's gonna happen already has my face aching from the possible punches thrown.

Maybe Matt punches me so hard, the pain ripples through time and space and hits me in the past. Which is right now.

I need to be prepared for worst-case scenarios here.

"Then let's do it," I say, proud I can keep my tone even.

"Tomorrow. Right now, I want to fall asleep in your arms."

"We'll miss dinner."

"I don't care," he says already half-asleep.

I kiss the top of his head.

Jet's laughter has never sounded so mocking which is saying a lot. "You look like you could puke."

"Not at all," I lie. "I wanted to tell them, remember?"

"Still doesn't mean you're not scared." Slowly, Jet approaches from the other side of the cabin and runs his hands over my chest and shoulders. "It's cute you're nervous, but it's not like you're 'meeting the parents.' They're your friends. They'll be happy for us. And if they're not, I'll throw a giant hissy fit and create a diversion so you can run away."

"That might be the sweetest thing you've ever offered to do for me."

Jet stares down at my crotch. "That can't be true. I've offered many sweet things." He rubs my cock over my shorts, and I grab his hand to stop him.

"Nothing to do with my cock has ever been *sweet*, and you can't get me hard right now when we're about to go tell everyone about us."

This makes Jet smile more. "I like it when you're grumbly."

When footsteps sound on the deck, Jet moves away from me. That alarm system is coming in handy with this whole secretly hooking up thing.

At the door, though, is Luce.

"He here?" he asks.

I step aside, letting him in.

"How was your night?" Luce asks Jet.

"Horrible. I had to spend it wrapped up in that." He gestures to my body. "Feel sorry for me!"

"You poor thing," Luce says sarcastically. "You live such a hard life."

"I know, right? But anyway, we have some news. Soren's coming with us."

Luce's gaze snaps to mine and then flits between Jet and me. "You're coming on tour?"

"I am. But I need to be back in Jersey in September."

"September," Luce murmurs and purses his lips. "Okay. We can work with that. It's actually kind of genius. And the label will love it. Harley has a beard. You having one too should calm the rumors."

"I'm not a beard," I point out and look to Jet for him to confirm that.

Instead, he grabs Luce's arms and jumps excitedly. "You want to come to breakfast with us? We're gonna tell my brothers that I'm fucking Soren. There might be bloodshed."

"You said they won't care," I say.

"Well, I mean, I believe my exact words were they *shouldn't* care."

"Great. Just great."

Jet entwines our fingers and drags me out the door. "You'll be fine. I promise. Besides, you're a hockey player. You're used to taking punches, right?"

"Uh, right." I guess. I'm not a fighter on the ice. All hockey players are to a certain extent, but I'm not known for it.

On the walk to the food hut, I keep telling myself that Matt didn't flip out at the idea the other day. Sort of. He said he couldn't see us together but didn't ask me to stay away.

"Is handholding too obvious of an announcement?" I lift our joined hands.

"Hmm, probably." Jet releases me.

As we enter, all sounds stop.

Literally.

Either I've gone deaf or some phenomenon is happening where the world has turned mute.

Then I get over my ego and realize the silence isn't for me.

"What's the verdict?" Matt asks Jet.

"I'm going back on tour."

There's a round of apologies and "that sucks," and then Jet looks at me.

I nod.

"There's something else," Jet says, his eyes still locked on mine. "Soren's coming with me."

More silence.

Talon, as if sensing the tension, goes for the joke. "What, like, as a backup singer?"

"No, dancer," Miller says. "Duh."

"No …" Jet waves me closer and puts his arm around my waist. Mine goes over his shoulders. "As my boyfriend."

Mouths drop open.

My stomach does a flip at the boyfriend label.

Matt, Noah, and Damon all try to glare me to death.

Matt and Noah would be thinking about Jet's well-being. Damon would be wondering what this will do to my public image.

"Twenty bucks on Matt kicking Soren's ass," Maddox says. When the glares are then sent his way, he cocks his head. "*Daddy's* ass? If Jet has to call Soren that, does that mean we do too?"

"Oh, for fuck's sake," I grumble.

Jet laughs.

Luce steps in. "The best way to keep Jet's ex off his case and the label off his back is by throwing his new boyfriend in everyone's faces."

"Oh, so it's fake," Matt says.

Jet and I look at each other. I want him to be the one to tell them no—that this is real. That's what I was offering last night when I suggested this. Not a beard or distraction for his label.

"We kinda, sorta, might've, maybe hooked up three years ago and never told you guys," Jet says. "And now we have this second chance, so we're taking it."

A relieved whoosh leaves me. For a second there, I thought he was going to tell them that it will be just for show.

"Three years ..." Matt says. "Three years and neither of you thought to say anything? Didn't think to say anything the other morning when I went to you and said, *hey, Jet has a thing for you*?"

Jet glares at his brother. "Oh, thanks for that by the way. There's nothing like big bro telling someone you're sleeping with that you've got a 'crush.'"

"You told him?" Matt booms at me.

"I was *there*," Jet yells back.

"Awkward," Maddox sings.

I wave my hands in front of me. "Okay, this is getting out of hand. Truth is, the night you guys came to my Stanley Cup final, I didn't know who Jet was outside of his band. I didn't know he was your kid brother, and stuff happened."

Jet's hand tightens around me. "Then I went on tour, and we haven't really seen each other since until this trip."

"And now you're together?" Noah asks.

"Well, no, but we're ... dating?" Jet says and looks up at me.

It's not how I'd describe it, but it's not like *serious boyfriend* fits either. "I guess that's the closest description."

"They're so fucking," Maddox says.

Damon puts a hand across his boyfriend's mouth. Thank God. "Stop trying to get the man killed."

"Killed?" Matt leans back in his chair and folds his arms across his wide chest. "Not gonna kill anyone." His voice is high-pitched and kind of scary. "Why would I need to kill anyone for keeping a secret for three fucking years?"

"That's why you're mad?" Ollie asks. "I thought it'd be that Soren's sticking it to your little brother."

I lean into Jet. "When do we leave for the tour? In the next six seconds might be a good idea."

"It's not like we've been dating for three years," Jet says. "I didn't realize I needed to inform you of all my hookups. Want me to write a list? According to the tabloids, I might need a whole legal pad."

"When do you leave?" Matt says, still edgy but now trying to cover it better.

"I'll handle it," Luce says. "Most likely, we'll be out of here this afternoon or tomorrow morning at the latest."

We can't leave right this minute?

CHAPTER EIGHTEEN

JET

"He's too old for you," Matt says while I pack my bags.

"Say it louder. I don't think he can hear you a hundred feet away."

"He's older than me."

"This may come as a shock to you, big brother, but I'm an adult." I gasp. "Fucking surprise! I grew up. And, as a side note? He's only ten years older than me. I've been with guys ten years older than *him*."

Matt puts his hands over his ears. "La-la-la-la-la."

"Age doesn't mean anything. Especially when you're as immature as Soren. Or you, it seems."

My brother looks confused. "He's immature?"

"Oh, like you wouldn't believe. He totally did a 'that's what he said' joke the other day. I was so proud."

"Stop talking about me. My ears are burning." Soren appears on the steps leading to my hut. "And I'm not usually immature. Jet brings it out in me."

"Because you're too old for him," Matt says.

"Fuck off," I grumble at my brother. "Always with the babying. How the hell do you think you're gonna do with an actual baby? Maybe you should worry more about that and less about me. I've been on my own for three years now. I can date who I want, and that includes any of your friends."

"Is he my friend though?" Matt raises an eyebrow at Soren. "Isn't bro code something like 'Thou shalt not fuck each other's siblings'?"

"In my defense, I fucked Jet before I was friends with you, so technically ..."

Ooh, brave move, Soren.

Matt steps closer. "We want to get into technicalities? Like how you *technically* lied to me for three years?"

"Put your dicks away before you start a pissing contest, okay?" I turn to Soren. "Babe. Go finish packing." I turn to my brother. "This is happening. Deal with it."

Matt throws his hands up. "Fine."

Soren kisses my cheek. "Fine." He lowers his voice. "I like it when you're bossy."

"And I like it when I can't hear shit like that," Matt says.

Soren ignores him as he leaves.

"You're going to have to get over this. You know that, right?"

Matt waves me off. "I know. And I will. I'm more pissed at the secrecy than you two being together."

"Then what's all the age talk?"

"An easy shot?"

"It is pretty easy."

Matt's brow scrunches. "The more I think about it, the more his behavior makes sense. I always thought he was semi-distant all these years because that was just him or maybe because Bryce was influencing him. Now I reckon it was because of what happened with you."

"He's a great guy. He cares about me, and he understands my music the way I wish all my fans would."

"And what's going to happen when he has to go play hockey?"

"He goes to New Jersey, and I finish off the tour."

"Then you'll be recording again and setting up the next tour. What kind of relationship is that?" He's not saying anything I don't already know, but it pisses me off all the same.

"That's for me and Soren to work out. Not you."

"You know if he hurts you, we get to kick his ass."

"Yes, yes, you're all big badasses who are violent and scary and fighty." I pat his cheek.

"JJ …"

There was a reason I didn't let the label make my new name JJ. It's what my brother calls me. Matt was my protector growing up. He fed us, looked after us, and I know it's natural for him to worry about me.

"Matt, I'll be fine. Soren won't hurt me."

He can't. He promised.

***

After an over-the-top goodbye with hugs all around from the guys, Joni drops Soren, Luce, and me at the airport to do the long-ass trip to the States. The flight to Fiji wasn't too bad because we had just finished the Asian leg before we were supposed to kick off the US tour.

Soren's presence by my side the whole way both eases my mind and makes me edgy.

I want him with me.

I love how he looks at me and the way we are with each other.

I wish Fiji could have lasted longer to explore this thing

between us, because bringing him into my real life is going to add pressure I don't need.

And then there's Harley.

When I'm away from him, I can pretend I'm strong. Either I'm really good at being in denial or he has some sort of hold over me in person because when I don't have to see him, I'm convinced I'm over him.

But I've been there before. All it would take is for him to turn up at my door, looking so damn broken, and I'd let him back into my life and my heart.

Soren shifts in his first-class bed, waking up from a long sleep on the plane.

His hypnotic amber eyes and that smile that makes him look boyish have me asking "Harley who?" which also scares me.

How will I handle both of them in one place?

Luce has already talked about running interference for us. We have a team of roadies, personal assistants, and a backup band to keep Harley away from us, but I don't hold too much faith. They were trying to do that the last few months, but we still found a way.

Maybe now that it'll be one-sided, it'll be easier to keep us apart.

"You didn't sleep?" Soren asks, his voice raspy.

"Not tired."

I don't tell him the only time I've slept more than a few hours in the last three years has been at home in New York, visiting with Matt, or the nights I've spent wrapped around him.

He reaches over and holds my hand while he puts his bed back into the seat position. "It's no private plane but still comfortable."

Luce snorts behind us. "We might have found you a man as spoiled as you are, Jay."

"NHL bucks," I retort.

"I'm sure that's chump change to rock stars."

I shrug. "I never see any of the money. We were given a black Mastercard and the label takes care of it all."

"You don't know how much money you have?"

"I have my own accountant. He knows that stuff."

Luce leans in. "Let's just say, ever since 'Someone Else's Perfect' went multi-platinum for Eleven, Jay doesn't have to worry about money for the foreseeable future. You know, unless he pisses off his label by pretending to have nodes and gets sued."

"Yeah, yeah, I get it. I fucked up. That's why we're here." I gesture around the plane.

"Getting nervous?" Soren asks.

"About Harley? Nah." About what I'll do when I see Harley? Yeah.

"Just remember I'm here for you, whatever you need. If you need me to be a friend or you need that escape you wanted ... I'm here *for you*."

My tongue feels thick in my mouth.

No one has ever treated me with the kind of respect Soren has since landing in Fiji, and doesn't that say something about me? Or maybe it says more about the people I hang around with and date.

Even Harley was known for being selfish—somehow always turning the topic around to himself.

Like this one time when I was being interviewed by some teen magazine and they'd quoted me saying some bullshit about being able to be persuaded by the other side if the right girl came along when I'd said it sarcastically and then mouthed off about how that's not how gay works. Yet, the article still made it sound like I was bi or pan, which there's nothing wrong with, but I was pissed she'd purposefully mislabeled me. To get more clicks online, to build controversy, I don't know, but the point is, when I was losing my shit over that article, Harley was there telling me about the time some other interviewer basically screwed him over years ago and how they almost fucked up his entire career.

Not helpful to my situation at all.

In a selfish world, voices get drowned out by everyone trying to out-woe each other.

Soren isn't like that. In fact, apart from a few comments about Bryce, he hasn't spoken much about himself at all.

Now who's the selfish one?

"Tell me about hockey," I say.

He looks confused. "What do you want to know?"

"What made you want to be a hockey player?"

Soren's face turns derisive. "Please, I'm Canadian."

I laugh. "Okay, but not every Canadian makes it to the big show. What makes you special?"

"My dad was a coach. I'm sure the first shoes I ever wore were a pair of skates."

"Oh, wow. Pressure."

"Not really. I loved every minute of it. He could be hard on me, sure, and there were times when I wanted to quit, but I never would have. I love it too much."

"How did he take it when you came out?"

Soren purses his lips. "It's a bit of a sore spot. Both my parents had known or suspected. I came out to them when I was twenty-five. Dad only said I was smart keeping it quiet from the NHL but apart from that didn't support or condemn it. He was sort of indifferent, and we don't talk about it. Mom was great. So was my sister. She's the one who dragged me to Noah's benefit that night the first time I saw you on stage."

"Ah. So I have your sister to thank for turning you into my very first fanman."

"Grace would love to meet you."

Okay, I didn't mean we should jump to that.

Soren laughs. "You look terrified. We can wait for the sisterly introduction. But just think, what if she hadn't been visiting or didn't make me go to that benefit? We might not be here now."

I don't want to even think about that, because even though Soren and I have danced around each other ever since we met, and I've been hesitant and holding back this Fiji trip, I couldn't be more thankful for him now.

We talk more about Soren's family and his life until we land at LAX.

Focusing on him is a good way to keep my mind off everything, but now, arriving back in the States, there's no fighting the inevitable.

Starting with the paparazzi waiting for us curbside next to what is no doubt our chauffeured Escalade.

"Couldn't have ordered a normal-sized car?" I ask Luce.

An Escalade basically screams famous person. Chances are, the paps don't know who they're waiting for, but once they see me, it's gonna be question after question about the tour and the "fight" with Eleven, which is the story mainstream media is running with.

"Joystar's fault," Luce says. "Here." He hands me his sunglasses.

Soren gives me his ball cap.

It doesn't help.

"You get Jay in the car," Luce says to Soren. "I'll put the bags in the back."

The driver helps him, and I'm quick to climb into the backrow seat, but that doesn't stop the shouts or cameras going off.

"Jay, why did Radioactive leave the tour?"

"Jay, is it true you got into a fight with Blake from Eleven, and they asked you to leave the tour?"

"Are you going into rehab?"

"Are you really sick?"

I don't answer any of them.

Soren shuts the door behind him, but the flashes keep going off even though they'd only get reflections from the tinted windows.

Luce opens the door on my side and takes one of the two seats in front of us.

"Okay, I've never had that many paparazzi after me. Not even after I came out," Soren says.

"See. I'm a real celebrity. You're just an athlete."

"Not anymore," Luce says. "It's going to take them three point two seconds to figure out who he is, and then they're going to want to know why a hockey player is with us."

I didn't even think about that side of things. "I'm sorry. I didn't think—"

Soren reaches for my hand. "It's okay. I did. And it's not like I'm completely new to all this. It's just on a much bigger scale."

Luce is on his phone, scrolling through something. "Okay, first stop is Joystar headquarters to grovel and talk about when we'll be rejoining the tour. Then home. Benji and Freya are already there."

"Home?" Soren asks.

"The band owns a place in the Hollywood Hills," Luce says.

"We bought it as a reward for hitting our first number one."

"And you all live there?" Soren asks.

"When we're in L.A. yeah, we live together. It's rare though. Benji and Freya go home to see Freya's family in New York a lot."

"You don't go with them?"

I share a look with Luce and wonder how much I should say.

"Not so much this past year, no." Because when we haven't been on tour, I've stayed in L.A. with Harley. That remains unsaid.

My life in L.A. almost feels foreign to me. It's not my real home. I always see Noah and Matt's place in New York, or even their Chicago penthouse, as home.

Home has always been people, not a place, so L.A. feels as empty as when I left it, but when I look at Soren, that same sensation that hit me that night he came to see me perform in Tampa is back.

He's a piece of home and sets me at ease.

I reckon I'm gonna need that to see Harley again.

CHAPTER NINETEEN

SOREN

Okay, I've stepped off a plane and right into the chaos that is Jet's real life.

There are more paparazzi outside of Joystar Records when we arrive.

"Don't say anything," Luce says. "Just get inside."

When I exit the car, questions are thrown to Roman, and I can only assume they think I'm Roman Josi. I pause in my steps.

Just leave it.

Roman and I get mixed up all the time. We're used to it. Still, it's annoying.

Jet slams into my back. "Keep going." That's when he hears it too. He grabs hold of my hand and drags me toward the building, but he gives a backward glance. "Do your research, boys. Wrong hockey player."

More flashes and yelling, and we don't get a break from it until we're safely inside where the paparazzi can't go.

What have I gotten myself into? This is just the beginning.

The question rings through my head, but with one look at Jet, I'm reminded of why I'm doing this.

I still don't know how things will work when I go back to hockey or even how long I'm still going to be playing. Perhaps Jet and I owe it to each other to take a few more years—him to experience all the success and me to retire.

But ever since the second he stepped off that helicopter in Fiji, all I've been able to think is this is our chance, and I'm going to take it—paparazzi, ex-boyfriends, and record labels be damned.

I follow Jet and Luce into the elevator, and we go up to the top floor.

When Luce points us toward a waiting room, he goes to speak to the receptionist.

"Sorry about that," Jet says. "I figured the paps should get their facts straight."

"I'm sure Roman is thankful."

"They should put you on the same team and call you twins. Ooh, you could swap jerseys and confuse people."

I laugh. "Thanks, but I have no desire to play for Nashville."

Jet's face falls. "Yeah, that'd be one way for me to dump your ass faster than you can say daddy issues."

"I know about your shitty family back in Tennessee. Your brother has talked about it some—mainly, how your parents basically sold Wade to Matt so he would pay off their debts."

Jet looks away and folds his arms. "Hey, at least they thought Wade was worth something. They threw me out and didn't care where I ended up."

Stepping forward, I wrap myself around him, and he buries his head on my chest. "Sorry, I shouldn't have brought it up."

"It's fine. I get the last laugh, right? They never supported me, so fuck them. They're not going to see a dime of my money. I don't know why Matt bothers with them."

I have a fair idea—that Matt being the oldest, he feels obligated to provide where their parents can't—but I understand the subject is touchy, and now's not the time to dwell on it. Jet has some groveling to do with the label execs.

When it's time for us to go in, the receptionist asks me to stay in the waiting area. I'm not allowed in the big boys' room.

I sit on the uncomfortable futuristic couch and flip through magazines that are months old. People come and go, some staring around the offices like it's their first time here, others seemingly upset as they leave.

So ... this is the music biz.

I take out my phone and call my sister to let her know I'm back in the States and email my parents who are on their own vacation in the Mediterranean right now.

And my list of responsibilities for the next few weeks is done.

If this is what retirement will look like, I can't say that I hate it.

Jet and Luce finally come back out with two suit-wearing old guys, and I stand, wiping my hands on my jeans, because with one look from them, I feel unwashed and dirty somehow.

It's not until Jet opens his mouth, I know why.

"See. He's real. Rumors of Harley and I stop. Harley goes back on stage, and everyone makes money. We good?"

"We're good," one of them mumbles, and they both turn and walk away.

"You two take the car home," Luce says. "I'm gonna stay and sort some shit. Eleven is finishing up a show in San Francisco tonight and the next stop is Seattle in two days. We'll meet them there, so be ready to leave by lunch."

"You're not coming by the house later?" Jet asks.

"Nah. Tell Marty I'll meet him at home. This could take a while."

In the elevator, I turn to Jet. "Sooo, how did it go?"

"It went. The label was happy for Radioactive to disappear for the rest of the tour, but Luce reassured them I've moved on and Harley and I will only interact in a professional manner lest I be dropped from the label."

"Just like that?"

Jet nods. "Just like that."

"Can I ask why Harley can pull diva tantrums to have you back on tour but you're getting the blame and being threatened?"

"Eleven is the label's highest-earning act. It gives them a certain level of power. They can pretty much demand anything they want so long as they keep bringing in the big money."

"Except come out."

"Exactly. Demanding an opening act is nothing to the label. As long as Harley's still toeing their line, he gets what he wants. End of story."

"Well, you don't have to worry about me being here or having to do whatever they want us to. Being forced to be your boyfriend isn't a hardship."

Jet's smile is tight.

"Though I get the feeling it might be putting too much pressure on you."

Jet pulls me close. "It's not you or us or even Harley. It's the politics of it all. Considering how open this industry supposedly is, it's ridiculous how many stars have beards, people are set up by their PR reps, and how certain relationships are good or bad for press. I understand the celebrity aspect of it—people thrive on thinking they know the real you and want to know everything about your life, but …" He lays his head on my chest. "It's exhausting."

"I know, baby. I'm here to make it better." I don't know how I'll do that for him, but whatever he needs, I'll give it.

I'm expecting to be hounded by paparazzi again, but when we get outside, the horde is gone.

"Guess someone more famous is around," Jet says.

"Thankfully." I pull open the door.

Jet climbs in first and goes to the bench seat in the back of the Escalade. "It's been a crazy week."

I can't help laughing. "No shit. I started my vacation worrying about contract negotiations and thinking I'd have to spend the entire two weeks trying to forget about being on a couples retreat alone. It's somehow turned into spending the rest of my off-season on a music tour with a guy I met a hundred moons ago. It's a mind fuck. I don't think I've wrapped my head around what the next two months are going to be like."

"Chaotic. Organized but chaotic. Good thing is, I basically get told where to be and when, and there's always someone there to make sure I get to where I have to be."

"And where you'll be, I'll be? Or will I be waiting on the outside a lot like back there?"

"Stuck like glue, my friend. Especially now the label wants to play up our relationship." Jet turns to me. "You're okay with that, right? Sorry, I didn't even ask. I just assum—"

"It's exactly what I want." I want to put everything into this and give it an honest shot.

Jet lets out a relieved breath, and that's when I notice the bags under his eyes and the all-around exhausted vibe he's giving off. He said he didn't sleep on the plane, so he's got to be dead on his feet.

"Come here." I gesture for him to lie down and put his head in my lap.

He comes willingly and puts his feet up on the window of the car. Warm, brown eyes glance up at me through thick lashes, but they flutter shut when I start rubbing Jet's forehead. "You know, I've seen Noah do this to Matt when Matt's stressed. If this is what having a boyfriend is like, sign me up."

"There're lots of perks to having a boyfriend."

"I can't wait to find out what else there is." He says that as if he's never experienced it.

"Harley never did stuff like this?"

Jet keeps his eyes closed as he talks. "We were more about stolen moments. None of this"—he waves between us—"tending to me when I was exhausted. Although, to be fair, we were both always exhausted."

"Guess it goes with the territory of being on tour."

His head moves across my crotch, and I have to remind myself to be good right now. He needs sleep, not me turning this into something sexual.

"You know how it is," he says. "You basically don't stop for eight months out of the year."

"See, I've trained my whole life to be your boyfriend."

"The University of Jet. Where you learn to deal with tour exhaustion, diva tantrums, horrible hangovers, and constantly being told what to do by the team of people surrounding you."

"Definitely sounds like the NHL. Also, where's that university? Sign me up."

Jet takes my free arm and pulls it across his waist. "You're already acing the classes."

He falls asleep with a smile on his lips.

I stare out the window the rest of the way, watching L.A. go by. I started my career on the West Coast, playing for Vancouver for my first few years and then Anaheim for a very short season before being traded to New Jersey. I'm familiar with the city, but not so much out here in the Hills.

Each house we pass gets bigger and more expensive until we pull onto a narrow side street and stop next to a black square building.

With very few windows, the house is boxy and modern.

I almost don't want to wake Jet up because he looks so peaceful.

"Jet," I whisper.

His mouth hangs open, and even his drool is cute.

"You're home."

The driver opens the door Jet's resting his feet on, which jolts him awake.

"Wha?" Jet sits up, and his head swivels from one side to the other.

"We're at your place. Apparently. Kinda looks like a warehouse."

He squints up at me. "You questioning my taste in real estate? Wait until you see the inside."

I wish I could bounce back from a nap as fast as Jet does. He's out of the car in a beat and even has a spring in his step.

Ugh. Young people.

There's no gate around his property, and it sits on a corner block.

"Isn't this a security risk? Like, do you have photographers lining this alleyway?"

"You sound like Luce when we decided to buy the place. Benji, Freya, and I didn't want to jinx us. We thought it might've been our only chance or it could all go away, and then at least we'd get a house out of it, right? But they haven't found us yet. Probably because the deed is in our full names no one really knows. I also don't see us living here much longer. At least, not together. Maybe Benji and Freya can buy out my share or something."

"You don't like it here?"

"I love it here. It's like my first real achievement, you know? Well, tangible achievement. Hitting number one on the Billboard charts is the biggest, but I can't hold that. Touch it. Live in it."

"Then why would you sell?"

Jet shakes his head. "Never mind. Forget I said anything. It's that part of me that always has doubts. The band will break up, the label will drop us ... I need to learn to ignore that voice."

"It doesn't help that the label is threatening to drop you."

"Eh. Same shit, different day. We were convinced that whole first year our contract would be torn up. It wasn't until 'Hat Trick Heartbreak' did anything that we found some stability."

"Well, in that case, you're welcome. Hey, do I get any royalties for that?"

"Do you think Taylor Swift pays any of her ex-boyfriends for being her muse?"

"Oh, she'd be broke, for sure."

"Exactly." Jet pushes open the door to his place, and he's right. The inside is amazing.

Hardwood floors, a set of wooden stairs to the right, small sitting area, but it's the wide windows and glass doors leading to a balcony overlooking the valley that takes my breath away.

My feet find their own way there. "Wow."

"Told you."

Commotion on the stairs catches our attention—a flurry of movement from a wispy thing of a guy.

He enters with an air of confidence for someone shorter than Jet. He's cute, kinda trendy, and has short brown hair and brown eyes. He looks to be in his late teens to early twenties, and I've got no idea who he is.

Then his stare drops dead cold. "You fucked it up."

Jet sighs. "Soren, this is Marty. He likes to bust my balls even though he claims to have loved me once upon a time."

"Yeah, then I met you."

"Ouch, Marty. *Ouch.* The pain is too much."

"Marty ..." I say. "As in Luce's—"

"Better half," Marty says with Jet-like attitude.

"How old—" I slam my mouth shut. "Sorry, never mind."

Jet laughs. "Marty looks young for his age. He's twenty-six."

How is that kid twenty-six?

"And Luce looks a lot older than thirty-four."

"Wait, Luce is only one year older than me?"

"It's the gray hair," Marty says. "Makes him look older."

Jet holds my hand. "See, age doesn't mean shit in Hollywood."

"So, who are you, anyway?" Marty asks.

I clear my throat. "Umm, I'm a hockey player."

Marty's mouth drops open. "*The* hockey player? Oh my God, am I standing in the same room as 'Hat Trick Heartbreak' and 'Someone Else's Perfect'?"

"Is that going to be how I'm referred to by everyone?" I ask.

"Yes," Jet and Marty say in unison.

Then Marty's voice goes high-pitched and squeaky while he jumps around like an excited puppy. "Oh my God, this is like meeting a celebrity."

"Hey, I am a celebrity," I protest.

"I mean a real one," Marty says.

"I don't think I like the music industry," I grumble.

Jet elbows me. "Well, lucky for you, you've only got eight weeks of it. If you even last that long."

"You're coming on tour with us?" Marty asks.

"Until hockey season starts."

"Okay, I'm no longer pissed about having our impromptu vacation cut short. The drama is going to be so worth it."

I cock a brow. "Drama?"

"Speaking of which," Jet interjects, "where are Benji and Freya?"

"Studio."

"Fucking or fighting?"

"Maybe both?" Marty says. "I never know with those two. All I can say is thank God for soundproofing."

Jet turns to me. "I'll show you the studio when it's safe."

"Your house has its own recording studio?"

Jet smiles. "It's small and not good enough for producing proper singles, but we use it to write music and see what works and what doesn't. I'll show you the rest."

Before we can move, Marty asks, "Where's Luce?"

"He said he'd meet you at home. He had shit to take care of at the label."

"I'll take off then. Have fun!" Marty leaves in the same speedy flurry he arrived in.

Jet takes me downstairs first where there's a large kitchen, large entertaining room with the biggest wide screen TV I've ever seen, and a deck with a firepit, leading to an aboveground pool.

"This is … this is nuts."

"I know, right?" he says proudly. "And I haven't even shown you the best part."

"There's more?"

"Lots more. Looks small on the outside, but it's built into the hill. It's four levels including the basement where the studio is."

"Okay, okay," I relent. "You're a 'real' celebrity."

Jet pulls me back up the stairs but keeps going to the top floor. He points to the right. "Benji and Freya's rooms are down there. Mine's this way."

He turns left and opens huge double doors to a master suite. It has its own bathroom, and its own balcony, and the same amazing view as downstairs.

"I can see why this is the best part." I move toward the big-ass bed and flop backward but lean up on my elbows. "Gonna show me what makes it the best?"

"Okay, I was totally talking about the double-headed shower, but this works too." Jet's shirt disappears, and then he's there, climbing on top of me.

"Double-headed shower? After that flight, maybe we should make use of that."

"I love how your mind works." He pulls me up and we strip as we race each other to the bathroom.

Under the spray, we're all hands and mouths, but it's fast handjobs and cleanup. I've been keyed up since back in Fiji, so it doesn't take long for me to tip over the edge. And once Jet comes, it's obvious the nap in the car only gave him a tiny boost and the orgasm knocked him on his ass again.

I hold him close. "Let's go to bed."

"It's midafternoon. We'll get jet lag."

"I'm already Jet lagged. Get it? *Jet* …lagged."

"I was wondering when the dad jokes would start. Because you know, you're old. Like a dad. Or … a Dadd—"

"Don't fucking say it."

Jet snickers.

We don't bother putting on clothes. We just dry off and climb into bed.

"So, this is your life …" I pull his body against mine.

I love the way he fits against me, the way his shaggy hair tickles my chest and how his callused hand scrapes over my abs.

"This is the tip of the iceberg."

I can't resist. "I promise I'm sturdier than the Titanic and can handle anything."

"Okay, Dad—"

I cut him off by kissing him goodnight … or afternoon.

CHAPTER TWENTY

JET

Soren says he can handle anything, but the paparazzi, going straight from the airport to a meeting to turning around and going back to the airport less than forty-eight hours later, it really is just the beginning.

Benji and Freya do a double take when they drag their asses out of bed the next day.

We've been awake since four thanks to passing out when we should've made ourselves stay awake.

"Hockey dude?" Benji asks through heavy-lidded eyes.

"Whoa, I'm surprised you remember him with how many brain cells you've killed in the last two years."

Benji looks like he wants to protest but doesn't. "Do we have shit to do today?"

"Nope. We're supposed to hide out until we make our reappearance in Seattle tomorrow and be all 'Surprise, I'm all better and have a new boyfriend. Go me!'"

"Do we have to hide?" Freya asks.

"I dunno. Call Luce. Soren and I are housebound though."

"We thought you were in your room sulking all night," Benji says. "Guess we know what you were doing."

"Yep, and wanna hear the dirty, dirty truth? We fucking slept. Fiji is *far*."

They laugh.

"We will be doing that all day though, if you two wanna go out." I don't give them a chance to respond before nodding for Soren to go upstairs.

"Nice to see you guys again." He makes a run for it.

Before I can follow him, Freya, the ninja jumps in front of me.

"What's the story?"

"Yeah, what's the story?" Benji asks.

"He's coming on tour with us. The label is worried about Harley and me, he doesn't have to report for preseason until September, so it's a win-win everywhere."

"Have you spoken to Harley?" Freya asks.

"Nope. Because that's what exes do. Don't talk to each other."

"So he has no idea you're with someone else?" Benji whistles. "And you say we're full of drama." He waves a finger between him and Freya.

She scowls at him.

I've seen how this plays out a million times. "You two should get married already. Now, unless you want to see a whole lot of gay sex, don't bother us."

"Will you judge me if I say I wouldn't mind seeing that?" Freya jokes.

"Judge, no, but I will tell the tabloids you have crabs if you come knocking." I kiss the top of her head and run upstairs.

When I get up there, Soren's not naked like I expect. He's pacing and talking to someone on his phone.

"Yeah, okay. I'll ask. Yep. I'll get you the number. Uh-huh

..." He spots me. "Damon, I have to go. Go back to your vacation." He ends the call and throws his phone on the bed.

"What is it?" I ask, deflated.

"We're big news already. Damon needs Luce's number or the number for your PR department at the label in case any damage control is needed."

"Damage control? Does it matter who you date?" I didn't even think of that.

"It's not a big deal. The media wasn't interested in me and Bryce because he was a no one. It'll be different with you, and I'm only contracted for this season, so it's just Damon being his usual cautious self. He's worried about how it could affect next season's contract negotiations."

"Why didn't you tell me? I never would've let you get tied up in my media bullshit."

Soren approaches and wraps his damn arms around me, making me melt into him. "I chose to be here. It's okay."

"What if you don't get another contract because of this?"

"I will."

"What can I do to make it better? We can tell everyone we're fucking around instead of trying to push some loved-up relationship on them."

Soren runs a hand through his hair. "That might be worse." He pulls me down so we're sitting on the end of the bed. "So, everyone knows there are all those puck bunny sites and single guys pop up there all the time partying with different girls. This is seen as relatively acceptable by the teams and the NHL in general because it's always going to happen. What they don't like to see is married guys on there. While they haven't explicitly said it, they've hinted about not wanting me on such a site with guys."

I frown. "I don't understand."

"Being gay in the league is scandalous as it is. Even three

years after Ollie and I have come out. We have morality clauses in our contracts, and you saw what that did to your brother when photos leaked of him with some guy on his knees."

"Meaning ..."

"The NHL would probably rather me not date you at all or ..." Soren lets me get to the conclusion myself.

"Or the opposite. Be in a fully-committed relationship."

"But that is way too much pressure to put on us right now, and I don't want to do that. So, we'll play this by ear. See what happens. Damon and Luce can keep an eye on the media coverage for us."

I don't think that's a good idea. "You know the media will run the story how they want to unless we control the narrative, yeah?"

"*Control the narrative.* Look at you talking PR lingo."

"Ignoring that condescension. Take your shirt off."

Cute lines appear on Soren's forehead. "Media ... narrative ... shirt off ... Yup, I'm not following that train of thought."

"Trust me." I reach back and pull my shirt over my head.

"Makes more sense now." Soren follows. He goes to pull me against him again, but I don't let him.

Instead, I reach for his phone and then climb behind him on the bed.

Wrapping my arms around his wide hockey shoulders, I stick my tongue out and take a selfie at the exact moment Soren cracks a smile at the camera.

I hit some buttons and post it to all his social media. Then I hand it back to him.

He looks at what I did and laughs. "*Nothing beats waking up next to him. Hashtag official. Hashtag Disney love.*" Soren bites his lip. "Disney love? Bit much, isn't it?"

I kiss Soren's cheek. His neck. "So, we're exaggerating what we are. We know our truth. Let them believe whatever so long as it helps both of us."

"Our truth. And what is that again? We kind of left Fiji without any real plan. Am I a friend helping you get through this tour? Are we boyfriends? Are we seeing if we'll even survive a few weeks on the road?"

Shit. "Umm …"

"It's okay if you don't have an exact answer for me. If you tell me all you can handle right now is a friend to distract you, I'll give it to you. I just want to know where we stand."

"I don't know what the rest of this tour is going to be like. Working with Harley again … it could be a disaster. I want this thing between us to work. I want to try … but fuck, my life's a mess right now."

"I don't want to put more pressure on you than you need. Just know I want you. All of you. Whenever you can give that to me."

"Do you think you can handle not having a definitive answer?"

"I can handle anything you throw my way, baby. I promise to be patient."

Shifting around so I'm no longer behind him, I straddle Soren's lap. "Don't make promises you can't keep."

He kisses me softly. "Never."

CHAPTER TWENTY-ONE

SOREN

I'm decked out with an all-areas pass as we're led into KeyArena in Seattle. Jet's edgy and kind of distant. I don't know if this is what he's like before a show or if it's because the inevitable run-in with his ex is going to happen tonight.

I've walked into empty arenas and stadiums and ice rinks a billion times, and it seems the atmosphere is the same whether it's set up for sports or a concert.

The ghosts of audiences past fill the space with phantom screams. Anticipation is built into the walls of this place and can be felt just passing through the corridors.

And as we hit the side stage area, I think I get the answer about Jet's headspace.

The Eleven guys are rehearsing or doing soundcheck or whatever they call it, and Jet's steps falter.

There's a moment where the whole group of us—me, Luce, Marty, Freya, and Benji—freeze with him.

The guys onstage keep going, but Harley locks eyes with us.

He and Jet stare each other down, and even though animosity

passes between both of them, I can't help noticing the heartbreak and unresolved emotion there. With one intense look.

"Let's go." Jet stalks off, heading for backstage.

"That was more brutal than I thought it'd be," Benji says.

Jet looks over his shoulder. "Heard that."

Benji has a point though. That was more than brutal.

I don't know how I'm supposed to react. I promised to be there for him even knowing he and Harley are in a completely different place than Bryce and me.

I have no reservations that breaking up was the right thing for us. I'm not sure Jet and Harley have reached that point.

And yeah, maybe I'm reading a hell of a lot into one look, but shit, their connection is fucking palpable.

"Babe?" Jet's voice snaps me back to him, and my feet automatically follow.

We're taken to a dressing room backstage, and Jet beelines it to a guitar case.

"My baby," he coos and immediately takes it out. "I've missed you."

"Should I be worried he's never spoken to me like that?" I ask. "He's been without it for, what, two days?" I haven't seen it since arriving at LAX.

Benji claps my shoulder. "Yeah, you'll need to give them a moment alone."

"Hope you don't mind sharing with his true love," Marty adds. "I don't want to know just how close he is with that guitar."

"Fuck all y'all," Jet says, but he's smiling as he says it. He takes a seat in the corner and strums his guitar.

The riff is "He's Mine." Jet glances at me and winks.

The room has a living room setup with couches and a coffee table full of snacks and drinks.

I grab a water and take the seat closest to Jet. Freya and Benji cuddle up on the love seat, Luce disappears and says something about stage time, and Marty scrolls through his phone.

Roadies and stagehands come and go, and when someone new enters the room, Jet's song freezes. It's for less than a split second, but it's every single time.

I grip his thigh and squeeze. He throws me a smile.

A voice comes from the doorway. "Couldn't stay away, could you?"

I take a deep breath. Here we go.

But Jet's face lights up at whoever it is.

I turn to find one of the other guys from Eleven.

Jet jumps out of his seat. "Ryder."

"Ride her? I barely even know her!" Ryder smirks. His light-blue eyes shine in mischief.

He and Jet hug. Guess they're close.

"So, what's this about leaving the tour then not leaving the tour? You're sick and now you're not sick …"

Jet turns serious as he says, "What can I say? Apparently, your whole tour was fallin' apart without the best fuckin' opening act in the world. Had to come save your asses."

Ryder laughs. "Well, I'm happy you're back even if others might not be."

"Others?"

Ryder avoids Jet's gaze. "I'm guessing Harley cutting out of soundcheck early had something to do with you guys turning up?"

"He left?" Jet asks.

Ryder nods.

The tension seeps out of Jet's shoulders as he relaxes.

Ryder sees it too because he scoffs. "Typical Harley."

"Typical?" Jet asks.

"You know him when he doesn't get his way. And I think forcing you to come back instead of letting you go was the ultimate temper tantrum." Ryder glances at me. "Bringing that with you was the perfect counter move."

"*That* is Soren." Jet playfully shoves him.

I shrug. "I'm cool with being treated like a plaything."

Everyone laughs at me, and then Jet's right there, climbing into my lap.

"Let's get one thing straight. You're not just a plaything."

"Aww, thanks."

"Let me finish. You're not just *a* plaything. You're *my* plaything."

"I'm here to look pretty," I say.

"Good boy." He pats my head like I'm a golden retriever, and I don't even care.

I lower my voice. "I would say isn't that my line, but then all the Daddy jokes will start again."

Jet pats my cheek. "Oh, babe. That implies they *stopped*."

"You're lucky you're adorable." I pull his face down to mine and kiss him, ignoring the groans from everyone in the room about PDA.

Jet's tongue teases my lips before he pulls away.

"When you're done with all the kissy face, soundcheck," Luce says from the doorway.

"I'd rather stay here," Jet says.

I kiss his cheek. "Go. Get to work."

Marty stands. "Come on, Soren. I'll take you to where you can watch."

I follow him back through a million corridors, and then we come out a door beside the stage.

"You'll be able to watch the show from here tonight too," Marty says. "It's a better view than from the side of the stage, but it's up to you."

"I don't care either way. I just love watching him."

Like right now. All that's happening is he's being fitted with earpieces, and I can't tear my eyes away.

"Aww, you guys are so cute."

"Thanks." I side-eye him. "You and Luce make a good team."

"We just know how to handle Jay. The job itself is brainless."

Luce appears behind us, wrapping his arms around his boyfriend. "Brainless for you." He glances at me. "Marty was a molecular engineer in a past life."

"Whoa, no way."

"I'll go back and finish my PhD one day, but until then, I'll pretend to be Luce's assistant instead of the real brains behind this band."

Luce kisses the top of Marty's head in the same way I would do to Jet if Jet said something similarly egotistical.

"You gave up your PhD to follow the band around the world?" I ask.

"Yep." Marty doesn't appear at all upset over that. "I mean, if we want to get technical, I did it so I could be with Luce, but the band is a huge part of my life. Has been since before I even met Luce or Jay."

"Marty played 'He's Mine' for me, and it made me want to rep the band."

I can't help smiling. "That's the song that made me fall for Jet —er, Jay before I even met him."

Marty's whole face lights up. "Me too!"

"Marty had a huge crush on your man." Luce grins.

"Until I met Luce." Marty winces and holds his hands up. "Please don't hit me."

I laugh. "I'm not a violent guy. Or all that jealous." Well, not *a lot* jealous.

"You play hockey, though," Luce says.

"Okay, I'm a little violent, but only on the ice. And barely even then. We have enforcers for a reason—they know how to fight."

Marty assesses me. "Note to self. Don't leave the hockey player in a room where Harley can get to him. He doesn't know how to fight."

"Oh, I can definitely hold my own if I have to." Not that I'll have to with Jet's ex ... right?

Before I can ask about the chances of that happening, Jet's guitar interrupts our conversation.

Then he's there at the mic, his hypnotic voice hitting my ears, and even though it's only a soundcheck, he brings the magic that is one hundred percent Jet.

Marty says something, but I don't hear it.

"What?" I ask, not taking my eyes off Jet.

He says something again that I miss, but I don't miss him turning to Luce and saying, "We lost Soren."

Yeah, they did.

Nothing can beat watching Jet on stage.

Not a crowd of hockey fans screaming my name.

Not scoring a goal or even a hat trick.

Jet in his element is *everything*.

"Thank you, Seattle!" Jet yells into his mic.

His audience screams. They really are *his*. He has everyone captivated.

During the band's whole set, the crowd has gone nuts for him and Benji. The entire stadium is full of fans. They may be here to see Eleven first and foremost, but they love Radioactive too. It's obvious. This was what Jet told me was his dream that first night we spent together.

He has worked his ass off for three years to get here.

"I know y'all are waitin' for Eleven to come out here." His Southern accent is more pronounced onstage than off, and yeah, that's adorable too.

Did I mention all those screaming fans are teenage girls? I hold my ears as they become even louder at the mere mention of the main event.

"But we've got one more song for you."

A roadie goes on stage with a stool, and Jet takes a seat.

"Everyone's been wonderin' why we disappeared last week, and the truth is, I had to pick somethin' up in Fiji."

Wolf whistles ring out, and Jet's loving it just as much as the fans are loving him.

"I'm sure all y'all know who Caleb Sorensen is by now. Apparently, we're trendin', baby." He glances at where I am down in the front but off to the side. I feel all seventeen thousand pairs of eyes on me. "And this one's for you."

Jet breaks into a slow, acoustic rendition of "Hat Trick Heartbreak," turning the upbeat song into Jet's style of anguish that cuts deep. When he hits the chorus, he picks up the pace, and the backing band joins in, kicking into the original version.

If it wasn't such a shitty reminder of what I did to him, I'd be able to enjoy it to the fullest, but like it always does, this song haunts me, and guilt takes over.

"This was Radioactive's first number one," Marty says in my ear.

"I know."

"Then stop looking like he's singing your obituary. This"—he gestures around the stadium—"Jay owes all of this to you."

"Doesn't make me feel any better about inspiring *that*." I point to the stage as Jet belts out the line about me being nothing but his heartbreak.

Then Jet makes eye contact with me again, and he smiles.

"Just don't break his heart again," Marty says. "Come with me. He's about to finish up and come offstage."

I follow him to the backstage area just in time for Jet to end his set.

I'm reminded of what he said back in Fiji. He wants someone waiting for him after his concerts.

I hold out my arms.

"I'm all sweaty." He ditches his earpiece and mic, handing it to a stagehand.

"Don't care." I remember that was a stipulation too.

Jet wants someone who's with him for him. Not for his music or the fame but for him.

He pauses only for a second before jumping into my arms and kissing the fuck outta me.

I groan into his mouth and pull back. "You were amazing, Jay."

"Nuh-uh." He shakes his head. "Everyone else calls me Jay. I don't want to hear that name on your lips."

"Whatever you want, *Jet*."

"That's better." He kisses me again and takes my hand as we're ushered with the rest of the band back to the dressing room.

I go for the couch, but Jet doesn't let me sit.

He pulls me through to the bathroom and shuts the door behind us. The lock clicks in place, and Jet's expression is downright devilish. "I like my plaything being on tour with me." He shucks off his sweaty shirt.

"That should make me feel cheap, and maybe I should care, but I don't."

Jet laughs. "Good. Now hurry up and get naked."

"Mmm, you think you're the one in charge here?"

"Yep. My tour, my rules."

"Your tour?" I grab Jet's wrist and spin him so he's facing the wall and then pin his hands above his head. My free hand trails down his back and lower. "But this is my ass, so I think I get to decide what to do."

Jet pushes back into me. "Fine, but whatever you're gonna do, just fucking do it."

"I love how you don't even dispute that your ass is mine."

"Why would I do that when all I've been thinking about all night is jumping off that stage and having you take it?"

I flatten my body against his and reach around to undo the button on his tight leather pants. "Performing does it for you, eh?"

Jet turns his head. "You watching me perform does it for me. I could feel your eyes on my every move."

"I can't help it when you're onstage." Or when he's off it, really.

Jet's presence turns me into someone I don't even know. I'm filled with a need to claim and possess him like some caveman.

I always used to roll my eyes at guys like that because I never understood it.

And then Jet happened.

I struggle with his pants. "Are these things painted on?"

"Pretty much."

They only get to his knees before I give up. "Fuck it." Pushing the middle of Jet's back, I force him forward until his ass is sticking out and he's braced against the wall in front of him on his forearms.

My fingers tease his crack, and he shudders.

"Caleb." Jet reaches back for me.

I press myself against him again. "I take it back. There're two times when you call me Caleb. When you're pissed off or when you need me inside you."

Jet grits his teeth. "Right now, it's both, so hurry up."

I reach for my wallet in the back pocket of my jeans that has the travel lube and a condom Jet threw at me before leaving for the arena this morning.

"For later," he'd said. I love a man who plans ahead.

I coat my fingers in lube and give Jet what he needs though I have fun while doing it. I tease his hole, pressing against it then pulling back.

The way he reacts, with such need and lust, it has my own body responding.

He bucks his hips backward, so his ass takes more of my fingers. "Babe. I need … need—" His chest heaves.

"You need my cock?" I breathe in his ear.

"Yes," Jet hisses.

I press against his prostate. "You sure? I need my fingers to do that."

Jet rests his head against the wall in front of him. "I'm sure. I need you filling me up."

Despite his begging, he still whines when I remove my fingers.

My hand fumbles with my pants and the condom until I'm covered. I use the rest of the lube to cover my cock.

"Bend over a bit more." I pull his hips back with one hand and push him down in the middle of his shoulder blades.

Then in one quick move, I'm buried deep inside him and letting out a moan so loud I'm sure everyone out in the dressing room can hear it.

I try to care about that, but it doesn't happen. The tight heat surrounding my cock would make it hard to care if there was an earthquake right now.

"Need you," Jet pants. "Harder."

I pull out and then thrust back in.

Jet grunts. He barely has time to catch his breath before I do it again.

And again.

I get a steady rhythm going and reach to grip his hair tight. It's all sweaty from his time onstage, and even that turns me on.

Jet's body accepts me willingly as I slide in and out of him, thrusting harder and faster.

With his pants around his knees, and mine around my ankles, it's the hottest and dirtiest fuck I've ever had, and I can already tell the orgasm building inside me will be just as awesome.

"Can you come hands free, baby, or do you need me to touch you?"

Jet doesn't even get a chance to answer before his body tenses. His ass tightens around my cock, and as his cum hits the tile in front of us, the rest of his body melts and relaxes.

I slow down. "I fucking love how responsive you are."

He turns his head. "Keep going."

"You sure?" I give a tentative thrust to make sure he's not oversensitive.

"I want you to come inside me."

I stop completely, wondering if he knows how that sounded or if that's even what he meant. "You mean—"

"No. At least, not this time. I haven't been tested in a while, but there's a doctor on the tour, and maybe ... eventually?"

My need to take him and claim him grows with just the possibility of going bare with him.

I lean over him and kiss along his spine, his skin tasting salty sweet. "Until then, you going to imagine nothing between us? Skin on skin, my bare cock inside this ass." My hands trail down his sides to grip his ass cheeks and pull them wider while I dive back inside him.

It's Jet's turn to moan so loud everyone outside could hear him.

"I'm close," I say. "You sure you can take it?"

"Fuck me until I can barely walk because, right now, I can barely stand, and it's pure will holding me up."

There's no more talking after that. Only me fucking him, our bodies slapping together, and my balls smacking his ass with every thrust. Sweat gets in my eyes, and my muscles begin to ache, but the need inside me keeps growing until it overflows.

"F-fuuuck," I scream as I come.

Jet still has his arms braced on the wall, and only when I stop convulsing inside him does he step away, pulling himself off my softening cock.

He smiles at me as he pulls up his pants.

I'm a little wobbly on my feet, not yet able to get my bearings, so Jet steps forward and takes care of the condom for me and then cleans up his mess on the wall.

My pants are still around my ankles when he comes back, and he helps with them too.

Smugness shines in his eyes. "You look wrung out when it should be the other way around."

I pull him to me and just kiss him because, after that, there are no words.

There's a knock at the door. "Now that you guys are done, Jay needs to come out here and deal with that comment he made onstage about Fiji." It's Luce.

"Damn," Jet says. "Thought that might've caused shit."

"It was kind of the truth though." I laugh. "You did come to Fiji to pick me up."

"Nuh-uh. I went to Fiji to escape my life. You inserted yourself into it instead."

"You sound so upset by that. I mean, what we're doing is so

... *hard* to deal with." My hands find their way to his now covered ass. I sigh at the clothing. I don't like it. It should be illegal for Jet Jackson to wear clothes.

"Let me take care of the press, and then we'll head back to the hotel, okay?"

"And then you'll make an appointment with the tour doctor?"

"Someone's eager."

"Always am when it comes to you."

Jet looks like he wants to say something to that, but instead, he gives me a peck on the cheek and walks out into the dressing room, only wearing his pants and no shirt.

I grab his shirt from the floor and follow him out, expecting to be totally annihilated by mockery for having very loud sex in a very small bathroom, but no one even bats an eye.

Marty must sense me waiting for the joke. "Don't worry. It's not a real rock tour if no one's fucking in the dressing room."

I could easily get used to this rock star lifestyle.

CHAPTER TWENTY-TWO

JET

Because Harley disappears after soundcheck in Seattle, and Soren and I disappear after Radioactive's set, we avoid the inevitable run-in with him.

The same happens in Vancouver.

It gives me a false sense of security, which is why in Salt Lake City, toward the end of my set when I take the opportunity in between songs to take a drink of water, I don't know what's going on when the audience starts screaming as if Chester Bennington himself came back from the dead and walked onstage.

I turn. Nope, not Chester Bennington. Just Harley Valentine.

"Hello, Salt Lake City!"

As Harley passes Benji and comes straight for me onstage, Benji takes a step back and mumbles something to him, but Harley ignores him and keeps coming for me.

The crowd is still screaming, the sound echoing in my ears.

This is the closest I've been to Harley in the week since we rejoined the tour, and he still has the ability to make my nerves get the better of me.

Messy, short brown hair. Growth on his chin that has a ginger tinge. High cheekbones on full display. Sad but beautiful dull-blue eyes that are green in some light. It should be a sin how pretty my ex-boyfriend is.

I plaster on a smile and speak through gritted teeth, making sure my mouth is nowhere near my mic. "What are you doing?"

"Putting on a good show?" He turns to the audience which is still too busy going nuts to calm down. "I was chilling backstage, listening to Radioactive rock your world, when I realized I hadn't officially welcomed them back on tour with us." Harley has to yell into the mic to be heard over the noise of the crowd.

The joys of boy band mania.

"Now, Jay here. I happen to know he's from a small town all the way down in Tennessee, so I figured a good ol' 'Tennessee Whiskey' toast might be in order."

I shake my head but play it off like "Aww, shucks" instead of "I want to fucking murder you." He used to hum this song to mock me. I always found it endearing until now.

"Know your audience, dude," I mutter. "No one here is gonna know that song."

"You know I'm all about educating youth on good music. You gonna start? Can't promise them something and then take it away."

With a huff, I play the opening chords and take my position at my mic, while Harley sings and shows off the more soulful tone of his voice.

He has amazing talent that doesn't always get to shine because of boy band dynamics, but it's his voice that made me fall in love with him once upon a time.

His voice is the reason I gave Eleven "Someone Else's Perfect." I mean, the royalty option helped in the decision-making, but it was Harley who sold me on it.

When we get to the chorus of "Tennessee Whiskey," I join in on the harmonies.

And this is the part where I hate having a connection to Harley. When we're singing and messing around with our music, there's an undeniable connection between us.

We complement each other, and I feel the emotion of the song in my bones.

I guess I'm lucky he picked a song that has negative connotations for me. Anything that reminds me of Tennessee and my upbringing is enough to turn me sour.

During the next chorus, Harley moves closer. Glaring at him and mentally telling him that's a bad idea goes unheard.

We come so close we share the one microphone, and I hate how magical it feels as we sing the powerfully effortless lyrics together.

The label is going to have a fit over this, and it's the type of moment that will go viral. But it's not as if Harley gave me a choice here. What am I supposed to say about him hijacking my stage? *Get back in your corner, bitch*? That'd bring more attention than singing with him.

We finish the song and breathe heavy, and he stares at me in the way that used to make it easy to get lost in him.

While we were singing together, I felt that bond I've always had with him, but right now, there's something missing.

That connection's severed.

It's like we used to be wired together, but when we were torn apart, we spent months trying to fix us the wrong way. Now, it's as if those wires don't even match up anymore.

Harley steps back, away from the mic. "You can't tell me you and your hockey player have even half as much chemistry. You can't *fake* what we just did."

My gaze flies to Soren, where he has stood for the last three shows. Even with his arms folded, pissed-off look on his face, and flushed red from jealousy or anger or maybe both, Soren makes butterflies swarm in my gut.

Harley's wrong about one thing. While Harley and I have undeniable chemistry, Soren and I have something fundamentally deeper. So much so I don't even know what to call it.

And Harley pulling this stunt might've put all of it in jeopardy.

Harley exits stage right after waving to the crowd again, and I'm left with a total mind blank. I need to do something. Like sing, maybe. I guess. Fuck, what song were we up to on the set list?

We can't leave the stage without singing our closing song, which is "Hat Trick Heartbreak," so my fingers do the work for me and start the song on my guitar.

Both Benji and Freya look at me weird because I know I've skipped over a couple of songs, but I need off this stage ASAP.

We kinda fumble our way through it. The backup band sings more than I do, but we get there in the end.

In a bit of a zombie state, I leave the stage unsure if I even tell the audience goodnight.

Just like in Seattle and Vancouver, Soren's right there, waiting for me. Only tonight, he looks unamused.

"Are you okay?" His frown is deep.

I try to shake off the encounter with Harley. "I'm fine. Just … taken off guard. Let's get out of here."

Luce appears out of nowhere like he always does. "Jay, there are reporters who want to talk to you about the impromptu duet."

"Damn it."

"They're in your dressing room."

We move as a group and meet two journalists waiting for us.

"Y'all are gonna miss Eleven's opening song."

"I just want a quick quote," one of them says. "Did you know Harley was going to do that, or was it spontaneous?"

"Definitely spontaneous, but that's Harley for you. He was probably bored backstage waiting for his turn."

"You sing amazingly together," the other says.

"We've become friends being on the road together for two tours now. We jam sometimes." Even I'm impressed with my casual tone.

"So, the rumors of a rift between you and Eleven aren't true?"

I huff. "I know not to bite the hand that feeds me. I don't have a problem with anyone from Eleven."

"But they have a problem with you?"

Ugh. Reporters.

Luce makes a slashing motion at his neck.

"If y'all will excuse me, my boyfriend needs me."

Luce pushes Soren closer to me, and the reporters turn and stare. Soren does this adorably awkward wave. It takes all my strength not to laugh at him.

"I'll let you guys get back to the concert." I take Soren's hand and walk out before they get a chance to ask any more questions.

Luce has a car waiting for us outside the arena. As soon as I'm through the door, I sprawl out on the back seat.

Soren slides in beside me. "Are you guys going to get in trouble from the label for the duet?"

"Harley might. It was out of my hands."

"It was kinda ballsy."

"It was a hissy fit. I'm surprised it took three cities for him to do it."

"You all right?" Soren's eyes are soft.

"Shouldn't I be asking you that? You looked like you wanted to kill him." It makes me feel guilty for letting Harley get to me the way he did during that song.

"Let's just say, he's lucky my mind isn't powerful enough to kill anyone, or he would've dropped dead onstage tonight."

I can't tell if he's serious or not. Then he smiles.

"Seriously, though. Are you okay?" I ask.

"I'm not happy about it, no, but there was nothing else you could do. It wasn't your fault."

"It's annoying," I say. "It's stuff I expected, you know? You've been helpful in keeping him away."

"He's made the first move. Do you think he'll keep trying?"

Ugh. "Probably."

"What about the interview back there? Will you get in trouble for that?"

"I'm always getting in trouble with what I say to the media. The label's used to it by now. I hate when they take everything out of context and twist it and then I look like the asshole. It's happened more times than I can count."

"It's happened to me too. The team actually has media training for all of us."

Just like when I'd complain to Harley about journalists, I prepare myself for Soren to turn this around to be about him.

"There's only so many times you can say 'we worked well as a team tonight. Pratt was on fire and carried us to the win' only for the media to print 'Sorensen says Morgan isn't a team player.' All because I mentioned Pratt. But you know what the biggest lesson I've learned is?"

"What?"

Soren puts his arm around me. "Fuck reporters."

I smile. I definitely wasn't expecting that. I was expecting him to maybe say it's part of my job or that I have to suck it up and deal with it like he does.

"Hey, Lennon's not that bad," I point out.

"You're right. He's not. And I'm sure there are other Lennons out there who don't spin things to sell articles, but I'm talking about the bloodsuckers. All they're trying to do is make money off *your* fame. You're amazing. Your music is amazing. You're bigger than them and bigger than life. Anytime one of these leeches come after you, just remember your worth. It'll save you so much resentment."

This is the reason I'm so drawn to Soren.

He's what a partner should be.

There's a difference between being there with someone and being there *for* someone.

Soren came on this tour for me and no other reason.

All those nights with Harley where he filled the loneliness were just that—a temporary fix for a bigger problem.

It was never about me or him or even *us*.

It was filling a void with superficial feelings that were easily confused as more.

Harley and I might have lit up that stage tonight and put on an epic show, but it's the here and now that matters.

When I need support, Soren gives it. He doesn't make everything about himself.

He's here for me in ways I wish he could be long-term, even if I know it's an impossibility.

"Why are you looking at me weird?" he asks.

I'm looking at him weird? Must be all the awe. "You're good at giving me perspective. That's all."

And I'm not talking about the reporters.

Soren keeps me focused by taking up most of my thoughts, keeps me professional by being stage-side for me every show, and keeps my insane thoughts at bay by fucking me until I can't think.

He's even great at scaring Harley off. There hasn't been an onstage or offstage attack since Salt Lake City.

Denver, Dallas, and Houston go smoothly.

In the very few instances when we've been in the same room, Harley has pretended I don't exist, and I've kept my eyes trained on Soren.

Not like it's been hard to do that. Soren lights me up just by fucking looking in my direction.

It takes seven days and three more venues to get here. Kansas City.

Soren and I disappear after Radioactive's set like we've been doing everywhere else. He has the ability to make this crazy schedule feel normal. He has a way of making the four walls of whatever hotel room we're in feel like home. And he makes this lonely existence of mine not seem so isolating.

"What city are we in?" Soren asks warily.

I laugh. "Kansas City."

He doesn't bother getting undressed before flopping down on the bed. "You know how we were arguing in Fiji about who's the better athlete?"

I strip off my shirt. "Yeah?"

"Rock stars win," he murmurs into the pillow.

"Bow down to your superior," I mock. "It's been two weeks on the road."

"Mmm."

"Be thankful we're not on the tour bus. Our first tour with Eleven, we bussed it everywhere. Overnighters, cramped bunk beds, little sleep. Be thankful for the jet, my friend."

If it weren't for my relationship with Harley, we'd be on our own headlining tour this year. There were discussions about it when Eleven's last tour ended, but Harley and I wanted to figure out a way to stay together. This was back when we were good at hiding our relationship. It didn't take much to convince the label Radioactive wasn't ready for our own tour yet and that being on stage with Eleven was the best exposure for us.

We did get a plane out of it though. We've had added press coverage this tour, so it was more conducive to have the band fly ahead to the next city to do local radio interviews and promote the shows.

Soren grunts.

Poor guy. He can play eighty-two hockey games in six months, but two weeks on a stadium tour is kicking his ass. Though, in his defense, we've been put through the media wringer since coming out as a couple.

The label's happy because it detracts from the Harley rumors and promotes the tour at the same time. Soren isn't part of the interviews, but his appearance on the sidelines is enough.

Arrive in a city, talk to a radio station. Interview for an online magazine, then go to soundcheck. We get a few hours of downtime after that if there aren't more reporters sniffing around us. Then rinse and repeat. Sometimes in reverse order. Some cities we play two nights, some just one.

"I'm gonna jump in the shower, and then we'll go to sleep," I say.

But when I get out of the bathroom, Soren hasn't moved. Hasn't even tried to get under the covers before passing out.

I find some sweats to pull on. Unlike him, I'm too wired to sleep. Some shows are so full of energy it takes a while to come down from them.

I climb on top of the covers next to him and turn on the TV.

I shouldn't have.

There on the news is a shaky video of Harley onstage tonight, getting down on one knee and proposing to a woman I've never seen before in my life.

Woman might be stretching it. She's a *girl*. Young. Cute but still hot. Or ... society's definition of hot. She's the perfect beard because she looks sweet enough to be everyone's best friend but pretty enough to be believable.

I hate her.

Okay, not *her*, I kinda feel sorry for her, but I hate the idea of her and the label's insistence on her importance.

It's complete bullshit.

Lyrics tickle the back of my mind.

I jump out of bed and find the notebook I keep for moments like this.

Words fly out of me in lines that probably don't make much sense. I curl up on the couch in the suite and keep writing.

The news plays that stupid clip on a loop. Over and over again, I watch Harley get down on one knee in front of a stadium of screaming fans.

"Thank fuck we left early," I mumble to myself.

"What, baby?" Soren asks in a groggy voice. His hand reaches out for me, but when he finds no one beside him, he sits up.

"Nothing," I whisper. "Go back to sleep."

He doesn't. He gets out of bed and makes his way over to me on the couch. His head lands in my lap. "Whatcha watchin'?" Soren's eyes close and he yawns.

"The news."

"Fun times."

"So fun." Maybe my dry tone is what catches his attention.

His eyes crack open.

"Look what we missed tonight." I nod toward the TV where it's on again.

"Wow. He went through with it, eh?"

"Yep. It makes sense they do it here."

"Why here?"

"Oh, so you read about Harley's real name but didn't know that he's from Kansas City? His family is here, so it's gimmicky for him to do it here."

I feel Soren's scrutinizing stare on me without taking my eyes off the TV.

"You need anything?" he asks softly. "To talk about it?" A hand travels up my thigh. "A distraction?"

"I don't *need* a distraction, but I'll never turn down a blowjob."

Soren laughs, but it fades when our eyes lock. I try to cover whatever the fuck I'm feeling by fake smiling. He doesn't buy it.

He sits up. "Jet, it's all right for you to think this sucks. If Bryce was getting married, I'd be hurt."

"He can do whatever he wants."

Loud knocking on the door echoes through the hotel suite.

"Expecting someone?" Soren asks.

"It'll be Luce wanting to yell at me for not hanging around for the meet and greet again." But something in the pit of my gut tells me it's not Luce.

"Jay!" The slurred voice comes with more knocking, and my suspicions are confirmed. "Jay bae."

Ugh. I hate that nickname. Harley loves it.

Soren stiffens beside me. "Want me to—"

"I've got it." Yet, I don't move.

Harley knocks again. "*Jay bae.*"

"He's drunk," I say.

Soren tries to contain a smile. "Whatever you say, Jay bae."

"Don't even start." Weighted with nerves, I make my way to the door and prepare to tell Harley to fuck off.

But as soon as it opens, there *he* is, and like the past few months, I can't shut him out. Only, this time, it's not because I'm weak. I understand now that our connection is only a kinship of two lonely people on tour. *That's* why I can't turn him away.

Even if I want to.

He hasn't shaved in a while, his ginger scruff more prominent. His brown hair is messy, and he has bags under his bloodshot eyes.

Déjà vu from the billion other times this exact scenario has played out runs through my head.

Only, this feels different. Things are unbalanced now.

"It's happening." He sways on his feet.

"I saw." I can't help feeling sorry for the guy.

"Because of 'Tennessee Whiskey.'"

"The song or the barrel of it you've had to drink tonight?"

"Because of us. Singing it. They weren't going to make me announce the stupid engagement until after the tour wraps. Now …"

I step aside and let him in.

A look of triumph lights his face, and I know immediately he's gotten the wrong idea, but before I can call him on it, he stumbles his way past me and freezes.

Harley frowns. "Why's he here when …"

"When what?" I ask. He doesn't answer me.

Soren glances between Harley and me and then stands. "I, uh, can go if you want me to."

It's obvious he doesn't want to leave me with Harley but is trying to be respectful. Well, fuck that.

"No." I approach and wrap my arms around Soren's waist. "You don't need to leave."

There's a three-way stare off until Harley's shoulders slump.

"I don't want to be here," Harley wobbles. "I don't want …"

"You're free to leave," I say bitterly. "You didn't need to come in."

Soren leans in. "I don't think he's talking about our hotel room."

"See, the hockey player gets it." Harley throws himself into the single armchair in the room. "My life shouldn't be like this."

"Yeah, massive stadium tours, millions of fans, and more fame than anyone could ask for. Your life is the worst." I cringe at my own dig because of everyone in the world, I know more than most the sacrifices he's made to have this life.

"And that comes at what cost?" Harley shakes his head. "It's too much. What they're asking of me."

"Then tell the label that." I pull Soren down onto the couch next to me.

"You know it's not that easy, bae."

I grit my teeth. "Don't call me that."

He flinches. "Sorry. Force of habit. But my point still stands. It's not easy."

"Neither is coming out," Soren says.

Harley's gaze flies to his.

"Deciding to be the first out NHL player was hard. I didn't know how the public was going to react or how it was going to affect my career. I understand the need to let the world know who you are and to live your true life, but maybe the label is keeping you quiet for a reason? You could lose everything you've worked for, and you need to be okay with saying goodbye to music if you do it. When I made my choice, I'd all but convinced myself I'd retire. It worked out for me, but your fans might abandon you. It's too unpredictable."

"I don't want to live this lie."

"Should've thought of that before you proposed publicly in front of billions of people," I say. "The whole world has seen it by now."

"I don't think that's helping, Jet," Soren says in my ear.

"What, you want to help him?" I ask incredulously.

"Does he look like someone who's doing this to spite you? Or to piss you off? He's clearly hurting."

Harley whines. "Damn it. Why'd your boyfriend have to be nice?"

"He's Canadian. He can't help it."

"Sorry." Soren shrugs.

"God, he's apologizing even though I'm in your room all drunk-like and complaining. He really is Canadian." His head kinda wobbles.

"Maybe you should go sleep it off," I say. "You'll be able to think more clearly when you're sober."

"If Ryder would hurry up and get the guts to leave already, we'd have a way to get out of our stupid contract," he rambles. I guess he's *not* going to go sleep it off.

"Ryder wants out?" I ask.

"He wants more time with Kaylee, and she's getting to an age where she needs routine and to be able to run around, and she can't get that on a music tour. If he leaves, the band breaks up, and we can all do our own thing."

"Every teenage girl's heart in the world just twinged, and no one knows why," Soren jokes.

"Oh, it's gonna be worse than when 1D broke up." I turn to Harley. "But why does Ryder have to be the first to leave?"

"He has the better excuse with his kid. If the rest of us do it, we're the diva and no one will want to work with us."

I try not to smile. "You *are* a bit of a diva."

"I'm sorry," Harley mumbles.

I blink at him. Harley Valentine doesn't say sorry.

"For forcing you to come back on tour. I … I didn't want to do it alone. But I know it's unfair to you, and I shouldn't even be here." He hangs his head in his hands. "I want everything to be like it was a year ago. Before everyone knew about us. Before it was drama. Before—"

"Before we got into the habit of repeatedly hurting each other by prolonging the inevitable."

Our eyes lock. "Exactly that. I'm just … sorry. And I'm sorry you had to resort to this charade for my sake."

"Charade?" I ask.

"Yeah. Isn't he just like my fiancée?" He shudders. "Everyone's been saying Luce set this up." He waves a finger between Soren and me.

"Harley, this isn't some random hockey player. He's *the* hockey player. It wasn't set up. This isn't fake."

Realization hits him. "He's 'Someone Else's Perfect'?"

"I'm going to start charging people every time someone calls me that," Soren says.

Harley slumps. "Well, shit." He runs his hands through his messy hair. "I should go." As he stands, he suddenly appears less drunk. His face is pensive as if a million thoughts are running through his head.

I walk him to the door, but Soren stays on the couch.

Harley spins at the last second. "Can I point out that this fucking sucks? Do you know how much it hurts to get up onstage every night and sing a song your ex wrote about someone else? And then to find out that he's now with that person?"

"I know."

"Sorry. Random blurtiness is blurty." His head shoots up. "Oh, one more thing. I'm supposed to tell you that you don't have to avoid the after-parties because of me. I'm supposed to promise to play nice."

"Ego much? I'm not avoiding them because of you."

Harley gives me a derisive look.

"I don't *need* to attend them. I'm not contractually obligated."

I glance over my shoulder at Soren who's trying to be subtle about watching us, but if the diaper commercial on the TV makes him look that worried, we have bigger problems than having to be on tour with an ex-boyfriend.

"People have been asking for you," Harley says. "If you don't stick around for some, you'll hear from the label. Contractually obligated or not, they'd prefer to keep all fans happy, and the fans want to meet you."

I huff. "Even though you hate the label, you're still doing their bidding."

"Yeah, well, I'm their puppet. But I mean, you don't have to avoid the meet and greets because of me. If nothing else, I know how to be professional. I promise to stay on my side of the room."

"I'll think about it."

Harley glances at Soren. "Yeah, if I had someone waiting for me, I wouldn't stick around either." He stumbles away.

I close the door and lean against it, wondering if that actually happened. "That was weird."

"Was it?"

"Yeah. He was ... rational. That's not like him at all."

"He seems lost. I was kinda hoping your ex would be a dick. So much easier to hate them when they're assholes."

"You heard from yours at all?"

"Oh, yeah. He says my midlife crisis looks desperate and sad. He also had a lot to say about my gallivanting all over the country with the rock star I was unhealthily obsessed with during our relationship to the point he suspected something was going on even though I promised that I just liked your music."

"Oops?"

Soren laughs. "Come here." He holds out his hand and pulls me into his lap. "Can I ask you something about the song?"

"'Someone Else's Perfect'?"

"Yeah. Why did you give it to Eleven?"

"The label said it was too much like 'Hat Trick Heartbreak' and refused to record it with us. So, they tweaked the melody, put a bopping beat behind it, and, bam, it became a pop song."

"Are you sure you're okay after that?"

I nod. "You don't have to keep asking if I'm okay. If I'm not, you'll know."

"Does this mean we have to stick around for the whole show now? Because I'm going to need a power nap in the afternoons or something."

"Aww, old man. I know being on the road can be rough—"

"Oh no. Being on the road playing hockey can be rough. Being on a music tour is fucking brutal. And the thing is, we're not even doing much. Well, I'm not. I follow you everywhere you go, and then you're onstage every other night shaking your ass. At least you're getting in some cardio. Preseason training is going to kick my ass because I'm getting fat and lazy and—"

My hands run over his rock-hard abs. "So fat."

"You know what I mean. There's hardly any time on the schedule to work out. I've been given maybe half an hour in two different cities. Hell, there's no time on the schedule for us to go sightseeing or even have some *alone* time. You're constantly surrounded by people, and they're always coming and going. It makes my head spin. You have one of the hardest jobs in the world. Dealing with an ex at the same time …"

As much as I appreciate the acknowledgment about how hard it is, freak-out soldiers march in my stomach.

I guess I didn't realize until this second that while I've been keeping naïve, heart-eyed Jet in check, he's still getting stupid ideas. Like Soren might want to stay on tour with me instead of going home. Which is really stupid because that *can't* happen.

He's under contract. And if it was an option, he wouldn't if he's not enjoying himself.

"You're not having fun?" I ask.

"I didn't say that." His lips touch mine. "I do love the time I get with you. I love watching you on that stage. There's nowhere else I'd rather be."

"Except maybe a gym?"

"Mm, maybe. But I'd *rather* be with you."

I make a mental note to fit in some time where Soren can go for a workout and where we can get away for a few hours.

Soren kisses me, long and deep, and I grind on top of him.

"Ready for that distraction now?" he rasps.

Instead of answering him, I climb off him and pull him toward the bed.

CHAPTER TWENTY-THREE

SOREN

Jet keeps playing up the serious relationship angle to the media and to his ex, and I want that to be real, but I'm not sure he believes it no matter how much I want him to.

It's obvious he's still hung up on Harley. If the way he was rattled by their impromptu duet on stage wasn't enough proof of that, how he handled drunk Harley would've tipped me off. He was trying to stay strong around him, but I saw the softness between them.

Their connection is obvious, and it's no wonder they couldn't keep their relationship a secret from people on the crew.

Part of me even feels guilty for coming between them, but at the same time, whenever Harley's been around, I've wanted to grab Jet and growl "mine" until Harley backs off. My want for Jet outweighs the guilt by a thousand.

Waking to a cold bed and empty room, I reach for my phone to see if Jet left me a message. Which he didn't. But social media notifications take up my whole screen like they have been ever since Jet made us publicly "official."

I really need to work out how to turn those off. I'd ask Jet but then he'd mock me about being an old guy who doesn't know how technology works.

I rub my tired eyes and get out of bed but only reach the couch before I lie down again.

I wasn't lying when I said touring is exhausting, and I'm not even doing the heavy work. But I wouldn't change it. No way. For the first time in a long time, I see my life without hockey in it. I'm living it.

All athletes have that fear of what will happen when we retire. Our careers have short shelf lives, and then what are we supposed to do?

Jet has made me realize I can do *anything I want.*

Something digs into my side, and I shuffle around to pull it out from under me.

It's the book I've seen Jet write lyrics in.

I don't mean to look because that would be like reading someone's diary, but it's open to a page where the words stand out and cause giant alarm bells to go off in my head.

On bended knee
Not in front of me
We couldn't promise forever
But we never said never

I gave you my heart
You tore us apart

Living a lie
Though I understand why
Living a lie

My heart breaks for Jet but possibly even worse for me. I don't know if I can compete with this—what he has with Harley.

I have no doubt in my mind that if Harley wasn't bound by his contract and he could be with Jet for real they would be together, and that doesn't sit right with me. But I can't let him go.

The door to the hotel room clicks open, and I don't have time to drop the book of lyrics.

"I wasn't reading it," I blurt out.

Jet laughs. "Yeah, that sounds believable."

"Okay, I didn't *mean* to read it. My eyes did it on their own."

"Unless you're plannin' to cut an album and steal what's in there, I don't care if you read it."

"Really?"

His eyes move to the page in question. "They don't mean anything. Those were rambling thoughts that came to me. Probably won't even become a song."

"They'd make a good song. Emotional."

"Meh."

I study his face, trying to work out if his indifference is genuine or forced, but I have no idea.

He takes the seat next to me on the couch. "Just because I have these thoughts, it doesn't change anything. It doesn't mean I'm pining for him. It doesn't mean I don't have real feelings for you or that I'm using you. It's just a song."

Hearing those words makes doubts about us even stronger in a way. Jet's music—his songs—is what brought us together the first time. He has publicly mapped out our past through his words, and it hurts, but it ties us to each other.

"Are the songs you wrote about me 'just' songs too?"

"Well, no, but both those songs went multi-platinum." Jet smirks. When I don't return it, his face drops. "Do you really want your songs to mean more? Pretty sure we wouldn't be sittin' here if I held on to those lyrics. Songs are emotions felt in a passing moment in time. Some mean more than others. I love my songs about you, but if I were to dwell on why I wrote them, I guarantee I wouldn't want to do this."

His arms wrap around me, he moves closer, and his mouth meets mine. Jet kisses me soft and meaningfully, and it's easy to forget Harley even exists in the same universe when his lips are on mine.

But doubt still lingers.

Jet must sense it because he breaks the kiss. "Think of it this way. The song you loved so much? That was about Matt and Noah. I wrote it when they were going through some stuff. They didn't think they'd survive it, but they ultimately did. That had nothing to do with me or where I was emotionally during that stage of my life. These words"—he picks up the book—"I wrote this while watching Harley propose to someone who wasn't me. It took me to all those months of being lonely on tour, of being used by band managers and groupies. Then when I found someone who made it not so lonely, the label took him away from me. It has nothing to do with how I feel about him *now*. Twelve hours later, I couldn't care less about Harley getting married because after this tour, I won't have anything to do with him. That's *my* choice."

I get it, I do. It makes sense. It still makes me uneasy though.

"Are we cool?" Jet asks.

"Yeah," I lie. "Thank you for explaining it to me." I pull Jet close and move in to kiss him again, but he holds off.

"Glad we settled that, but we don't have time for this."

"Why don't we have time? I thought we had this morning off?"

"We do, but I spoke to Luce, and I did something."

My eyes narrow.

"I know the tour is insane and always on the go and people are always barging in or dragging me to interviews and we haven't had a lot of actual time alone other than in bed."

"Definitely not complaining about the bed part." I move in to kiss him again, but he pulls back.

"Get dressed. We're going out."

"In public? Where we'll be mauled by paparazzi and fans?"

"Just get dressed. Trust me." The mischievous gleam in Jet's eye shouldn't make me nervous but it does.

I get changed quickly, and we head down to the chauffeured car that has been shuttling us from the hotel to interviews to concert venues and back.

Paparazzi are camped outside the hotel, but we're both decked out in hats and sunglasses. This has been our life since arriving back State-side.

We rush to the car to give them as few photos as possible, and then we're off to God knows where to do God knows what, but Jet looks excited about it.

I want to bug him for more information, but I get the feeling his excitement comes from surprising me rather than where we're going.

We leave the city and not long after pull into a practically abandoned parking lot leading to a nondescript building.

"You're abandoning me here and making me find my own way to the airport?"

"No, but that's a great idea for the next leg of the tour. Come on."

I follow Jet to the entry, and he looks so damn proud.

"Last night you complained that people keep interrupting us and we don't have real alone time. So ..." He opens the door, and I see it in big block letters behind a reception desk.

ESCAPE ROOM.

"So, we're going to be locked in a room for two hours. No interruptions." He bounces on the balls of his feet.

I'm stunned and a little taken aback. "I can't believe you came up with this."

"Is that a dig at my intelligence? I'd argue with you, but I have no doubt that we're going to need the full two hours to get out of here if I have to use my brain."

I squeeze his hand. "I didn't mean that. At all. I meant ... last night, when I complained, I was just exhausted. I didn't mean for you to do all this or for you to worry I'm unhappy."

Jet flushes and glances away. "I know touring is hard, and I want to make sure you have fun."

I wrap my arm around his shoulders. "I'm having so much fun, but this is a perfect break."

A throat clears behind us. "Are you ready?" the receptionist asks.

We nod.

"Which room would you like to escape from?" She points to the options.

We look at each other and then back at her without an answer. It doesn't matter because it's not the actual activity we're interested in.

She eyes us, our arms wrapped around each other, and then she smiles. "I think I know which one you'll love."

The room in question has a setup that doesn't make much sense at all. There are random knickknacks, bookcases, an old desk, a giant globe, and a whole heap of incohesive furniture. It looks more like someone's storage room than a planned mess.

The attendant explains how it works—that we get clues which lead to a key to get out of the room and we have two hours to do it.

As soon as the lock turns and shuts us in, a light on the desk flashes.

"Hey, question," I say. "Wasn't there a horror movie about this? If we don't figure out the clues, we die?"

Jet looks horrified. "And you thought to bring that up now after getting locked in here?"

"A hockey player and a rock star using their brains to save their lives."

"We're fucked," Jet says, and I laugh.

"Hey, not all hockey players are dumb."

"Okay, Mr. Smart Guy. Where's our first clue?"

"I'm guessing the flashing light on the desk."

"Ooh, look who's paying attention."

I press it, but nothing happens. It's just a light. "Okay, so there's the light, but what do we do with it?"

"Not so easy now, huh?"

"You want to maybe help look?" I bite back.

Jet smiles. "Maybe this wasn't such a great idea. It's going to end in a fight. I can see it now."

"Never. I'm cool under pressure. You've seen me on the ice." I bend to look under the table to see if anything's underneath the light.

"Umm ... Sure."

I stand straighter. "Wait, you have seen me play, haven't you?"

He runs a hand through his shaggy hair. "Of course. There was that Stanley Cup game. I was there for that."

"Hold up. That's the *only* game you've watched? I've been stalking your career, and you've never once seen one of my games since the night we met?"

Jet becomes flustered. "Uh, maybe check the drawers. There

might be a clue in there." He rounds the table and reaches for the handle, but I close in on him and grab his wrist.

"You haven't seen me play," I say again.

"You say that as if it's because I don't *care*. I do care. I care *too* much."

"What does that even mean?"

"It was hard enough hearing the gay brigade talk about you. I didn't want to watch you. I had too many what-ifs flying around in my head. It wasn't until what happened in Tampa that I finally accepted we would never happen, and then I didn't want to watch your games because I was mad at you."

"Jet—"

He turns to face me. "Don't. It's all water under the bridge or whatever, but yeah, that's why I haven't seen you play. We don't need to get into it."

"I wasn't going to say anything. I was going to do this." I cup his jaw and kiss him, soft and sweet.

I could do this for the full two hours. I could use this time to savor him while also convincing him this is happening. I'm here.

I'm here for him.

When I pull back, Jet lets out a cute whine.

"I'll watch every single one of your games from now on. Just keep kissing me."

Well, if he insists ...

We go back at it until we're breathing heavy and groping at each other.

I press Jet against the desk, and I'm about to push him down on his back when a voice echoes around the room.

You have one hour and forty-five minutes left.

I slump and pull back. "We better get to it. You check the drawers on that side."

There's nothing in them.

"What about the phone?" Jet points to a flashing light on the phone.

It's flashing in time with the light on the desk.

I pick up the receiver and press the hold button where the light is.

"I'm a word that ends in 'U-C-K'," a recording says. "I'm needed when you get too hot."

I repeat it to Jet.

"A fuck?" he asks. "Are we supposed to look for porn in here?" He looks around. "What kind of room did she put us in?"

Another clue is said in the phone, and I repeat it to Jet. "I often have a lot of guys inside me."

"Slut doesn't end in U-C-K."

The knickknacks catch my eye. "Firetruck."

I hang up the phone and rush over to the antique toy firetruck in amongst other classic metal cars.

There's another clue stuck to the bottom.

"After you turn me on, I get hot. I'm of no use until you screw me. If I'm not in tight, I could fall out."

"Seriously?" Jet asks. "Is it me or are these clues super dirty?"

"I think that's the point. They sound dirty but have normal answers."

"Okay, so we're not looking for a vibrating butt plug. Got it."

"Something you screw," I say. "Like a drill? Or a nail?"

Jet glances above my head. "Light bulb."

"Perfect."

There's a single dark light bulb hanging from the roof, but there's nothing on it. No clue, no letters …

"Do we have to unscrew it?" Jet asks.

I shake my head. "It's fixed."

"Maybe turn it on?"

I pull on the chain, and it illuminates the room in a bluish hue, but nothing happens.

"I don't get it," Jet says.

"Neither."

Our next fifteen-minute warning sounds before we can figure it out.

"It's a black light," I mutter. "But what does that have to do with anything?"

"Let's go back to making out on the desk," Jet says.

"Giving up on only the third clue?"

He shrugs.

"Black lights show things you can't see without them." I step away, and on the ground is … I squint to try to make out what image it is. "Is that …" I cock my head.

"It's a dick," Jet supplies helpfully.

"It's not going to be a dick. It looks like one, but it's going to be something not sexual."

We split up and look through all the junk in the room. There's so much stuff in here it could be anything.

"What if we look under everything?" Jet asks. "Statistically, we have to come across another clue somewhere."

I glare at him. "You don't play by the rules, do you?"

"Never."

"I'm making a mental note right now."

Jet picks up a random snow globe and looks under it. "You're taking notes on me?"

"I'm going to remember that if we ever play a game, I'll have to keep an eye on you to make sure you're not cheating."

"Cheating makes it fun."

"Well, yeah, winning is fun. Which is why we need to find this cock-shaped … whatever."

"Maybe there're cameras in here, and they want one of us to whip out our dick, and then they'll give us the next clue."

"By all means." I gesture for him to go first.

He gets as far as unzipping his jeans when I see it on the shelf next to him.

"Cactus plant."

Jet glances up from his crotch. "Huh?"

"Beside you. Cactus. Looks like a dick."

"Are you sure I don't have to take out my cock?"

"I didn't think this through."

Jet zips up his fly again. "You've seen it plenty."

"I'll never, ever see it too much. Just FYI."

"What if we joined a nudist colony?"

I involuntarily growl. "No one gets to see that but me."

Jet seems to like that. Our eyes lock, his deep-brown eyes on my lighter ones, and suddenly, I can't remember what we were supposed to be looking for.

Jet breaks first and as if reading my mind, he says, "Cactus."

"Right. Cactus."

We move through more clues, all dirtier sounding than the last, but always with a normal answer.

It takes us an hour and a half to find the key out of the room.

I flip it in my hands. "Should we use it now or enjoy the last half an hour of no interruptions?"

"Let's get out of here. I have another surprise for you."

"Well, aren't I lucky?"

"No, you'll get lucky later tonight. This afternoon, you might wonder if you still like me."

It's not until we arrive back at the hotel and, instead of going up to the room, he drags me down to the basement that I understand what he means.

"You've brought me to a gym."

"I know you haven't had much time to work out, so I spoke to Luce, and he's going to schedule some bigger blocks of time for you in each city while I'm doing radio interviews."

"Is this because I complained about getting fat?"

"Sort of, but no." Jet turns to face me. "I kinda feel like I dragged you from a vacation in Fiji to practically working on my tour, and I know you were tired last night, so it was mostly whining, but I want this to work for both of us. You need to be ready for the season, and I don't want it to get to a point where you have to go home early so you can focus on training. I'm trying to find a way we can both get what we need while getting you to stay on tour with me."

The things Jet does shouldn't stun me. I shouldn't be surprised by how thoughtful he is.

Perhaps it's because of this outlandish persona he has even with the rest of the gay brigade and his band. He puts on a show for everyone, but this—this caring guy who wants to fix whatever made me go on a tired rant—this is who Jet is deep down. And that guy is someone I could so easily fall in love with.

I love his snark and his energy and his public persona, but I love this other side of him even more. I don't think he shows it to many people, and my heart feels full knowing that I'm one of the few who gets to see the real Jet.

I just wish I didn't have to leave him in six more weeks.

I don't know how I'm supposed to walk away from him.

Not again.

CHAPTER TWENTY-FOUR

JET

Routine becomes easy once I know what it is Soren needs from me. Since our escape room and gym date, he's been able to still have a sense of normal in his life.

Every couple of stops, I make sure to get Soren out on a date-like activity where we can break away from the craziness that is the tour.

Sometimes we've had to cut them short because of paparazzi or fans recognizing us, and not every activity we do can be private like the escape room, but we try.

I don't get much free time, but I make every spare minute count.

Soren works out in the hotel gym while I go do interviews, but he's always, without fail, at the side of the stage for every soundcheck and show.

Despite Harley telling us to go to the after-parties, we don't because other than keeping fans happy, I don't see the point of them. The people pay for VIP passes to meet Eleven, not us. If we were headliners, we'd have no choice, but I do get a choice, and I choose to escape to my hotel room with Soren.

With the new sense of normal between us, it's the first time in touring history I can say I'm completely, one hundred percent, happy.

Soren brings something extra to my life: stability in this insane celebrity lifestyle.

He calms me.

Brings me out of the clouds.

Makes my mind less fuzzy.

It's not the sexiest thing in the world—even the word *stability* makes me cringe—but fuck knows I need it.

As the concert dates pass, cities blur together. We move through the motions, we get it all done, and then we fall into bed next to each other every night. It means I develop an awareness of him. Of his body.

Which is why when Soren starts to become unsettled, I notice. He covers it well during the day, but it's obvious in his lack of sleep that only seems to grow with each city we're in. I'm a light sleeper, so I know every time he rolls over, sense when he's not actually asleep, and I feel the loss every time he stops touching me or gets out of bed.

We make our way through the Midwest and then the South, but it's when we fly to Montreal that I sense him really beginning to pull away and finally have to say something.

He's staring out the window of our hotel, looking pensive.

"Home sweet home?" I hedge. I hate how unsure I sound because I'm usually nothing but confident—even when I'm faking it.

The tension that's been building between us scares the shit out of me because our time is running out, and I'm thinking he's pulling away for a reason I don't want to hear.

Soren turns, and his lips quirk. "Do I need to get you a map? Montreal isn't Toronto."

"Wait, Canada is *not* all the same? High school geography lied!"

He pulls me close. There is absolutely no better feeling than being in Soren's arms. Not eighteen thousand fans screaming for more or the adrenaline of being in front of a large crowd. Not even coming home to Matt and Noah after a long tour and getting a good night's sleep.

The best feeling in the world is Soren.

"I wish I could be there when you guys hit Toronto," he says. "Although, I'm guessing you're happy to get out of meeting my family seeing as I won't be there with you."

You'd think that, but I'm disappointed the schedule didn't allow for him to be there when I am. I want to meet his parents.

Which is insane. I don't know how to talk to someone's parents. I don't even talk to my own.

I practically choke on the question I don't want to ask. "Is that why you've been kinda weird lately? Because there's only two shows left before you leave?"

"I've been acting weird?" Have to admit, Soren's convincing at pretending to be confused.

"You haven't been sleeping well. Kinda been pulling away."

"You're perceptive."

"Damn. I was hoping I was reading into things."

"Sorry. I didn't want you to worry. There are a few things going on. Mainly to do with hockey and getting this contract extension. I have to play well this year, and now that preseason is getting closer, I'm realizing the type of pressure I put on myself by signing the one-year deal instead of the three."

"Why did you only sign the one-year deal?" I tell the hope blooming in my stomach that it might've had something to do with me turning up in Fiji, but I remind myself that this is about his career. Not us. And he signed it before we started hooking up.

"It came with a no-trade clause. I have Damon and Ollie close by in New York and a good support network. Thinking about getting traded makes my stomach twist."

"I get it. Being traded could be great or it could be bad, but it's the not knowing that'd kill you."

"Exactly. I figure it's better to stay where I am, but now there's extra pressure."

"Is … is that all that's been bugging you?" I have a gut feeling he's holding something back.

"Yeah. I'm just … reassessing. Maybe I need to accept that this could possibly be my last season."

I'd totally be okay with that, but I can't say that to him.

"Are you ready to retire?" I ask because that feels like a safe thing to say as opposed to "please retire and be my tour bitch forever and ever."

"No? Maybe? I don't know. I want to retire on my own terms—when I'm ready. Not when they tell me I'm too old to keep up. Sometimes I think I've had a great career and should get out while my body still works. Other times, I think I can't quit until I have that championship title. When we made it to the Cup final a few years back, it was the closest I've ever come to winning it. I got a taste and thought it would happen for the team, but the last few seasons, we've barely made it to the playoffs let alone to a championship. I really want that win."

I can't take that away from him just because I'm falling hard and want him to follow me around the world on tour.

I want Soren with me for that but not at the cost of him saying goodbye to the career he's been working at since before I was even born. "Then you should forget about next year for now and go focus on the win. Keep going until you get it."

Soren leans in to kiss me. "I should be thankful they're

offering me anything with how crappy the last few seasons have been. Plus, I'm old."

I snort. "So, *so* old."

"Shut up."

"Kiss me."

Soren exaggeratedly rolls his eyes. "If I have to."

"Whatever, you love it." And so do I. Probably too much considering I have to say goodbye to him after the Ottawa concert in three more days.

I become a different person on stage, and no matter what has been going on in my life, I've always been able to tap into that. Sleazy managers, loneliness, forced breakups, I've been able to hide them all and do what I have to do on that stage.

But during the Ottawa concert, knowing tomorrow morning Soren gets on a plane, I can't summon it.

I hit the right notes, I play the right chords … there's just no heart in it.

Benji can tell and sends me questioning looks throughout the set, but about halfway through, he gives up and decides he needs to perform for both of us.

His over-the-top antics are a welcomed sight because they'll at least take some of the focus off how I'm fucking this up. They also make me laugh, so, hey, at least I'm bringing some personality to the stage.

In between songs, Benji takes his shirt off, and the crowd screams so loud I have to wonder if Harley is commandeering the stage again. But no, it's because my bass player's abs and muscles are on display.

Can't say I'm complaining. Benji is hot and nice to look at, and he's the perfect distraction for the crowd right now.

I sweat so much onstage that I generally change my shirt about now, but I can see Luce in the wings, scowling at me, and I don't wanna have to go and explain myself.

But when I look over there again, Soren has joined him. In the eight weeks he's been on tour with us, he's never once watched the show from the wings. He's always down in the front and off to the side, just inside the barricades that keep the audience in their place.

Soren's brow is scrunched in worry or confusion, so after I finish the next song, I run offstage and hand Luce my guitar while I strip off my shirt so I can assure them I'm fine even though I'm not.

"What is going on out there?" Luce asks.

"My head's not in it." I throw a fresh shirt over my head.

"Since when does that ever stop you?" Ooh, yeah, Luce is pissed.

"Can we have a sec?" Soren asks Luce.

"Literally a second. He needs to go back on."

Soren steps closer as Luce moves away. "Baby?"

The term of endearment makes tears spring to my damn eyes. "I'm fine."

"I was kinda hoping the last show I'd get to see would be more energetic."

I laugh. "Way to kick me while I'm down."

"What can I do to make this better?"

Don't leave me.

But I can't say that. He can't stay even if he desperately wanted to. Just like Harley couldn't come out for me even though he desperately wanted to.

All my adult life, I've had faith epic love was out there for me. I had no doubt I'd find what Noah and Matt have. Yet, the two times I've come close, something's always gotten in the way.

With Harley, it was our record label. With Soren the first time around, it was ex-boyfriends and big dreams. Now, it's the NHL and our stupidly busy schedules.

This is the end of us. I can feel it deep down.

"I don't want you to leave," I whisper.

He leans in. "What?"

I shouldn't repeat it, but I can't help myself. "I don't want you to leave."

"I don't want to go. But—"

"You have to. I know."

"We'll talk about this later tonight, okay? You need to get back out there."

I turn to go, but he grabs my arm.

"Please make the rest of the set count? I want to remember this show for being the best you've ever played."

Every part of me wants to break down instead of going out there to put on a good show, but I'd do anything to give Soren everything he wants. I want to make him happy. So, I shake off the emo part wanting to already wallow in self-pity and sing my fucking heart out.

I still don't think it's enough.

CHAPTER TWENTY-FIVE

SOREN

The talk Jet and I should be having gets delayed when we realize this is the last night we're going to have with each other for a while and the revelation that neither of us want me to get on that plane tomorrow.

When he told me the other day that I should chase the Cup and focus on the win, I admit it gutted me. Having his support means the world, but I kinda wished he'd asked me to retire next year.

Which is unfair to put on him, I know, because if he did that and then I retired and regretted it, I could easily blame him for it.

All I want to do tonight is lay him down and worship his body that fits perfectly with mine. I want to bring him unforgettable pleasure until he won't have any choice but to pine for me while we're apart.

We stumble into our hotel room, all mouths and tongues and hands.

He hasn't showered since he finished his set—we've been leaving the venue right after every show and he's been showering at the hotel—so I push us into the bathroom and start the water while refusing to let him go.

"There's so many things I want to do to you tonight, but I don't know where to start," I say against his neck.

I breathe in his sweaty scent.

I'm used to smelling man sweat—you can't be an athlete without knowing what a man's body smells like—but there's something about Jet that's so uniquely him, and I know I'm going to miss it.

He smells like the last eight weeks, and it'll be ingrained in my memory forever.

"Can you just hold me?" he asks.

"Aww, baby. I'll do anything you want me to." It feels physically impossible to hold Jet any closer.

We stand under the water with our arms around each other for I don't know how long.

Jet's strong and steady heartbeat pounds against my chest, and in a weird way it soothes me. I could stand here forever and happily never leave.

But eventually, the water between us runs cold.

I turn off the shower but keep one arm wrapped around Jet.

He hasn't lifted his head, which is buried in my shoulder.

"Come on, let's go to bed."

Jet holds on tighter.

I pull back and lift his chin with my finger. "Jet?"

"Why do I have 'Like I'm Gonna Lose You' by John Legend playing in my head?"

"I don't know that song."

Jet grimaces. "Do you live under a rock?"

"Pretty much. I only know Radioactive songs. You might have heard of them. Their lead singer is kinda hot. Heard he's a loudmouth pain in the ass though."

Jet laughs, and apparently, that's all it takes for him to let go of needing to go slow and to start devouring my mouth.

He presses against me and kisses me harder.

My skin flushes, and it's hard to breathe but not because of what he's doing. It's because of what he's not doing. The weight of me leaving hangs between us, and the switch in him from wanting to be held to wanting to be distracted is obvious.

And I don't think I have the heart or the balls to put a stop to it.

I can slow it down, though. I need to try to slow *him* down.

My hands find the back of his head, and I pull it back, breaking our kiss and exposing his sexy as fuck neck. I didn't know necks could be sexy, but Jet's is.

I trail my tongue down his skin. "Make love to me," I murmur against him.

"Isn't that what we're doing?"

Nope. He wants a fuck.

"You know it's not," I say. "I want you to make love to me. I want to go slow, and I want you inside me."

Over the last two months since we've been on tour, I haven't bottomed again for him. It's not for any particular reason. I think Jet's and my preferences align similarly. We're both vers, but I prefer topping, and he hasn't complained or asked to top me again.

"I want you," I say again.

"We should go to bed." Jet pulls me out of the shower and grabs a towel. When he starts patting me down, I laugh.

"I can dry myself."

Jet sinks to his knees. "You always take care of me when you fuck me, so I'm going to do the same to you."

Okay, so he won't admit that this is so much more, but that's okay because he's right. I do take care of him, and him wanting to do the same for me is as much an acceptance of what we have as if he'd said it out loud.

I don't need words.

Actions speak louder.

And our bodies are saying they don't want to be apart from each other.

Jet goes slow drying me, even slower laying me on my back and prepping my hole, and by the time his cock is lubed up and sliding inside me, I have to wonder how long has passed. The reminder my alarm to leave will go off early in the morning pings in the back of my head, but I ignore it.

If this is the last time Jet and I can be together for a while, I want to make it last.

We move together. Jet's thrusts are long and slow. His hands and mouth wander, tracing every inch of my skin. My fingers make their own path over Jet's tattooed sleeve.

He hovers above me, his eyes piercing mine.

His deep-brown gaze is so expressive, and even though he's trying desperately to hide his pain, I can see everything.

I want to reassure him. I might be leaving, but I'm not leaving him. No matter what I say, though, I know I won't be able to change the stubborn thoughts running through his head.

And like a rubber band coiling tighter and tighter, something finally snaps.

Jet pulls out of me. "Roll over."

I do as he says without hesitation, and then he's right there, filling me up, only he's not going slow anymore.

Maybe he was too close to letting out something he wasn't emotionally ready for, and this is a way to put that barrier back up between us—the one I've been trying to pretend doesn't exist.

I don't think Jet truly trusts that just because I'm walking away tomorrow that doesn't mean I'm not coming back.

I will always come back for him.

Always.

Because I'm not going to make the same mistake again.

Jet moans his release, and I feel it inside me. I've been too lost in my thoughts to come.

Jet knows it and pulls out again, flipping me over onto my back once more.

Without words, he slides down and leans over me, engulfing my cock in his mouth.

"Oh, fuck—"

Two fingers breech my slick and used hole and press right against my prostate, shutting me the fuck up.

It takes a total of twenty seconds for me to come with Jet's name on my lips and confusion clouding my head.

What was I worried about again?

My phone alarm going off competes with my groan. I don't want to wake up. I don't want to unwrap myself from Jet, and I really, really don't want to get on a plane today and go to the team skate tonight.

Preseason is always grueling. Training camp brings out early competitiveness, reconditioning, and the offensive coach for New Jersey even has the superstition that if we lose the first game, our whole season is fucked.

I'm not just leaving Jet; it feels like I'm leaving an entirely different world. One I've loved being a part of.

Now, I'm going back to the only world I've known since I was a kid, and the idea of it sits wrong.

I try to pull away from Jet, but he holds me tighter.

"No." His voice is firm.

"I have to."

"I know." He reluctantly releases me.

"Just think, you've only got seven more venues. Three and a half more weeks. And you're in New York for three of those days."

"But you're at an away game for two of them," he mumbles.

"Technically, it's only overnight. We'll still have two whole nights together." It's like the universe is working against me. I'm in Boston when he's in New York. I come back, and then two nights later, Jet goes to Boston.

"Three and a half weeks is nothing. We went three years without each other."

Jet nods. "True."

"Then Luce says you'll have a couple of weeks off to unwind before they get you back in the studio. So, it's not like this is goodbye or anything."

"And what happens after that?" Jet's voice is small, and it makes me want to crawl back into bed with him and promise him I'll never leave. "We have a few more weeks, and then what? You'll be busy with hockey, and I'll be in L.A."

"I don't know. Maybe I can join you on tour during the off-season."

"You'd spend your vacation time on the road again?"

"If I got to be with you, I'd go to the fucking moon."

Jet looks all cute-like and confused. "Why would I be on the moon?"

"Because in the future, you give up your music career to become an astronaut. Duh."

"Damn it, don't make me laugh. It'll make me miss you more."

I can't hold back this time. Jumping back on the bed, I climb on top of him and kiss his cheek. "Three." I kiss his other cheek.

"And a half." A soft kiss on his lips this time. "Weeks. Three and a half weeks is nothing."

Jet pulls my head down, crushing our mouths together.

I'm thankful I had the foresight to pack what little I have last night after Jet fell asleep because that means I can enjoy this moment for a while longer.

We kiss like it'll be the last time, which is ridiculous because I literally just said three and a half weeks is nothing. It'll be easy.

But when the knock at the door comes and Luce says my car is outside the hotel waiting, all that's left of me as I force myself away from Jet is the overwhelming feeling that I'm leaving my heart on the road with him and going home to a life that might not fit me anymore.

That sense of wrongness lingers with me all the way to the airport, all the way through waiting for a flight that gets delayed twice, and it's still with me when I land at Newark and Uber it straight to the practice rink, because now, I'm late, thanks to the delays.

Here's the thing though. The minute I step through those locker room doors, I'm hit with the memory of why I do this.

The smell of the rink, the halls that I've walked for the last four years … the place that's been like a second home for so long.

Suddenly, leaving Jet this morning makes sense because this—*hockey*—is where I've belonged forever.

I've had an amazing career, but the idea I was ready to let go this morning is now all but gone. I'm not done yet.

I'm also not done with Jet though.

How can our relationship survive if we can't see each other for almost nine months of the year? Six months if the team doesn't make the playoffs, but that's not the point of me re-signing. The aim is the Cup. Always the Cup.

Then a small voice that sounds a hell of a lot like Jet's fills my head. "It's just a cup. It's not like it's filled with dildos and party favors. It's an empty cup."

Is it too greedy for me to want both? Jet and a Stanley Cup win?

Because I'm late to the rink, I'm late onto the ice.

Under normal circumstances, that would mean I'd be walking into mockery. When I've been on the road and in tabloids with a rock star? It's a bloodbath.

I expect it from my teammates. Hell, them breaking out into "Hat Trick Heartbreak" isn't all that surprising. It's funny but not surprising. What does get me is even the coaches get in on it.

When they finish yelling the chorus at the top of their lungs, I not only miss Jet already but can't help feeling like it's a welcome home of sorts.

"So y'all know, you can't see it because of the gloves, but I'm giving each and every one of you the finger."

"Oh my God, did he just say 'y'all'? The Canadian is talking like a Southerner and it's so dang cute," Morgan says.

I aim my glove his way but turn to my offensive coach. "Is that welcome punishment enough for being the last one to practice?"

Coach Wexler shakes his head. "Aww, that's even cuter. Go. Suicides now. Let's see how living the life of a rock star has weakened you."

Motherfucker. I look around at the rest of my team when I notice something. "Hey, Copeland's not here, so I'm not the last."

"Dude, you really have been out of the loop," Morgan says. "Copeland signed with Carolina. He's gone."

Well, shit. "Who's replacing him?"

"If you'd been here for the prospects showcase, you would've seen the new kid from the farm team," Morgan says. "Faster than all of us combined."

"High praise from you, Morgan," Coach says. "We'll see how fast the kid still is under pressure. Still waiting on those suicides, Soren."

"Welcome back," I grumble.

"And remember—" Coach says, but I cut him off.

"Yeah, yeah, no vomiting on your ice."

Oh yeah, I'm home.

CHAPTER TWENTY-SIX

JET

I want to go home.

Even my mind is whiny. Apparently, I've been an emo little bitch since Soren left. Benji's words, not mine. And when I call him on being an insensitive asshole, Marty informs me, no, Benji is an *accurate* insensitive asshole.

It's not my fault I'm grumpy. I've gone back to hardly sleeping because I can't get comfortable. I don't know why I have issues sleeping, but it's been like this ever since we signed with the label. Whether it's pressure to do well, the unfamiliar surroundings and countless hotel rooms, or maybe it's that I don't have something or someone grounding me from the ever-buzzing energy coursing through my veins.

Soren did that for me.

Interviewers are asking how the separation is going seeing as the NHL preseason has started, and that doesn't help with the grumpiness.

Add that to the fact now that Soren's gone, Harley has taken it upon himself to be present for soundcheck and watches my set from the wings. For four cities now.

He's doing what I thought he'd do when he called me back on tour. He's trying to tempt me with longing glances and warm smiles.

Bless his heart.

A few months ago, I would've caved the second he turned up to a soundcheck.

Now? He's shit outta luck. Harley's move comes across as desperate, and I can see how little self-respect I had during all those months when I let him back into my life. We both knew it couldn't happen, but we kept doing it anyway.

If Soren has taught me anything, it's that love shouldn't be messy. Sex, yes, definitely messy. Love? It should be selfless and compromising. It shouldn't leave you cold.

Ooh, song idea.

I go to search for my notebook, but there's a knock on my door followed by Luce's voice.

"Soundcheck."

Damn. I grab my phone off the bedside table of yet another hotel in another city and go to open my notes to get my ideas down in there, only I'm surprised by a notification popping up.

Soren and I have been texting back and forth since he left, but it's his first preseason game tonight, so I haven't been expecting to hear from him.

My stomach flips when I see a "Break a leg" text.

I quickly type out a reply: GUESS I CAN'T WISH YOU THE SAME THING WITHOUT BEING CONSIDERED CRUEL. GOOD LUCK TONIGHT. GET IN FIGHTS AND LOSE SOME TEETH!

His response is immediate: PLEASE WATCH ONE OF MY GAMES. YOU SHOULD KNOW YOUR MAN DOESN'T FIGHT ON THE ICE. JUST KICKS ASS AND SCORES GOALS.

I laugh as I open the door to meet up with Luce, while internally preening that Soren called himself my man.

Luce steps back. "Whoa, it smiles."

"Whoa, you're still an asshole."

Luce grins. "Please, I'm the nicest person on tour."

"Sadly true."

We start toward the elevators to meet the others and go to soundcheck.

"What's the hockey player saying?"

"He's got a game tonight. We were wishing each other luck."

"That's sweet." Luce's words seem genuine, but when his lips turn into a flat line as if he's forcing himself to say nothing more, I have to know what he's thinking.

"What's with your face?"

"My gorgeous, irresistible face? It's just my face."

"You're holding something back."

Luce averts his gaze.

I stop in my tracks. "Go ahead and say it."

He keeps avoiding eye contact as he says, "I figured when Soren went back to hockey that you guys would break up. I'm surprised is all."

"What? Why?"

"When are you even gonna get to see him? For a week or two after the tour while he's coming and going for away games?"

He's not saying anything I haven't thought, but Soren and I haven't discussed it either. We're talking about the next time we'll see each other, not the time after that.

I push my way forward again to the alcove where the elevator banks are. "We're taking it as it comes. We'll look forward to the next time we can see each other and put our heads down and focus in between."

"Okay, but are you allowed to hook up with guys in between or—"

"Why, you and Marty wanna have some fun?" I quip.

"No. I mean—"

"You mean you're asking about something that doesn't affect you?" I push the elevator button harder than I need to.

"Fair enough. I'm sorry for caring about you not getting heartbroken again like with Harley, but hey, your life."

"Exactly. It's my life."

Only, I'm scared Luce has a point.

A big one.

Soren and I didn't specifically say we're exclusive. I just assumed it's a given. And if he can't keep it in his pants for three and a half weeks, then fuck him and his dick.

Still, that doesn't stop me from reading over Soren's words again: *You should know your man doesn't fight on the ice.*

My fingers fly across the screen: IF YOU'RE MY MAN, ARE YOU FUCKING ANYONE ELSE NOW YOU'RE HOME?

Luce must be reading over my shoulder because he scoffs. "Subtle, Jay."

"Subtlety is for people who are too scared to be direct, and when have you ever known me to be anything but blunt?"

"Point taken."

Soren doesn't reply, but he could be on the ice now for a skate before the game.

We head to the arena for soundcheck, which goes smoothly, but the whole time, I'm itching to check Soren's response.

Once we're done and we go to Radioactive's dressing room to wait it out until our stage time, I throw myself in a single armchair while Benji and Freya take the couch.

I put my hand out to Luce, but he refuses to give me my phone.

He and Marty stand, refusing to sit.

"Why can't I have my phone?" I whine.

"Because you need to get your head in the game. You can't

afford another stage fuckup like in Ottawa. We're still fielding bad reviews in the media because of that show."

"That one show. People need to get over it."

"No, you need to remember your fans made you. They deserve the best show you can give them. You're already getting a reputation for being a snob by not turning up to the VIP meet and greets."

"They're here for Eleven. What's the point?"

"They're not all here for Eleven," Benji says. "I always get asked where you are."

"Same," Freya interjects.

"Okay, fine. I'll go to the meet and greets. Just give me my phone."

Luce folds his arms across his wide chest.

Marty grunts next to him and fishes my phone out of Luce's pocket. "He's trying to keep you from freaking out. Soren hasn't replied."

"I'd rather he not reply than to respond with 'Oh, shit, I wasn't supposed to fuck the flight attendant on the way home?'"

"He wouldn't say that," Freya says.

"Even if he did do it," Benji adds.

Luce is close enough to slap him across the back of the head for me.

Freya rubs my arm. "Ignore him. Soren left here smitten with you, and it's been two weeks. Unless he's a complete jerk, he wouldn't have had sex with someone else yet."

"Yet ..."

"I didn't mean it like that."

"He'll reply," Marty says.

He doesn't.

And no matter how many times I glance at Luce during the concert, while I sing and dance my lungs out, giving two hundred fucking percent to keep Luce happy, he always shakes his head.

Still no reply.

Maybe his phone died, I try to tell myself. That'd make sense. That would mean he can't contact me until he gets home from the game.

His game was at seven, and it was a home game against Boston, so ... two hours for the game, twenty minutes to shower and get dressed after is being generous, and then going from the rink to his place, though I don't actually know how far he lives from the arena ...

God, I feel like I'm in one of those high school math problems. If a hockey player is fucking someone but covering it up, how long does it take him to travel X miles and plug in his damn phone?

When he hasn't replied by the time the meet and greet comes along, even though he'd definitely be home by now, I'm not only confused, I'm fucking pissed. Not being able to go back to my hotel room makes me even angrier. I have to stand here and take photos with fans while Harley watches from the other side of the room.

"Twenty more minutes," I complain to Luce when my ass is grabbed by yet another fan for a photo.

"Would it kill you to smile?"

"I am smiling."

"No, you're gritting your teeth. Stop it."

Another fan approaches so I open my mouth wide like a clown and give Luce a thumbs-up.

He tries to keep a stoic and stern face because, let's face it, dealing with me is like dealing with a toddler. If you laugh at my antics, I will never respect you again.

His lips quirk, and I know I have him.

Then his face falls completely when he catches sight of someone else approaching.

The fan screams her head off, and I don't even have to turn to know who's there.

"Mind if I join you for this photo?"

Fucking. Harley. Valentine.

I grit my teeth harder and smile for a photo with them, making sure the fan stays between us.

Harley's arm brushes against mine behind the fan's back, and I'm surprised at how much I want it off me. Not because I wish I could have more like I would've a few months ago, but because I've reached a place where I know he doesn't deserve me. Any part of me.

He doesn't get to keep messing with my head and my heart, confusing me and making me want what he can't give me.

I even want to be mad at him for it, but I don't think he's doing it on purpose. It's practically routine with us at this point, which just makes this whole situation sad.

And I've moved past it.

This time apart where we haven't fallen into old patterns has made me step back and see the bigger picture. There's nothing other than regret with a side of heartache toward him now. The kind you can't and don't even want to try to recover from. There are no ill feelings. There's ... nothing.

The fan is moved along by security, and I turn to Harley.

People are taking photos of our interaction, so I keep my expression friendly.

"Shouldn't you be on your side of the room?"

He waves to the crowd and does the whole *Hey, it's you!* to someone who clearly thinks they should be recognized. Security keeps the next in line back while Harley and I talk, but we're totally on display. "I came over to make sure you're okay. You're at a meet and greet."

"I'd be a lot better if you were on your side of the room like you promised."

"What, friends can't show concern for other friends?"

"On what planet are we friends?"

"Easy there." His fake smile never falters. "Getting a bit loud."

Someone yells from the line of VIPs waiting for their photos. "Can you two stand closer together? That duet was awesome. You should work together."

Harley steps closer and throws his arm around my shoulder.

We're the same height and similar build, and I remember I used to like that. Now? I miss Soren's bigger body. He's not as big as Miller or Ollie, or even Talon, but he's bigger than me in all the ways that count, and when he touches me or wraps me in his arms, I can't help melting into him.

And I already miss it.

More than I ever missed this with Harley.

"Working together sounds like a great idea," Harley mutters under his breath. "And it's actually what I've been trying to talk to you about."

"Is that why you've been watching my sets again?"

We continue to smile for the cameras, talking through gritted teeth.

"Well, that, and I'm wondering what's happening with the hockey player now he's gone."

"He's at training camp. He's not gone. We're still together and happy." I think …

"Okay fine. Just thought I'd ask. What I actually want is for you to think about your career. Ryder says he's gonna do it.

Eleven's breaking up, and I *need* Radioactive on my solo album. I can be professional if you can."

Flashes continue to go off in our eyes.

"You can't afford me," I say.

Harley laughs. "We have boy band money. We could probably buy the whole label if we wanted to. Which would mean I'd own you."

"Not collabbing with you either way, so don't even try. We need to get back to the fans. You're holding everything up."

"This conversation's not over." Harley finally stalks away to let me get back to the job, when my phone vibrates in my pocket.

Finally, Soren's replied, but his words don't bring me any comfort:

Do you want me to?

Wait, I ask him if he's fucking anyone else, and he asks if I want him to? Why in the hell would I *want* him to be with someone else? Unless *he wants* to be with someone else.

Do you want me to want you to? I reply.

"Jay," Luce says. "Phone away."

I do as I'm told. "Fifteen more minutes, and then I'm gone."

I knew staying away from these things was a good idea.

CHAPTER TWENTY-SEVEN

SOREN

I read over Jet's text for about the billionth time, while I ice my knee and my side.

First preseason game? A fucking bloodbath. If I wasn't killing myself trying to keep up with the new kid, I was trying to keep Tommy Novak—still a legend in the league and pushing thirty-seven—and his impressive line from scoring.

News flash: it didn't go well.

We lost, and even though preseason doesn't count for standings, superstition and the fact we got our asses kicked 4–0 doesn't bode well for what's to come.

I'm achy and exhausted, feeling old as I stare at my phone again.

Do you want me to want you to?

What does that even mean?

Is he seriously asking if I'm fucking anyone, or is this some roundabout way to ask if *he* can fuck someone?

The first text was confusing enough. Now I have no idea what's going on.

I had a feeling when I was leaving that we should've talked

about rules and stuff—that maybe it's unfair of me to demand exclusivity when we're going to be apart for long stretches—but I figured it's only three and a half weeks this time, and the thought of letting Jet be with someone else makes me want to both vomit and hurl things across the room. Maybe beat the shit out of my pillow with a hockey stick.

Not being a caveman or anything.

I don't understand where this is coming from, and the last two weeks have been grueling and hard without seeing him, but we've been texting daily when we can, sending pics … Well, he's been sending photos of each city he's in. I've replied with photos of the gross food our coaches have us eating as our preseason diet. But we've been cool.

At least, I think we have.

I'm kicking myself for not forcing a conversation face to face, but I also thought we didn't need it.

We were both on the same page—he didn't want me to go, and I didn't want to leave.

Sitting here right now in pain, I'm wishing I *hadn't* left.

What I don't know is why he's suddenly asking a random question about having sex with other people.

Cautiously, I ask: D<small>O YOU WANT TO FUCK SOMEONE ELSE?</small>

I have to switch ice packs, so I get up and amble toward the freezer. It's times like these I'm glad none of the gay brigade are here to see this.

I'm sure if they could, my joints would creak like an unoiled door. I'm the tinman from *The Wizard of Oz* right now.

Jet hasn't replied by the time I hobble my way back to the couch, but he should be at his hotel by now.

My phone pings, but it's not a message from Jet. It's a daily Google alert email I set up about Radioactive and their lead singer.

Bryce said it was obsessive, but I've loved watching Jet evolve over the last three years. From his early performances and interviews where he'd say the wrong thing to the rock god he is now where he still says the wrong things in interviews.

The Google alert is for numerous news articles and social media posts from tonight's concert. And right on the first page of Google images is a fan photo of Jet posing next to Harley with their arms around each other.

What the fuck?

They've got a backdrop behind them and the room is busy with people, so I assume they're at the after-party, but he told me he was still avoiding the VIP meet and greets.

So, why tonight? Why, after sending me that text, did he go out instead of going back to his hotel?

It's not that he can't go out—I'm not trying to dictate his life—but ever since I read that text this afternoon, I haven't been able to shake the feeling that something's off.

He still hasn't answered my question, so I'd like to blame my next move on impatience and the pain I'm in from being back on the ice.

I forward the photo of him and Harley and say: *Do what you want.*

A groan falls from my mouth as I drop my phone on the couch and lie back with the new ice packs in place.

I love my job, but this is the downside.

I close my eyes and imagine myself not in pain. I think of being back on tour with Jet, watching him from the side of the stage and just admiring the fuck out of him.

I must fall asleep, because, even though it only feels like a few minutes, I wake up wet from the melted ice packs and cold. But that's not what startles me to consciousness.

It's the banging on my front door that rouses me.

My achy body stumbles toward the door.

I have no idea what time it is or who it could be. The entire gay brigade is on the list with my concierge at the front desk, along with a few of my teammates, but if I had to guess, I'd say it'll be Ollie to rub it in that his bestie, Tommy, kicked my ass tonight.

Only, when I open the door, I'm proved wrong.

So fucking wrong.

"Baby?"

Jet stands there, his hair loose and curly, his cheeks flushed, and a look of pure anger on his face. He's wearing a leather jacket that makes my sweet man look like the rock star he is to everyone else. "What the fuck, Caleb?"

Caleb. Ooh, yeah. He's mad.

I'm still trying to get my bearings and make sure I'm not actually still asleep on the couch and dreaming this.

I blink.

Jet's still there. He thrusts his phone at me, hitting me in the chest. "What. The. Fuck?"

"Aren't you supposed to be in DC? Wait …" I look around my apartment. "How long was I asleep? How did you get into the building?"

"The dude at the front desk recognized me, but that's not the point. The text is why I'm here. Really? *Do what you want?* What the hell is up with that?"

I squint and rub my eyes. "You might need to bitch slap me awake or something because I don't know what you're talking about."

"Don't tempt me with the bitch slappin' because I'm tellin' ya I'm two seconds away from losing my shit." With his thicker than usual accent, I can't help thinking we're already past that.

"Umm, I think you were there five seconds ago."

He thrusts his phone at me again, only this time I take it.

Our texts are open, and the last one was sent by me, telling him to do what he wants under the picture of Harley and him.

"Okay, I can kinda see how this is passive-aggressive now," I say.

"Passive-aggressive? How about stupid and out of line? I ask if you're fucking anyone, and you turn around and accuse me of … what? Wanting to sleep with Harley? Not only that, but you tell me to go for it? What the fucking fuck?"

"Whoa, whoa, whoa, slow your roll for a second. I didn't know what you meant. I didn't know why you were asking me if I was fucking anyone when I thought it'd be obvious that I'm not interested in anyone but you. You're the one with the ex still sniffing around you, and it's obvious to anyone with eyes that you two have dynamite chemistry. Your duet went viral, for fuck's sake. You were in love with him only a few months ago."

"Yeah, well, anyone with eyes would be able to tell that I'm in love with you now, you … you … I'll use language your Canadian ass will understand, you big, dumb *hoser*!"

I blink at him again. "I think … But … Huh. The team doctor said I didn't have a concussion, but now, I'm not so sure …"

Jet's angry vibration stops suddenly. "Concussion?" Concern etches its way onto Jet's beautiful features.

"Still haven't seen a game of mine, then?"

"Luce made me go to the stupid after-party, which is where that photo was taken, by the way, and then as soon as I saw your message, I knew I had to see you, so no, I didn't see your fucking game. I was going to stream it when I got back to my hotel, but I went straight to the airport. What's this about a concussion?"

I shake my head. "It doesn't matter. I'm fine. You … you flew here? From DC?"

"Had the band's plane take me. What happened at the game?"

"I'm old. That's what happened in the game." I step forward and pull Jet against me, cupping his jaw and lowering my forehead to his. "You said you love me."

"I also called you a hoser."

"I am a hoser. I read into that text and thought ... I dunno, I thought you were fishing for something."

"I was. I wanted to know if you were fucking anyone. Luce even said it was blunt."

I step aside to let him in. "Come in. We should talk about some stuff. About what we want."

Jet grips my shirt. "I just want you."

He kisses me hard and pulls me close, but his arms put pressure around my middle where I'm still sore.

I wince.

"Seriously, what happened at the game?" he asks.

"I took a nasty hit at the end of second period. Hit my head and bruised my side, but they checked me out and said I was fine. I still played the third. I'm just a little tender."

Jet runs his hands over my shoulders and down my chest. "Let me take care of you."

Hmm, sex or talking about what we should've talked about two weeks ago? Tough call.

"Fine, but afterward, we're talking."

"Mmhmm, sure." Jet kisses me again. "Talking." Lips land on my neck.

Okay, I know where this is leading, and I'm not making the same mistake we did the last night I was on tour. "Fuck it, we'll talk right now and get it over with. Jet, I want you to be my boyfriend. Like, my proper, not just dating, not putting on a show for the media, boyfriend. I want that to be our truth. I don't want anyone else touching you. Ever. Because this"—I grab his ass and pull him against me—"is mine."

"There." He slaps my chest. "Was that so hard to put in a text? Would've saved me a flight. You had me thinking you wouldn't care if I hooked up with someone else."

"I didn't know what to say because I was sure 'If Harley touches you, I know about ten different ways to kill a guy with my hockey gear' would've scared you off."

"Not at all." Jet's voice gets all raspy.

"You like it when I'm jealous?"

He nods.

I go to kiss him, but he stops me.

"Really though? Ten different ways?"

"Clubbing. Obviously." I lift my finger and start rattling off ways while counting. "Using the stick to choke him is another. Snapping it in half and stabbing him. Do you want me to get started on my skates? Those fuckers are sharp."

Jet laughs. "I don't know if I should be terrified right now or not."

"I did warn you."

"I still love it."

I grin. "You love me."

Jet's cheeks turn pink. "Maybe."

"Nu-uh, you said it. You can't take it back."

"Wasn't going to take it back, but I am wondering why I love you right now."

"Because I'm handsome."

"That's my line." Jet pouts.

"And I'm awesome. We can't forget awesome."

"Also, my line. Considering we've spent the last two weeks apart, you sound an awful lot like me."

I take Jet's hand. "Come on, I have something to show you."

"If it's your dick, I'm all for it."

My arm on my good side goes around his shoulders. "You

might want to hold off on the jokes because it might ruin the moment we're about to have."

Jet follows me as I hobble toward my spare bedroom to search for something I've had all this time but didn't want to tell him about because I feared he'd think I was creepy.

"Umm, did your legs get injured too?"

"No. My knees just think they're fifty instead of thirty-three."

Jet laughs again, but it dies when I push open the closet door.

I point at him. "Make a Narnia joke right now, and I swear I won't show you what's in here."

He puts his arms up like a busted perp.

I pull out a guitar case and wait for some sort of reaction from him. All he does is eye it suspiciously.

"Do you remember after 'Hat Trick Heartbreak' hit number one, you donated your guitar to charity, and it was auctioned off online?"

Jet's eyes widen. "Y-yes ... I ... fuck, I tried to find out who bought it because I regretted it as soon as I donated it. With my first royalty check, I bought the most expensive acoustic guitar I could find and gave away my old secondhand Yamaha because I'm a dickhead." His gaze goes to the case. "Please tell me—"

"I wanted to remain anonymous." I lift the case and put it on the bed. "You wrote that song—our song—on this guitar. And even though our night in Tampa ended disastrously, a part of me always held on."

Jet stares at it as if trying to convince himself that what he's seeing is real. "From memory, the winning bid for this guitar was over twenty grand."

"Twenty-four."

"My Firebird cost a quarter of that. You got ripped off."

"No, I didn't. Because if I couldn't have you, I could at least have something to remember you by."

"Can I?" He points to the case.

"Of course."

Jet unzips the case and pulls out the black guitar, laying it on the bed as softly as he would a baby. His fingers run along the strings in a slow caress.

"You need me to give you a minute alone with your old lover?"

Jet ignores my joke, and his eyes lock with mine. "Why? I mean ... I don't understand why, when you wanted nothing to do with me back then."

"That's not true. I thought I could never have you and that we wouldn't work out, but never, not once, did I stop wanting you. I knew that was wrong because I had Bryce, but I've always, always had this pull toward you that I can't fight. It's been there ever since the first time I saw you on stage. I don't know why I bought the guitar. I can only tell you why I'm showing it to you now."

"Why?"

"Because you've always held a piece of my heart, but I'm giving all of it to you right now. I love you, Jet."

Something happens to Jet in front of my eyes. Not a transformation but a shift. His rigid shoulders relax, and he lets out a loud whoosh of air as if he's breathing without pain for the first time ever. His eyes are glassy as he looks up at me.

"Say it again," he whispers.

I smile. "I thought I loved you before I left the tour, but these last two weeks without you have only made me realize how deep I am in love with you. I want to make you mine."

"I want to be yours." Jet pulls me toward the bed, and I shove my twenty-four-thousand-dollar guitar out of the way. He gasps. "Hey, careful. She's precious."

I laugh and move it across the room and lean it against my desk. "Better?"

"Much." Jet moves toward me with a predatory look in his eye. "Now, I think I remember saying something about taking care of you because you're old and broken."

My mouth opens to protest the old remark, even if my body whole-heartedly agrees, but Jet lands on his knees in front of me, his mouth teasing me through my sweats, and I groan instead.

"Bed," I rasp.

"Because of your grandpa knees?"

"Fuck you."

"I wish, but I've got to take care of my man, and my man is in pain." Jet stands back to full height and leads me to the bed.

My back hits the mattress, and then his lithe body is on top of me.

We kiss, all tongues and devouring, while Jet's hand makes its way between us to undo his jeans.

"I'll go easy on you," he says.

We manage to get naked, and then Jet straddles my thighs.

"Lube?"

"We're in the spare bedroom, one I never—wait—" A thought occurs to me. "How did you know this was my apartment?" He's never been here before.

"How do you think?" Jet smirks.

"Ollie?"

He nods. "I wish I could ride you and then go back to Washington with your cum in my ass, but seeing as there's no lube and you're broken, I won't do that."

I want that too even if it'll hurt.

The way he's with me right now is similar to the night before I left the tour. He has longing in his eyes and shows love in the tender way he's taking care of me.

"Love you," I say because now that I've said it once, I don't want to stop saying it.

I'll remind him every single day if I have to.

"Love you too."

I close my eyes and let his words wash over me.

Falling in love wasn't the exact plan when we up and left Fiji, but I'd hoped for it. I wanted him to give me a real chance, but I guess I've still had alternatives running through my head.

Until now.

What we have is real, and it's so us.

Impulsively getting on a plane to yell at me is totally something Jet would do, and I wouldn't have him any other way.

Because he's fighting for *us,* just like I have been since he reappeared in my life.

Jet licks his hand and shifts so his hard cock is against mine, and his calloused grip wraps around both of us.

He grinds on me until we're sweaty, panting, and there's a giant pool of cum between us.

His body slumps on top of me, and I can't even bring myself to care about the ache in my side.

"I've missed you." His voice is so quiet.

"Me too, baby."

"It's only been two weeks. How are we going to survive when I'm back in L.A.?"

"I don't know yet, but we'll make it work. No matter what."

"Yeah?"

"We'll text, we'll video chat, we'll do whatever we need to until my season's done, and then I'll come to wherever you are."

"Six months," Jet says on a sigh.

I poke him. "Eight. We're gonna win the Cup."

He moans. "That's even worse."

"Let's not think of it as eight months. Let's think of it as a week because that's when we'll see each other again. And then you'll finish the tour in Boston a few days later and come straight back to New York. We'll take it one visit at a time, and before you know it, eight months will be over, and we'll have the entire off-season together."

"Eight months," he murmurs, sounding sleepy.

"What time do you have to leave in the morning?"

"Early."

"Go to sleep." I don't even make the effort to clean up or even move into my room. "We'll see each other when you play New York in a week."

"Mmm. A week."

CHAPTER TWENTY-EIGHT

JET

"What do you mean I have to record with Harley? I don't gotta do anything." Yes, I'm being petulant.

I pace the dressing room trying to get all my excess angry energy out.

"The Eleven split is happening," Luce says. "They're announcing it after the last night of the tour, which means it's going to be a scramble for the four guys going solo to fight it out to be the next Justin Timberlake. If it's Harley and you have a collab on his first solo album? It could be amazing for the band. It's an opportunity you can't turn down."

"But he's recording right after the tour."

"And?"

And I want to see my boyfriend in New York. Yeah, okay, that sounds like the lamest excuse ever.

"We're famous enough," I argue.

"Your headlining tour only goes ahead if your next single does well."

"The label won't go for it."

"I've already got word from the big guns that they'll sign off on it."

Of course. When I actually want them to keep us apart, they don't. Maybe now they know there's absolutely nothing between me and Harley, they don't see us as a threat. "He's my ex. It's weird."

"You both know how to be professional if you put your minds to it. You've managed for months now."

"Benji and Freya hate him."

"No, they don't, and where are they? You're going on soon."

"I think they're fucking in some storage closet somewhere."

"Fine, I'll go find them and get them to the stage, but they're not the reason you don't want to do this."

"Fine," I relent and tell him the real excuse. "I don't want to go to L.A. two weeks early to record a song with him because I want to go see Soren."

"There we go." Luce throws up his arms. "There's the truth. And how does it feel to say it out loud?"

I hang my head. "Stupid and childish."

"Good chat. You're doing the collab." He leaves the dressing room, and even though he can't see it, my middle fingers follow him.

My break before needing to go to L.A. just disappeared, which means Soren and I only have tonight and tomorrow night together until the next album is finished.

That could take the entire hockey season because we don't have enough songs written for it. The plan is to lock ourselves away until it's done. We all contribute to writing for the band, but with Benji and Freya always fighting, most of the songs that land on our albums end up being mine because they're too busy bitching each other out to work as a team.

I write better on my own anyway.

But it's only been three weeks without seeing Soren, minus my impromptu middle of the night visit a week ago, and it's fucking hard.

I don't like it.

Being on the road when you're single is lonely enough, but at least then you can have warm bodies filling your bed. It's empty and always leaves you feeling worse the next morning, but it eases the pain momentarily. Touring while in a couple, long distance, is even more isolating, and while it's a different type of loneliness than what I'm used to, I ache for him. I miss him.

I don't know how we can make it eight months.

Even if I convince the band to take weekends off, flying across the country to see Soren for a few hours only to fly back the next day will be torturous.

Pulling myself away from him a week ago was damn near unbearable.

Maybe that makes me needy and clingy, but when you've lived a life surrounded by people who don't think you matter—parents, record labels, boyfriends—all you want to do is hold on tight to anyone who fills that void in your heart that's telling you you're not worthy of true love.

Soren not only makes me feel worthy of it, but he makes me want to give him the same thing in return.

Not by making overt romantic grand gestures or posting our relationship status online for the world to see.

He's who I want to see with a smile on his face whenever I leave the stage. He's the one I want to hold me at night while we sleep.

I don't need over-the-top romance.

I just need him to be there.

I need more of those eight weeks on tour.

I need things I can't ask of him because taking him away from his job—his NHL dream—would be hurting him and his career as much as me turning down this opportunity to be on Harley's solo album would hurt mine.

Luce is right, I know that. I can't turn down Harley's offer. This could be the thing that tips Radioactive from *that band that has a couple of number ones* to *that Grammy Award-winning band*. It could be our shot into superstardom.

I throw myself onto the couch in the dressing room and run my hands through my hair. Soren's supposed to be here any minute, along with Ollie, Lennon, Damon, and Maddox. I always get the gay brigade tickets when I'm playing in New York.

And after the concert tonight, I get to go home to Noah and Matt's empty townhouse and sleep in my bed in the only place I've ever considered my real home. I only lived there about a year, but Matt and Noah made it a home.

I only wish they could be here instead of in Chicago.

The door opens, and I push all the wallowing down and put on my Jay mask.

It almost slips out of place when I lift my head and see Soren in the doorway, but I lock that shit down.

We literally have two nights together for the foreseeable future. He'll be at practice tomorrow, and I won't even get to see him then, so I'm going to make the most of it. Spending our time together whining will just make us both depressed.

I stand and run to him, jumping into his arms and wrapping my legs around his waist. I cling to him like I never want to let him go.

Because I don't.

Ever.

I attack his mouth, kissing him with maybe too much excitement.

He laughs against my lips. "Missed you too, baby, but uh—"

"Oh, hell no," comes a voice from behind Soren. A voice that shouldn't be here. "I'm all for you two being together, but that is not something I want to see. I prefer to think of Jet as a virgin, thank you very much."

"Noah?" I squeak.

"Surprise," Soren says and taps my leg.

Oh. I'm still wrapped around him.

I slowly lower myself to the ground and go to hug my brother. "What are you doing here?"

A towering giant steps into the room. "And a virgin? Jethro ain't been a virgin since I was in diapers, probably."

"Wade?" Holy shit, when did my baby brother grow up? And when did he get so tall? He's skinny like me, but fuck ... I don't think I've seen anyone taller in real life before.

"Double surprise," Soren says awkwardly.

I hug my little brother who's not so little anymore. Then I reach up and slap him upside the head. "And don't call me a slut. When you were in diapers, I was, like, eight."

Wade laughs.

"Ollie and Lennon couldn't make it because Ollie has a game," Soren says. "I figured those two extra tickets could go to someone else."

"You're supposed to be in Chicago." Duh, Jet. Way to point out the obvious.

"If Matt could've taken time away from the team, he would've come too," Noah says. "We're heading back tonight after the concert." He throws his arm around Wade's neck and forces his head down. "This little one has school in the morning."

"Shut up," Wade grumbles.

"I can't believe you guys are here." And I will not start sprouting tears, damn it. I turn to Soren. "You did this?"

He shrugs. "I just asked if they wanted to come seeing as Ollie and Lennon couldn't."

I wrap my arms around him and bury my head in his chest. "Thank you."

Soren cups my face so I'm looking at him. Without breaking eye contact, he says, "Noah, shield your eyes."

When Soren's mouth meets mine, softer and more controlled than when I mauled his face, the doubt disappears.

He makes me believe this can work because we love each other enough to try, to put in an effort, and make it work no matter what.

I still don't wanna do it though.

I groan when he pulls back. "Time apart sucks."

"I know, but just think, three more days, and we have a couple of weeks together."

"About that—"

Noah's phone goes off. "Oh my God. Oh my God, oh my God, oh my God."

"What?"

"She's going into labor. The birth mom. She's ... she's—"

Wade's hand lands on Noah's shoulder. "Breathe."

Noah does as he says.

Huh. Guess Wade might be good for Noah even if there's like a weird parental role reversal going on right now.

"Her water broke. Matt said he's driving to Indiana to meet her. She was supposed to come to Chicago for the birth, but our baby is two weeks early." Noah approaches and hugs me again. "Sorry, kiddo, we have to go."

I hug him again. "Well, thanks for dropping by, I guess."

"Sorry."

"I'm kidding. Go, go!"

"She's two weeks early!" he exclaims again as if he can't believe the baby didn't abide by their parenting timeline.

Ooh, yeah, it's going to be so much fun watching Noah and Matt try to be parents. I mean, they'll be great at it, but it'll be an adjustment for sure. And he or she—wait ...

"*She?*" I ask. "*She's* two weeks early? You're having a girl?"

"Crap. That was a secret. Don't tell Matt I told you all."

Wade starts pulling Noah away. "Come on, *Dad*. We have to go."

Dad. Jesus. Alternate universe right here.

"I'll come visit the baby on my way to L.A. in a few days," I call after them and then wince when I feel Soren stiffen beside me.

"A few days?" he asks, his voice soft.

"I'm sorry. I just got told myself. Harley wants to collab for his new solo album, and Luce is making me do it."

"You. And Harley."

"The *band* and Harley. Benji and Freya will be there at all times."

I can tell he's still upset.

"I'm really sorry," I say. "If the Harley thing is a problem for you, we can record separately on different days or whatever—"

"I trust you. I just ... I hate he gets to spend time with you and I don't."

"Maybe I can talk to Luce about taking a break in between writing and recording Harley's song and the band's next full album. We can still have our few weeks, but just a couple of weeks later."

Soren kisses the top of my head. "We'll figure something out."

"I wish L.A. wasn't so far away."

"Hey, that rhymes. You should put it in a song."

I shove him. "How about you leave the songwriting to the professionals."

"I'm super good at rhyming. Love, glove, shove, dove, flove."

"Flove ... *Flove*. I cannot believe you just said the word flove to me."

"You know, like, *flove*. Fucking love."

"I know what it means. Geez. It's just, someone from Gen X saying it is weird."

"Hey, fuck you. I'm a millennial."

I side-eye him.

"I swear. I'm not *that* old."

"Mmhmm. You're lucky you're good-looking. That's all I'm saying."

Someone rushes into the room, startling us. Maddox stands there, panting. "Noah and Matt are about to be parents. The world is fucking ending."

Damon strolls in behind him, calm as ever. "Was that really necessary?"

Maddox loses the panic. "Yeah. It was fun."

I can't help laughing at him. I don't think anyone can help laughing at Maddox, honestly. "Hey, guys. Thanks for coming."

We do the handshake, man-clap on the back thing.

But then Damon turns to Soren, and my stomach sinks when he says, "We need to talk."

I don't know why, but I get the feeling this can't be good.

CHAPTER TWENTY-NINE

SOREN

I had a feeling this talk with Damon might be coming.

The new kid, the one I'm struggling to keep up with on the ice, is going to be a huge star. And beside him, I look like a tortoise wearing skates.

I'm about to get a lecture on upping my game.

"They're ready for me," Jet says and kisses my cheek. He gives me a concerned look as he walks out, and I try to give him a reassuring smile in return.

"I'll …" Maddox looks between his boyfriend and me. "I'll go find my spot out there."

As soon as Maddox leaves, I cut Damon off.

"I know I've been sucking."

He holds up his hand. "Don't want to know what you and Jet get up to—"

"Dude—"

"Sorry. I spend way too much time with Maddox. But yeah, your preseason game is struggling. At this rate, you might become the highest paid player in the AHL. With a no-trade clause, they can't trade you, so the only way to go is down."

I grunt. "I keep telling myself it's only preseason and I'll get my mojo back the more I'm on the ice, but it hasn't happened yet."

"If you want that contract extension, you're gonna have to do something."

"Good thing I've got all season to find my game, eh?"

"Think you're in the right headspace to do it?" Damon glances around the lavish dressing room at all the band's equipment.

"Subtle, man. Real subtle. What would you say if I told you I'm starting to regret even signing for this season?" Hockey may have been my home at one point, but now I'm split down the middle between hockey and Jet.

"That maybe you've found something more important than hockey, and there's nothing wrong with that."

"I'm sure you're hoping for the ten percent of a multimillion-dollar extension contract, but thanks for pretending you're not picking a side."

Damon cocks his head. "You should know me better than that by now. I'm not picking a side. And, if you are ready to retire, I can look into other types of jobs for you. Endorsements or maybe speaking events around the country that might happen to coincide with a certain rock tour …"

My gaze flies to his. "Am I that obvious?"

"That you're head over heels in love? Yeah, you are."

"Am I stupid to consider early retirement for a relationship?"

"It's not really *early*, old man."

I point at him. "I'm only three years older than you, asshole."

Damon laughs.

"I thought I'd have a few more years."

"And you can have it—if you pull your head out of your ass

and get back to work on the ice. Guess you need to decide what's going to be your priority. Your career or Jet's."

When Damon leaves, I take a seat on the couch in Jet's dressing room, and a billion things run through my head.

Never before have I taken someone else's life into consideration when it came to my NHL career.

I don't want to make the same mistakes I did three years ago.

On the other side, I don't want to walk away from hockey unless I'm one hundred percent sure.

Once I'm done, I'm done. There are no comeback tours for athletes. Any who try inevitably retire again soon afterward.

Radioactive is on the cusp of becoming one of the biggest bands in the country, and I can't ask Jet to step back for a few years while I finish out my career.

If I can even turn this season around and save my career.

Gah! This! This is why I'm fucking up on the ice.

Something's going to give eventually. I don't want it to be Jet, but am I ready to let go of hockey?

Music filters in from the stage, and Jet's loud voice carries through the building.

I shake off the confusion and indecisiveness of my future and tell myself the same thing I have been since preseason started. There's nothing I can do about it in this moment, so no decisions need to be made.

I'm going to go out there, enjoy my man's show, take him home and make love to him, and then do it all again tomorrow.

Then when I have to say goodbye, I'll put on a brave face and try to convince both of us that we can do this long-distance thing.

It's only eight months. And that's if we make it to the Cup.

We can do it.

We can totally do it.

When the hell is this convincing thing supposed to kick in?

Right now, with Jet in my arms, my hands trailing down his naked skin, I'm more than ready to say *fuck hockey*.

I've had a good career. A long one. Fifteen years is a *great* career.

I may not have a Stanley Cup win, but neither does Dino Ciccarelli, Pavel Bure, or Phil Housley, and they're all in the Hall of Fame. More players walk away from the game without one than with.

"What did Damon want to talk to you about?" Jet asks.

I've been waiting for it but wasn't sure if he'd ask. "He wanted to lecture me about my game. With the way preseason's going, the contract extension's not going to happen."

"You've still got the whole season ahead of you."

"I know."

"But you're worried."

"I'm struggling to get my head in the game, but it'll come to me. It always does. Don't you ever get in a funk and it looks like there's no end in sight, but then something clicks and you're back at the top of your game … uh stage game … is that even a thing for musicians?"

"For writing songs, I go through those phases. Especially when the label breathes down my neck to force out songs for an album. But the only time I've been kinda absent onstage was in Ottawa. The night before…"

"The night before I left."

Jet buries his head on my chest and nods.

I don't want to think about what that means because my initial thought is we're great at messing each other up professionally, and I don't want to open that can of worms.

"This distance thing is gonna suck," he says.

"Yeah. It will."

Jet groans. "So will working with Harley."

"Because you still … I mean …"

Jet leans up on his elbow. "Still what, Caleb?"

"I mean, *why* will it suck?" I almost accused him of still having feelings for the guy, and I think he knows that's what was about to come out.

"Because he's so particular about his music. He never wanted to do the boy band thing. It's the label who threw those guys together, and he says the other guys don't care how they're famous, just that they are. Harley's obsessive. I reckon it'll take longer to record his one song than our entire album. He's particular and—"

"And that's why you fell for him."

Jet grimaces. "What?"

"Because you're exactly the same with your music."

He lifts one shoulder. "I guess, but there's a difference between being able to relate to it and having to work with it."

"It'll be worth it, though. I'm assuming."

"Harley's the only one strong-willed enough to make it on his own. Ryder has the most talent, but Harley wants it the most. I don't know the other three too well. Being on Harley's album will definitely give the band more exposure."

"Then you have to do it. Even if the thought of you two in a recording studio, spending hours writing and playing music, makes me uneasy."

"Because you think something will happen? I have to admit, if Bryce up and joined the NHL and you had to work with him, I wouldn't be as cool as you right now."

I pull Jet down on top of me. "Please don't mistake my composure as an *I don't care* attitude. I do care. A lot. And not because I think something will happen. I trust you. Like you said, it's not something I'm comfortable with, but I know you have to do it, so there's no point in fighting about it because it has to be done."

I *hate* it, but sometimes hard choices need to be made, and turning down an amazing opportunity for his band isn't something I'd want him to do just because I'm a little ... okay, a lot insecure.

"Wow. You're so ... like ... levelheaded."

"If you say it's because I'm old, I will spank you."

Jet cracks up laughing. "Sure thing, Big Daddy."

"Oh, really. That's how you want to play it?" Without warning, I tackle him and roll us over so I'm on top.

"I have to say, if this is supposed to be a punishment, you suck at it."

"Yeah? What if I was to do this ..." I reach between us and take his cock in my hand and stroke slowly.

"Still not seeing the punishment." Jet throws his head back, exposing his slim neck, and I have to lean in and kiss it.

Jet lets out a moan.

And that's when I pull away. I sit up, straddling him, and stare at his anguished face.

He whines. "Oh my God, no, you did not just do that."

"More of a punishment yet?"

"Yes! Fine. Just come back." He tries to reach for my hands, but I widen my knees and use my legs to pin his arms to the bed. "You're evil."

"Evil is better than old, I guess." My hand takes hold of my cock. "And now you get to watch while I come all over you, and there's nothing you can do about it."

Jet licks his lips. "We're back to you not knowing what a punishment is."

"Did I mention you can't touch yourself or get off?"

"I hate you."

"That's not what you said an hour ago when I was balls deep inside your cute little ass."

"My ass is not cute. It's, like, ass-tastic."

"That too."

Jet's glance falls to where my hand is slowly stroking my dick, and he bites his plump bottom lip.

"Stay just like that," I rasp.

Jet's light skin practically glows in the dark, giving him this ethereal quality that encompasses everything that's so him. But in this light, underneath me, he's the most beautiful thing I've ever seen.

It doesn't take much for me to be on the edge of coming. All I have to do is look into Jet's big doe eyes, look at his shaggy hair across his forehead and small curls around his neck, and think about being deep inside him like I was earlier, and I'm achingly hard.

I can't get enough of Jet.

Never will.

Ever.

His chest rises and falls, and his own, untouched cock points upward, the tip glistening with precum.

Leaning over him, I put one hand on his pillow next to his head and stroke myself harder and faster.

His breathing matches mine as he watches. Jet's smaller body wriggles underneath me, trying for friction, trying to get his arms free, but it's the pleading coming from his mouth that pushes me over the edge. "Caleb …"

My body tenses. My load hits his skin. I can't catch my breath, and I collapse on top of him.

Jet's hard cock digs into my stomach, but I'm too busy basking in the aftershocks of my orgasm.

A callused hand moves down my back and up to my shoulder again.

"Soren?"

Oh, I'm back to Soren now. Someone's sucking up. I smile but don't lift my head so he can't see it. "Uh-huh?"

"Can I ask you to do something?"

"Yes, I'll take care of you." I roll my hips. "I'm not that much of an asshole."

Jet shakes his head. "No, that's not it. I …"

I lift up to look into his eyes. "What is it?"

"Can we, like, promise not to let us get in the way of what we have to do these next few months?"

I hesitate to ask for clarity, but that's what got us in trouble before. "What do you mean?"

"Missing you is gonna suck. Being away from you is gonna suck. But I don't want your game to suffer because you're too busy missing me."

"Jet—"

"I can't afford timewise to jump on a plane every time we have a misunderstanding to yell at you."

I snort. "Yeah, that might've been extreme."

"I reckon we should make our careers our priority for the next few months."

Wait … is he … trying to break up with me?

My face must fall or something because he's quick to keep talking.

"Maybe I'm not explaining this right. I love you and want to talk with you and Skype and do all those things we've promised. I still want to be a couple even though we're apart. Every day I'm in that recording studio, I'm going to be missing you and thinking about you—it'll make for some good songs on the next album—

but even though I'll be hopelessly grumpy as fuck without you, I'm not going to let that get in between me and the album."

"I wouldn't expect it to."

"Just like I don't want it to mess with hockey."

I can't help smiling. "You're worried you're bad for my game? Baby, no. I have no idea if my disconnect on the ice has anything to do with us or not, but even if it does, I wouldn't change us or what we have."

"Just promise me something."

"Anything."

"Make this your best season ever."

That's a big ask. "I promise I'll try. If my knees get on board, I'm all for it."

Jet gets that mischievous glint in his eye I'm coming to love. "Now that's settled, you can get me off."

"So demanding." I move my way down his body and get to work.

I'll do what he asks. I'm going to make this my best season ever because I'm pretty sure it's going to be my last.

CHAPTER THIRTY

JET

I finish Radioactive's set on the last show of the tour three days later and don't bother sticking around for Eleven's big announcement or the nightmare of an after-party because it's going to be ugly.

How the label thought it would be a good idea to announce the band breaking up where riots and stampeding teenagers could happen is beyond me.

I'll be landing in Chicago by the time that happens.

I have twenty-four hours to meet my niece and hang out with my brothers, and then it's straight into the recording studio. Harley's determined to get his track out first, so while the others are all doing media appearances, he'll be working.

That's how Harley is.

Matt and Wade are waiting for me at the airport in Chicago, and seeing them together, the oldest of us Jackson kids and the youngest, one tall and wide, the other taller but skinnier, I can't help thinking that we survived it—our childhood.

If CPS found out how often we were left alone, I don't know if we would've made it through without being put in the system.

Matt protected us from that, and now he's taken in our fifteen-year-old brother so he can have the best education his genius mind deserves.

He's going to an Ivy League, Matt's in the NFL, and I'm a rock star with fans and a headlining stadium tour coming up.

We not only survived our childhood, but we're succeeding. And I know most of my success belongs to Matt because without his support, I wouldn't even be here.

I make a note to thank him one day, but I can't pass up an opportunity to mock him. Especially when he looks like he could fall asleep standing up.

"You look like shit."

Wade laughs.

Matt grumbles. "Jackie screamed all last night and most of today."

Thank God, I can only stay twenty-four hours. "Is that normal?" I ask.

"It's normal," Wade says.

"And you would know how?"

"I got bored and read all the parenting books Matt and Noah bought."

"The first night she was so good," Matt says. "Then, I dunno what happened. Whose idea was this baby thing? Because I can't remember. Memory function is all but gone with how little sleep I've had."

Wade leans in. "He's complaining now, but wait until you see them with her. They're so sickeningly in love with her already." He turns to Matt. "I told you. She's cluster feeding."

"The books say that only happens with breast-fed babies."

My brothers argue all the way to the car about the behaviors of breast-fed babies versus bottle-fed babies, and I don't know when I entered an alternate universe, only that I need to get used to it.

Matt is a *father*.

I take out my phone and text Soren.

Me: *Landed in Chicago. Have fallen into a world of breastfeeding and screaming babies, and I haven't even met the kidlet yet. It has scarred me for life. Just FYI.*

Soren: *I seriously hope Matt and Noah aren't breastfeeding that poor baby.*

Me: *LOL. Miss you already.*

"How's Soren?" Matt asks from the driver's seat, eyeing me.

I put my phone away. "Good."

"That's all you're gonna give me?"

"Yup." Because I don't want to hear lectures about how long-distance relationships don't work. He and Noah couldn't even make Chicago to New York work before deciding they needed to be in one city. Noah moved for Matt, but he's also a billionaire with basically no ties to anything and can do what he wants.

Both Soren and I are under contracts we can't get out of, and even if we found a way out, we'd be sacrificing at least one of our careers.

I fill the drive from O'Hare to Matt and Noah's penthouse apartment by asking Wade questions about school so they can't ask me about Soren.

We enter the apartment to a frantic Noah slashing at his throat with his hand and then putting a finger to his lips.

"She's asleep," he whispers.

"Good. Because I'm exhausted and need to sleep too," I say back. "I'll meet her in the morning."

It's a short three hours later when I meet my niece, thanks to the munchkin's lungs.

I stumble into Matt and Noah's kitchen, grumbling about kids coming with a mute button. And speaking of buttons, I flick the coffee machine on. I'm up now. I'm gonna be up the rest of the night most likely.

"Hey, it's only one night for you." Noah moves about, preparing a bottle for the baby. "Apparently, we're going to be living with this for the rest of our lives."

"*This* is your daughter, and she has a name," Matt hisses while he holds Jackie close and kinda bounces her up and down. She quiets, but the second he slows down, she starts wailing again.

I wait impatiently for the coffee and speak through a yawn. "About that. Jackson Huntington? You gave her a boy name."

Noah folds his arms. "We didn't realize names had genitals."

I throw my hands up in surrender and turn back to the coffee machine. "How is Wade sleeping through this?"

"Noise-canceling headphones," Matt says.

"Wow, baby bro really is a genius."

Jackie won't take the bottle and keeps screaming her little head off.

"Okay, give my niece to me." I have absolutely no experience with kids, but what the hell, I'll give it a whirl because my head already hurts from how hard the thing is crying.

"Support her head," Matt says as he passes her over delicately.

She looks up at me with big, wet eyes and a pouty bottom lip. It trembles, her chin shaking, and it's as if she's waiting to decide if she likes me or not.

The main thing is, she's stopped crying.

"Hi, baby Jackson. I'm your Uncle Jet, but just like your daddy, you can call me JJ." I start walking around the apartment, trying to replicate the bounce thing Matt was doing.

He passes me a bottle. "Keep talking to her. I think it's working."

"Umm ... okay."

Matt shows me how to hold the bottle properly, and she starts drinking like a champ.

"Hmm, what to talk about. Well, you're gonna have to know that I'm going to be your favorite uncle. Wade may be a genius, but I can get you awesome concert tickets. And hockey tickets. I know, I know, don't roll your eyes at me. Hockey is not football, but I have a secret to tell you. Hockey players are hotter than football players."

"Hey," Matt whines.

I shush him. "I'm having a moment with my niece here." I turn back to her and talk her ears off about what a great family she has, how much support she'll have from not only her daddies and uncles but the whole gay brigade too.

When I run out of random things to say, I start singing.

My songs. Eleven songs. And then I move onto the classics like Queen.

Her little eyes get droopy, and she stops sucking on the bottle.

"She needs to burp," Matt says.

I look up to find him lying on the couch and Noah nowhere to be seen. "Where's Noah?"

"You lost him around the time you started singing boy band songs."

I give him the finger.

"I told him to get some sleep while he can." He stands. "Here. Hold her upright so it's easy for her to burp. Oh, and she'll probably spew on you."

I shrug. "I've had worse on me."

"Don't want to know."

"You know, I don't know what you're complaining about. This baby thing is easy."

"If I wasn't so tired and thankful she's being quiet right now,

I'd totally tell you to fuck off, but I won't because I'm seriously questioning if I've gone deaf."

"Do you think if I sit down, she'll start screaming again?" I ask.

"Give it a try. She only weighs eight pounds but she sure gets heavy after a while."

I sit in the recliner and wait for the crying to come back. Jackie looks up at me with warm, brown eyes. "Are you sure you adopted her and didn't accidentally impregnate someone? I swear she has the Jackson family brown eyes."

Matt laughs and takes a seat on the couch. He continues to watch us, and while I'd put it down to being an overprotective father, I know something else is bothering him.

"What's up?" My tone is exasperated, and he can tell.

"Are you and Soren good? For real?"

"Ah. Nice time to bring this up because I can't yell."

"I'm just askin'. I know I didn't react ... umm ..."

"Sanely. The word you're looking for is you didn't react *sanely* when you found out about us."

"I just didn't see you two together, but I know when to admit I'm wrong. I wanted to talk to you while you're here because I know you guys are doing long distance, and—"

"If this is going to be a lecture on how it won't work—"

"It's not. Look at Talon and Miller. They did long distance for the first six months of their relationship. They're one of the strongest couples we know. I have faith you guys can pull it off, but you might need help to do it. So, we're offering you the Gulfstream to use whenever you want."

I try not to break into laughter, but it slips out. I worry about disturbing Jackie, but when I look down, she's sound asleep on me.

"What's funny?" Matt asks.

"Doesn't that feel weird to you? Like the words are foreign coming out of your mouth? 'Hey, if you need to get anywhere, take our plane.' Like it's no big deal. If you'd told us that fifteen years ago, you think we would've believed it? Maybe you would have because you were always good at football, but wanna know what I almost replied with? 'Thanks, but I've got access to my own.' I mean, it's the label's, but I can still use it if I need to."

Matt chuckles. "I'll admit, it took a long time to get used to."

"Thank you for the offer. I'm not saying no. It's comforting to know I have options."

"You and Soren will make it. I'm sure of it. And I'm going to say one more thing, but then we can erase it from our memories."

"Oh, God, I'm terrified of what's about to come out of your mouth."

"Talon and Miller always say the key to a long-distance relationship is … uh … naked Skype calls. And now we're pretending I never said that."

I laugh. "Noted."

CHAPTER THIRTY-ONE

SOREN

My phone beeps as I reach the locker room, and as I pull it out of my pocket and stare at the pic that's been sent through, my chest warms. I don't know if it's because of the photo or the caption. It's obviously a group text with the rest of the gay brigade, but the fact I'm included in it means Matt and Noah must actually be okay with Jet and me.

It's a photo of Jet asleep in their recliner with baby Jackson on his chest.

Better up your uncle game, bitches.

It's the most adorable thing I've ever seen in my life, and a voice in the back of my head says that photo could be our future if we wanted it.

We can have anything we want.

"Whoa," Morgan says beside me as his looming presence hovers over my shoulder. "Please tell me your boyfriend didn't steal a baby."

"It's Jet's niece."

"Cool. So, listen …"

I sigh. "I know preseason has been a mess. Don't need to rub it in."

"Your man is a distraction."

"Would you be saying that if I was dating a woman?"

"Fuck yes. The number one reason for losing a Cup is dick distraction. It's scientific fact."

I laugh.

"But I'm not trying to give you a hard time. I was going to ask if you wanted to stay back after practice today and try to get out of the funk you're in. Sometimes, you've gotta let go and forget about doing well and just mess around to get out of your head … or, you know, distract yourself from whatever's distracting you." He nods toward my phone.

"Thanks, man."

He claps my back. "See you out there."

Practice goes about as well as the rest of preseason has.

I struggle. I struggle hard.

The coaches yell at me, and my teammates grumble under their breaths.

"Need to turn it around, Sorensen, or the fans are gonna be screaming for you to ditch your boyfriend," Pratt says. "Remember when they thought Grant's girlfriend was a bad luck charm? It was a mess."

Grant got traded two seasons ago, so I can't quite remember what happened with that.

"Didn't he marry her?" I ask.

"Yeah, to show the fans they were wrong and his relationship was serious. Dude got divorced after thirty-five days."

Figures. "Well, thanks for the warning. I'll be sure not to marry Jet to prove a point." If I was going to marry Jet, I'd do it to prove a point to him, not our fans.

Morgan skates up to me. "We still hanging back?"

"Yeah. What're you going to make me do? Suicides in full gear like Coach?"

"How's that going to get your mojo back? All that'll achieve is it'll make you like me less."

"That's true."

Morgan picks up the puck on the blade of his stick and tosses it in the air a few times. "I was thinking we could have a good ol' fashion game of shinny."

A grin takes over my face. "Hell, yes."

"No checking. No icing. Let's do this."

Messing around with Morgan reminds me of Fiji with the guys. It doesn't feel like work because it's *fun*, and I forget what I'm supposed to do, where I'm supposed to be, and how hard I have to skate.

I just fucking play.

"That all you got?" Morgan taunts. It only spurs me on. Which makes him go faster. "Come on, old man."

I groan. "Not you too. I get enough of that from Jet."

Morgan changes direction, taking the puck with him. "Then I approve of the kid."

"You're not exactly a spring chicken yourself. You're pushing thirty ... old man."

"Still younger than you," he sings.

"Asshole," I hiss but laugh as I do it.

He pulls his stick back, preparing for a slapshot, but I kick it up a notch and get to the puck first.

It lights that fire in me—that need—and my movements become more natural. My skating is smooth, my puck-handling soft, and anyone watching wouldn't believe for a second that I'm in a slump.

My coach must agree because ... "Where the heck has that been, Sorensen?"

Morgan and I pull up short and turn toward the chute where the offensive coach stands.

"I told him he just has to get out of his head," Morgan says.

"Think you can bring that in two days?" Coach asks.

I fucking hope so. I don't say that, though. I say what you're supposed to when your coaches ask something of you.

"Of course, Coach."

The first game of the official season is an away game against Winnipeg. The pressure to do well after our shitty preseason is the most intense I've experienced in my entire career, or at least it feels like it in this moment.

The coaches give their usual pep talks while the team gets riled up.

I'm too nervous to get fired up like the others, which is ridiculous. It's my fifteenth season playing professional hockey. Nerves happen every now and then, but this is beyond normal butterflies.

This is *I may vomit on the ice* nervous.

It could be because of the rocky preseason, or maybe it's something bigger. Maybe, it's because retirement has always been a future thing to contemplate. Whereas now, I'm ninety percent sure this will be my last first game of the season ever.

The beginning of the end.

Hockey is still my home. It always will be. I'm sure I'll still attend games, maybe even do workshops for peewee hockey or something.

I thought retiring meant having to say goodbye to the sport, but that's not true at all.

The more I think about the possibilities, the more I realize there's so much more I could be doing that doesn't have me stuck in this tight schedule. Leaving the NHL doesn't mean leaving hockey.

The nerves get the better of me for the first seven minutes of the game. I make easy mistakes, and it's the disaster that's been the past month all over again.

When the coaches call for a line change, I sit on the bench, my leg bouncing erratically.

Something hits me over the back of my helmet, and I turn to find Morgan's red and angry face.

"Get out of your head," he yells over the noise of the crowd and loud atmosphere of a hockey game. "Think of something *fun*, and then go out there and live it."

The most fun I've had since Jet left was with Morgan the other day. Before that it was ... shit, any time I've been in Jet's presence.

I picture the way his curls fall into his face and think of his unapologetic attitude.

Just his passion for life makes me feel complete. His joy is contagious, and it's impossible to be in a bad mood around him.

I must make a face because Morgan smiles.

"That. Right there. Hold on to that."

I get back on the ice, thinking of Jet, picturing the photo of him and his niece that Matt sent the other day, and I think about how much fun we'll have next year when I'm no longer doing this.

Make this your best season ever.

Jet's voice rings through my head so loud and clear I'd swear he's out here on the ice with me.

Pratt, a D-man on my line, wrestles for the puck. His opponent goes down, and Pratt gets the breakaway.

The rookie, Ivanov, the one I've been barely able to keep up with, chases after him.

One of Wayne Gretzky's famous sayings is: *A good hockey player plays where the puck is. A great hockey player plays where the puck is going to be.*

So, I don't skate to catch up to Pratt. I skate to put myself in the perfect position.

And it's like fucking magic.

I'm where he needs me to be the second he needs me to be there.

He passes backward to me, and I take my shot. My slapshot to the top right of the net is always on point, but everyone in the league knows that about me by now. It's my signature move and has been for years. That won't do this time. Not if I'm going to make this season my best. That's why I deke the goalie out of position and let him think I'm taking the slapshot. He prepares to catch it in his glove and blocks the right side, which is why he's taken off guard when I change direction and send the puck sailing past him.

The lamp lights up for the first time tonight for either team.

Pratt gets to me first with a massive hug and backslap, and then the rest of my line catches up and does the same.

My mojo is back.

After that, there's no stopping me.

I get an assist for Ivanov's first-ever NHL goal.

Another assist.

Then a goal.

Assist.

And to top it off, in the last minute of the third period, I pull off the fucking hat trick, and we walk away winners of the game 7–3.

Six of those points belong to me, and I don't think I've had a solo game that great in at least five years.

Nothing can bring down this high. Not even when our head coach says, "So glad you finally caught up from your vacation, Soren."

"I figured saving it all up for when the proper season starts would be smart," I say, and the entire team laughs.

After I shower and get dressed in my post-game suit, I take my phone out.

My stomach flips.

Jet: *My man scored a hat trick. Congrats, babe. You were on fire tonight.*

Me: *Wait ... are you telling me you saw one of my games? Like MY game. Me. One of my games ...*

Jet: *I told you I would. And hey, I totally streamed your preseason games but there was nothing in them to brag about.*

Me: *You're lucky I'm on such a high right now even your snark can't bring me down. I wish I didn't have a roommate tonight so we could Skype.*

Jet: *Ugh. I'd love that, but we can't anyway. I'm still at the studio. Will be all night at this rate.*

Me: *Still?*

I tell myself not to hate that. He's *working*. And it's not like he's there with Harley alone ... I don't think.

Me: *Are Benji and Freya there?*

I'll be lucky if he doesn't ream me for that one.

Me: *Sorry. I do trust you, but I don't like it.*

Jet: *Hey, I wouldn't like it either if I were you, so I understand. Benji and Freya aren't here, but Marty and Luce are. They've been running interference with Harley.*

It's fucking entertaining, but it's getting painful. We still haven't even begun laying down our track, and it's been two weeks.

Me: *Apart from that, how's working with him?*
Jet: *Don't get me started.*

CHAPTER THIRTY-TWO

JET

I grit my teeth. "I'm gonna kill him."

"You can't," Luce says.

"Sorry to every teenage girl in the world, but your precious Harley Valentine is a dead man."

"Jay ..."

"What?" I snap.

"You can't kill him. You're too pretty to go to prison, and sex is only fun when it's consensual."

"Damn my boyish good looks."

Marty snorts.

"Maybe I could chop off all his hair? He won't still be that good-looking with a shaved head."

"Still considered assault," Luce says. "Still risking prison time."

I grunt. Maybe I should be thankful he's working his way through a shit ton of songs for his album because the asshole took over our recording time in the studio. The sooner he's done with his album, the sooner Radioactive can start on ours.

I turn to Luce. "Any word from the label about getting

recording time at another studio?" I pitched the idea that we'd get an album out sooner in a familiar environment. Like New York where we were discovered. Yeah, they saw right through that one and shut it down. Recording studios are a dime a dozen in L.A. and therefore cheaper. The ones in New York are expensive, and the label heads refused. Apparently, we're still not big enough to demand stuff.

"They're still a firm no on that one," Luce says.

"Damn it."

Harley comes out of the recording booth smiling because he's recorded yet another single. A single that's not ours. "Sorry about that. I gotta go where the inspiration is, you know?"

"Yeah, and all your inspiration since you got here has been for other songs on your album and not our collab."

The song he recorded the day after the announcement that Eleven was breaking up was released out into the world not a full thirty-six hours afterward. It's already at number one.

He's done the pushing part. He beat out the other guys in Eleven, and now he's riding the number one wave while he gets his first solo album done.

"You said you'd only need me for a couple of weeks. We haven't even started. What is it? What do you want from me?"

Even though I'm only yelling, Luce holds me back in case I follow through on my death threats.

"I want a number one hit from you. That's what I want. What we've been writing ... it's ... blergh."

"Blergh? *Blergh*?" I turn to Luce. "Please tell me he did not just say my lyrics are *blergh*."

"I'm staying out of this," Luce mutters.

And if I'm honest, I can't say I blame him. Or Harley.

I have been half-assing it when it comes to this collab. I'm throwing out words in hopes some will stick. I don't know what the label is hoping for, but I'm pretty sure we can't write about our relationship, so what does that leave us with? Love is off-limits, heartache is off-limits, and I don't want my new boyfriend to have to listen to me sing that kind of song with my ex. That means everything coming out of me is shallow and weak.

"Can we have a minute, guys?" Harley asks Marty and Luce. "We don't need babysitters."

Luce raises an eyebrow at me.

"If you must, you can keep watch from out there." I point toward the foyer of the recording studio. The big glass-paneled doors in this place don't give much privacy, but I prefer that. For Soren's sake. I know nothing will ever happen between Harley and me again, but I wouldn't feel comfortable with Soren being in a room with his ex by himself, so why should Soren have to suck it up?

I respect that it makes him uneasy, and I don't ever want doubt between us, so Marty and Luce keeping close doesn't piss me off like it does Harley.

As soon as they're out of the room and the audio engineer and his producer follow, Harley doesn't hold back.

"Are they really necessary?"

"Well, one is my manager, and if you remember correctly, Radioactive is supposed to be using this space to record our next album, but a fucking boy band broke up, and now, *someone* has taken over the entire studio."

"Okay, I get it, you're pissed, but … Can we sit?"

We take opposite ends of the plush leather couch behind the mixing board.

"What happened with us?" He sounds so serious that I can't help myself.

I laugh. "Hmm, let's see, big white dress, a promise of forever, matching rings—"

"That can't only be it. It's a sham engagement."

"That sham engagement meant that we could never have anything *real*. And that's all I've ever wanted. Someone real. Someone honest. Someone who makes my day brighter just by being in it. Soren is that for me. What you and I had ... We turned to each other when we were lonely and on the road. Maybe even the secrecy of it all added to the confusing feelings. Put two gay dudes on a music tour for eight months and tell them not to bang. It's impossible."

"Trust me when I say it's entirely possible."

My eyes widen. "Luce said not all you Eleven guys were straight, but I still can't figure out who. And I don't exactly want to ask because, you know, rude and stuff."

Harley smiles. "Since when do you care about not being rude?"

"True. But damn, my gaydar is so broken."

"Let's just say, it's the person you'd least suspect because he has the best cover story."

The best cover story. Like a wife isn't the best ... Wait ... a daughter?

"Oh, shit, I guess I wasn't subtle enough because from the look on your face, you've worked it out. Can you pretend I didn't just out one of my best friends to you? I don't think he'd care. At least, not with you, but it's not my place."

"Yeah, of course. Is that the real reason Ryder wanted to quit Eleven?"

"Nah, his main reason was Kaylee. When we left the press conference, we all hugged, and he joked about seeing us at the reunion tour when we're forty. I think he just wants a break."

"A break sounds good right about now."

"You'll get one as soon as we work through this block of ours."

"Harley …" I don't want to be a dick, but he can't keep doing this. "We don't have a block because there is no *us* anymore."

I see the moment it really clicks for him, and I hate that I'm causing that look of hurt on his face. I'm pretty sure it's how I used to look every time he left me alone in a hotel room on the road after sneaking out in the morning.

"What is it about the hockey player that made you forget about the eighteen months we had?"

"Do you really want to do this?"

"I have to do this because I've never felt this way about anyone else. Ever."

"You're confused. We were both confused for a long time. We thought comfort was love. We thought that full feeling we had when we were together meant something. You know what it meant? That we weren't so alone anymore. Being with Soren? Even though he's on the other side of the country right now, I'm not lonely."

"You don't miss him?"

"It's hard, and I miss him like crazy, but that void that was in my chest that you temporarily filled on tour isn't there. Which is why I want to get this album done so I can go see him. Hint, hint, I'm telling you to hurry the fuck up."

Harley reaches for the pen and paper on a side table next to the couch. We've got papers strewn all over the room as we write draft after draft of songs. When Harley's been working on his own stuff, I've been writing for Radioactive, so it hasn't been a complete waste, but I want to get this one song with him over and done with already so I can truly focus on my band.

He scribbles something down and shushes me when I ask him what he's writing. Eventually, he shoves the paper at me.

Confusing love with isolation

Holding on in desperation
I thought I'd found my one
The one I'm meant to keep
But that's not how it works
And now I'm in too deep

I don't want to let go
Even though I have to

You help me escape
A life I can't lead
A life I need to hide
I want you there with me
For the entire ride.

I thought I had it all
But what we had was nothing
Take it with you
I don't need your exclusion
Leave me with our ever-lasting confusion.

"There's our number one hit. 'Confusion' by Harley Valentine featuring Radioactive."

My mouth hangs open. "Harley, the label will never go for this. It's one thing if you sing it on your own. It could be about a girl. You'll practically out yourself in this if we record it together."

Harley stands. "Don't care. Do your thing, work your Jay magic and tweak whatever you need to tweak, and then we'll record it."

It's not the first time I've helped him with his lyrics, and some of our best times were doing just this—passing songs back and forth to make them better.

"You might think our love was confusing, but I know that wasn't the case for me," Harley says. "The label can go fuck themselves for taking you away from me."

I want to argue that we would have ended eventually anyway because I definitely would have run into Soren at some point, and from the moment I met him three years ago, I've never been able to fight the pull he has on me.

We're meant to be, and there's no doubt in my mind.

I don't want to belittle what Harley and I had because he got me through some rough times on the road and through doubts about my career.

I stand and put my hand on Harley's shoulder. "Things have worked out the way they were supposed to. One day you'll see that."

"I see it now," Harley says quietly. "I don't like it. But I see it." He walks toward the door where Marty and Luce are practically pushed up against it, but he turns back at the last second. "Oh, by the way, after our song's recorded, I'm kicking you out of this studio."

"W-what?"

"I own it. I bought it when Ryder started hinting about leaving Eleven. I'm also blackballing you from every other recording studio in town. Eleven and Radioactive's feud is all over the news, you know."

I'm confused as fuck. "What in the ever-loving hell—"

"I'll use my clout to get you the studio time in New York you've been asking for. Really think about what I'm saying here before you yell at me."

It finally registers. "Y-you'd do that for me?"

"Record this song with me and go home to your man, Jay."

"Harley," I croak.

He holds up his hand. "Don't. I'm doing a good job of being the bigger person right now, and I don't want to blow it by taking it all back and begging you to pick me. We both know you won't. I'll get over you eventually. Just ... make sure the hockey player is worth it, okay?"

I don't say anything because I don't want to rub it in that I already know Soren is worth it. He's *everything* to me.

CHAPTER THIRTY-THREE

SOREN

As we stand for the national anthem at a home game, I'm trying to get in my zone. My streak has continued, and I'm having the best season of my entire career, but I can't get comfortable. Not now. It's still too early.

I'm so distracted by my thoughts of the game and trying to suck the atmosphere into my lungs that I barely register who they introduce to sing.

"Please welcome Jay from Radioactive to sing the national anthem."

The crowd does its usual screaming thing, just like they always do when he's onstage.

Morgan nudges me, but my eyes are locked on Jet walking out onto the carpet they've laid across the ice.

"Did you know he was coming?" Morgan asks in my ear.

"Had no idea," I murmur.

I glance up to find my face on the giant screen. Not an odd occurrence during a game, but this is different.

Jet's eyes find mine, and his smile softens to something that's just for me. "Love you," he mouths.

The crowd goes wild again because they must've caught that on camera.

Jet's here.

Here, here.

And in perfect timing, this is our last home game before we hit the road for eight days.

I laugh because it makes me want to cry. We leave for Carolina tomorrow, and I don't know how long Jet's in town for.

Only the first line is out on the ice. I'm stuck in the team box when all I want to do is jump over the railing and skate for him.

Jet's decked out with a headset and microphone, and he's holding his black guitar. *My* guitar. After his middle of the night visit, I told him to take it with him. It's his baby. But now instead of using his pride and joy—his acoustic Firebird he bought with his first royalty check—he's using ours. And I know it's for me.

The entire arena goes quiet to listen.

Whether it's the acoustic version of the national anthem, or perhaps it's the way he sings it, Jet's voice has his Southern lilt, making it sound country.

I want to blow off the game and take my man home and worship him in the best way I know how, but my team would hang me by my skate's laces if I did that. I'm the highest scorer of the season so far.

Jet finishes the song, hitting every note flawlessly with that rasp I love so much, and then he gives me a wink, leaves the ice, and I'm left wishing the game was already over.

Morgan hits me in the back of the head. "Don't let this distract you. Your man's here. Show him in person how you've been kicking ass."

He's right. I can't let Jet's surprise appearance distract me, and when I hit the ice, I'm surprised at how easy it is to block it out.

Superstition is a big part of hockey, and any change in routine can be a disaster. Not that I actually believe good luck or bad luck is real; it's all mind over matter. Anything that can get into your head has the ability to affect the game.

But knowing Jet's here watching me, it inspires me instead of hinders.

By the end of the first period, I have a goal and an assist.

When the new kid started, I thought he was going to outshine me, but it turns out we make a great team.

We leave the ice and head down the chute when my eye catches on someone hanging over the railing from the stands. Jet's an inch or two away from falling over the thing.

Lennon gives me a wave behind him as Ollie holds on to Jet's tight jeans so he doesn't fall. Lucky Ollie doesn't have a game tonight, or my boyfriend would be broken in many places.

With my skates and how far Jet's leaning over the barrier, it almost brings us face to face when I reach him. "You couldn't have given me a warning?"

"And spoil the surprise? Hell no. I just wanted to give you this." He leans in to kiss me, but I pull back.

"I'm all sweaty."

"What do you say every time I leave the stage and warn you about my perspiration?"

"That I don't care."

"Exactly. Now kiss me, then go kick some ass. I'll be waiting for you after the game."

"What ... I mean what are you even doing here? How are you here? Not that I'm complaining, but—"

"Soren," Coach Wexler says. "Stop socializing and get your ass in the locker room."

"After the game." Jet kisses me quickly. "We'll talk."

I hurry into the locker room where I'm welcomed with a round of ribbing and a stern warning from the coaches.

For the rest of the game, all I'm focused on is getting shit done so I can be with Jet, even if it's only for a few hours. We have to hold on to everything we can get.

I get one more goal in the second but come up short of a hat trick in the third.

Still, three points and taking home a win for the team is still a good night.

I'm down the chute and in the shower before any of my other teammates, and I curse not being able to get dressed in jeans and a T-shirt and leave when I'm done.

Instead, I stand at my cubby, tackling my tie and trying to look presentable.

"Soren, they want you for the press conference."

My face falls, and I turn to my coach. "Why? I mean ... why? Pratt scored more points than me." I want to get to Jet.

Coach's face breaks into a grin. "I'm messing with you. Go, get out of here."

A relieved whoosh leaves my lungs, and I'm out of the locker room before most of my teammates are out of the showers.

I push my way through the reporters waiting outside the locker room to get their post-game interviews before the press conference. They throw questions at me about my boyfriend's performance and I answer something about it being a great surprise. If I give them a soundbite, they should leave me alone.

I move like lightning down the hall, but I don't know where Jet will be. As I pull out my phone to text him, three figures step into the corridor, and we almost collide as we cross paths.

My gear bag drops to the ground, and a smile spreads across Jet's face.

He goes to say something, but I cut him off by pulling him to me, our bodies slamming against each other, and then I ravish his mouth before he gets the chance to even get a word out.

His tongue keeps up with my demanding one, and if I wasn't positive we were being filmed or watched by the reporters down at the other end of the hall, I'd push Jet against the nearest surface and just keep doing this.

When Ollie and Lennon clear their throats and one of them, not sure which one and don't really care, singsongs, "Awkward," I finally pull away.

"Hi," I say.

Jet lets out a little laugh. "Hey."

"You're here. Like, here, here."

"Great power of observation you got there."

"Thanks. Hockey players are known for their smarts."

Jet's hand runs down my cheek.

"How long are you here for?" I ask.

The grin that takes over his face is blinding. "Until the album and or your season's done."

My heart skips a beat, but I tell myself not to get my hopes up. "What? How?"

"Harley blackballed the band from all the recording studios in L.A."

"He what? I'll kill him. Those ten ways are about to come in handy."

Jet's still grinning.

"Wait ... we're happy about this?"

"He did it for us."

"I'm confused."

"He gave me the opportunity to come to New York to record the album. I'm staying."

Jet's staying.

"Staying. In New York."

Jet's staying in New York.

"Please tell me you're not fucking with me?"

Jet shakes his head. "Not fucking with you. The band is here until we record the album and release our next single. And then we'll talk touring, but then during the off-season you can be with us on the road, and next year we can try to record in New York again, or—"

"Next year won't matter."

"Why not? You've been killing it. They'll offer you an extension for sure."

"I already decided I'm not taking it even if they do."

"Whoa, you're retiring?" Ollie butts in.

I turn to him and Lennon. "Can you guys give us a minute?"

They take their exit but glance back at us with matching concerned expressions.

"You're quitting hockey?" Jet's voice is small but so full of hope.

"No, I'm retiring. Not quitting. There's a difference. Not only that, I'll be retiring on a high. If things keep going the way they're going, I could have the highest-scoring season of my entire career."

"Exactly. Which means you should keep doing it. You can't retire for me. What if it's too soon? You'll hate me in the end."

I lower my forehead to his. "Jet. My sweet Jet. I could never hate you, and I'm not retiring for you. I'm retiring for us. For me. I'm done after this season no matter what. Remember how I said I wanted to retire on my own terms and not on the NHL's time? This is my choice. My time."

"What happens if you don't win the Cup?"

"Doesn't matter."

"Soren—"

"I love you. I want a life with you. A future. I want *forever* with you. I've had my career, and it's been an amazing and fulfilling one. Now it's your turn to have yours, and I want to be there for it."

Jet's warm eyes blink up at me. "I guess I must be your hat trick, huh?"

"No."

Jet pouts.

"You're so much more than that. You're a goal in the last minute. A five-on-three powerplay. You're the crowd screaming for the win."

"I don't know what that means, but good to know."

I laugh. "Jet, you're everything. You're my Stanley Cup."

Jet smiles. "I guess that makes you my Grammy? I don't really know what metaphor we're going for here."

I hold him close. "I'll put it the easiest way I know how to say it. You're the most important thing in my life and being with you forever is my only goal."

Jet's eyes get shiny. "I want to help you achieve that goal."

"Then we'll do it."

I seal our promise with another public display of affection that I'm sure is being photographed by the media.

Welcome to the rest of our lives.

CHAPTER THIRTY-FOUR

JET

THE KIDLET TURNS ONE

The door to Matt and Noah's apartment swings open, and Matt stands there holding the baby, who's got a flowery headband on while wearing a New York hockey jersey.

Soren gasps. "Ollie beat us."

I snicker. "He's been good at that lately."

Soren's hand flies to his chest. "Wounded! Help! Do you *have* to rub my professional failures in my face?" He huffs, but I know he doesn't care. I mean, not really.

He's disappointed his team didn't make it to the Cup game, but he left with his highest-scoring season under his belt and his head held high. New Jersey offered him three more years with a no-trade clause because of it, and he still turned it down to follow me on tour.

Hashtag *real* Disney love.

He still has a few connections to the sporting world. He's agreed to feature on Lennon's ever-growing podcast he started about six months ago, and Damon's also been talking to him about scheduling talks and appearances all over the US to coincide with the band's touring schedule.

Soren might've said goodbye to his career in the NHL, but he'll always be involved in sports in some way.

"You guys are late, so everyone's beaten you to presents," Matt says.

Soren and I glance at each other out the corner of our eyes. Yeah, there's a reason we're late. Might have something to do with a life-altering decision followed by a quick pitstop at the county-clerk's office.

"Give me my niece." I reach my arms out for her, and she comes to me easily.

We've only managed to come to see her a handful of times with Soren's team making it to the playoffs and Radioactive's tour kicking off, but she still loves me, and I remind her every time I'm her favorite uncle.

"Happy birthday, kiddo," I coo.

We enter the apartment to find the rest of the gay brigade and Wade in the living room.

"Hey, guys," I say casually but I don't take my eyes off Jackie. She's so cute with her big brown eyes.

She looks up at me with a furrowed brow as if she's trying to work me out, and I'm only mildly offended that she doesn't remember how awesome I am.

Soren takes the seat next to Ollie, who's sitting there with a big frown on his face and his arms folded. Probably has something to do with the giant moonboot he's wearing.

"How's the ankle?" Soren asks.

"Broken," Ollie grumbles.

Lennon rolls his eyes. "It's a hairline fracture. In your foot."

"I'm out for at least the next six weeks."

"Aww, poor Stanley Cup winner." Soren pats Ollie's head.

Soren couldn't be happier for Ollie, and because New Jersey was knocked out by the team who then went on to win, it makes Soren feel less bad about it not being him who got to hold the Cup up at the end.

And after that triumphant win, Ollie gets tripped during preseason and somehow manages to break his ankle. Or foot … whatever.

"Thanks for the perspective, retiree," Ollie says.

"I may be retired, but I didn't break a bone during a preseason game … well, ever," Soren taunts.

"Have to tell you, crying into the Stanley Cup makes me okay with that."

Maddox groans from across the room. "Even when you're all retired, you guys are still going to smack talk each other, aren't you?"

"Hey," Miller cuts in. "Just because Soren and I are retired, doesn't mean we're no longer athletes."

Soren reaches forward to high-five Miller. "How are your first few weeks of retirement?"

Miller sniggers. "I get to sleep in while these two get up for training." He points to Talon and Matt. "I'm loving it."

Miller's retirement came after he had a rough season with the leg he injured a few years ago, but clearly, he's not overly upset about it.

Soren turns to me. "See. Miller's retired, and he gets to sleep in."

"You get to sleep in."

"After staying out until *should-be-asleep* o'clock."

Everyone in the room makes an old man comment. I'm pretty sure Jackie even tries to say "old man." She's smart, this one.

"So, uh …" I glance at Soren who nods. "We have some

news, and I can't remember the last time we were all in one room together—"

"Talon and Miller's wedding," Matt and Noah say in unison.

"Okay, so yeah, this kinda can't wait a few months, so I'm sorry for hijacking your one-year-old's birthday party, but …"

Soren and I look at each other again.

He stands and makes his way over to me, putting his arm around my shoulders and bopping Jackie on the nose with his finger. "I asked Jet to marry me."

Before everyone can jump in, I add, "And seeing as we're hardly ever together as a group anymore, and we're about to hit the European part of the tour, we figured we should make the most of this. So, we're doing it tomorrow."

Everyone's excitement drops a little.

"Tomorrow? As in tomorrow, tomorrow?" Matt asks.

I cock my head at him. "No, as in the day after today. That tomorrow."

"We got the marriage license today, booked to get hitched at the courthouse tomorrow, and I've already bought flights for my parents and sister to fly in from Toronto."

I tell them the best part. "And because it's such short notice, the paparazzi won't be fucking crazy like at Talon and Miller's wedding."

That was insane. There were photographers jumping fences to try to get a shot of the grooms.

"It's all we want. Our closest friends." I glance at Ollie and Lennon. "Our chosen family." I turn to Damon, Maddox, Talon, and Miller. And then I turn to Matt, Noah, and Wade. "And my brothers."

Soren clears his throat.

"Oh, and his family too, but I've met them, like, once, so that's more for him." I pat Soren's chest.

The room is silent apart from Jackie, who's starting to squirm and fuss in my arms.

"You want to get down and crawl, baby girl?" I look up at Matt as I put her on the floor. "Is she walking yet?"

He doesn't answer me. He just keeps staring at me. Even when his daughter crawls her way toward the coffee table and puts someone's wallet in her mouth. Have no idea who's it is.

I reckon everyone in the room must be taking their cue from Matt.

I sigh. "Go on. Say it."

Matt at least averts his gaze as he says, "Isn't it ... fast? It's fast."

I balk. "Fast? Says the guy who married Noah after *a few months*. Soren and I have been together for over a year. Known each other for four." *Technically.* We'll pretend those few years of avoiding each other count.

"Yeah, I married Noah after a few months, and now I'm stuck with him."

"Hey," Noah complains.

Matt turns to his husband. "Love you." But now his focus is back on me, and I hate—hate, hate, hate—that he's making me feel like a kid again. I thought we were past this, but nooooo. "I'm sorry," Matt says, surprising me. "I'm happy for you. It's just hard to let go. You're not old enough to be married."

"Need I remind you that you were my age when you married Noah? And you did it the exact same way we are. Courthouse wedding with the only people who matter to us."

"I'm offended," Talon says. "We weren't there."

Matt ignores him. "I know you're not the kid I left back in Tennessee, but sometimes I need reminding." Matt steps forward and hugs me tight, and then the rest of the guys follow with rounds of congratulations.

The guys mutter, "You hurt him, I kill you" and other variations in Soren's ear, but he laughs them all off.

I lift my head to look at Soren behind me. "Are you sure you want to marry into this? You can still get out."

"Not on your life. I'm not going anywhere. Never will."

CHAPTER THIRTY-FIVE

SOREN

FOREVER LOVE

The best thing about a courthouse wedding?
No frills.

We're both in jeans and button-down shirts. Jet's wearing a leather jacket, and I'm wearing a tie, but that's as formal as we get.

It's legal and that's all we need.

Jet and I don't need big declarations of love because what we have is complete confidence in each other and our relationship. We just want to make it official.

Our epic love is inside him. Inside me. It encompasses us as a couple and as individuals.

So, when the judge tells Jet to place the ring on my finger, it's like the last piece clicks into place.

Getting married doesn't change anything between us. It doesn't change how I feel or how I see Jet. I understand Maddox and Damon's and Ollie and Lennon's decision not to take this step, but for me and Jet, that wasn't an option.

Jet has lived a lonely existence, and the ring on my finger is a promise he never has to do that again.

With Damon planning appearances for me and being part of Lennon's podcast, there will be times when we're apart, but with our marriage vows, I promise Jet will always know I'm his.

"I now pronounce you husbands," the judge says.

When we kiss, I can hear my mother blubbering and can't help but laugh into Jet's mouth.

"First kiss as a married couple, and you're laughing? That doesn't bode well."

"I'm sorry, but my mother is ridiculous."

"First kiss as a married couple, and you're thinking of your *mother*? That's even worse."

Our small group snickers.

"I'm sorry." Mom sniffs. "I'm just so happy my Caleb has found a loving family to be a part of when he's not with us."

When I stare around the room at the gay brigade and their warm smiles, I realize I really am a part of them.

I have been in some way for the past four years, but not being with Jet made me hold them at arm's length.

"He's one of our brothers," Matt says. "And not just because he married JJ."

We reach the steps of the courthouse when Noah says, "I booked us a table at Sky. It'll be the last time we're all together in one city for a long time."

With Matt and Noah now living in Chicago permanently, Talon and Miller only coming to New York to see Miller's family during the off-season, and Jet and me on the road for at least the next four months, it will be a while before we're all together like this again.

We're all moving on, all finding our own lives, but we know

that no matter what, if any of us needed something, we'd all be there in a heartbeat.

Not because we have to out of some sort of obligation, but because it's what chosen families do for each other.

I squeeze Jet's hand. "I've been thinking. After the Europe leg of the tour, maybe we should go on a honeymoon."

"Where'd you have in mind?"

I want to take Jet somewhere that changed both our lives. It gave us our defining moment. It was the first time I'd heard Jet's song the way it was supposed to be heard, the first time I saw how much we had truly affected each other's lives, and the whole place means so much to me and to *us*. "How about Fiji?"

Jet answers in the most perfectly Jet way.

His lips curve up into his trademark smirk—the one I always want to take away by covering his mouth with my own. And now that we're together, and I'm his husband, I can. Always. I will never get enough of kissing him.

Jet's head rests on my shoulder at the dinner table. The restaurant is in the highest building in Chicago and overlooks the entire city.

The views are amazing, and it's perfect for our wedding dinner.

Low-key but beautiful.

Jet's lips hit my cheek. "I'll be right back."

I watch as he walks away, but my sister's hand on my arm brings my attention to her.

"We really do love him."

The only other time my family has met Jet was when Radioactive played in Toronto not that long ago. They came to the show, and I knew they'd fall for him, just like I had, without even properly meeting him. Even Dad was vocal in approving of Jet, which is more than he's ever been when it's come to my sexuality, so I'm taking it all as a very big win.

Jet's on the shy and awkward side around them, which is weird for him, but he says it's because he doesn't know how to act around real parental figures seeing as how he never had any growing up.

I'm sure it won't take long for him to show his true self, and now that we're married, my family has to love him no matter what.

Too late, suckers.

I'm assuming Jet's gone to the bathroom, but then his voice cuts through the noise of the restaurant.

"Geez, does he carry microphones around with him?" Talon asks.

I laugh. It wouldn't surprise me if Jet did.

We turn and find him sitting at a grand piano on a tiny stage in the corner of the restaurant.

"Does someone want to get out their phone and record this for me?" His eyes lock on mine. "We're about to go viral again, babe."

Damon moves his chair to the side of the group and gets out his phone. When he nods to Jet, my husband starts playing a melody on the piano.

My husband.

Yeah, I don't know if I'll ever get used to that.

Jet looks at me while he plays. "Even though we didn't have a traditional wedding with any vows, I wrote some down anyway."

Of course, he did.

Then he starts singing, and I fall for him all over again.

Insecure
Unsure
Faking confidence
You see it all

I'm not myself
A little off
You know immediately
When times are rough

I cannot lie
You'll see right through
And this is why
I love you

You want me for me
And not for Jay
You know my heart and soul
And love me anyway

Forever, is what you said
Forever love ...

He pauses and looks me dead in the eyes as he says, "I wrote this last line for you, but there's no way it's going on the official single."

Forever, is what you said
Forever love
Our epic flove.

He wrote me a love song. Not one about heartbreak, or pain, or the new one on their latest album about missing me. It's love.

Epic *flove*.

AFTERWORD

Thank you all so, so, so much for loving these guys and this universe so much that one little idea of a straight guy pretending to be gay for his entire hometown turned into five books about friendship, love, and chosen family.

Maddox was the beginning of this journey and it ends with Jet—the character I knew I had to give a voice the second he appeared in book two but didn't quite know what his story was yet.

While this is the last full-length novel in this series, these guys weren't quite ready to let go. I decided to give them a bonus epilogue each to let you all get a glimpse into their lives now.

Want to see how Matt and Noah gain custody of Wade and adopt baby Jackson?

Or witness Maddox's disastrous proposal in Fiji?

An update on all the couples is coming in *Final Play*. To learn more, you can join my reader group here: https://www.facebook.com/groups/absolutelyeden/

Alternatively, you can join my mailing list: http://eepurl.com/bS1OFH

AFTERWORD

Want to read how Marty and Luce met and how Luce became Jet's manager? Their story is in *Winning You*, which is part of the *Fake Boyfriend Breakaways* collection along with two other short stories about side characters from this universe—Aron & Wyatt from *Trick Play* and Max and Ash from *Deke*. Available here: getbook.at/Breakaways

The beginning of Marty and Luce's story was originally published in the Heart2Heart anthology in 2018 **but has since doubled in length and story.**

NOTES ABOUT HAT TRICK

Rua Daulomani Island isn't a real place. Sad face, I know. Neither is the dirty escape room with seemingly sexual clues.

Songs that inspired Jet and I listened to on repeat while writing:

Lewis Capaldi
Someone You Loved
Forever

Morgan Evans
Young Again

Andy Grammer
Don't Give Up On Me

Colby Bennett (YouTube) version of Imagine Dragons
Radioactive

EDEN FINLEY BOOKS

https://amzn.to/2zUlM16
https://www.edenfinley.com

FAKE BOYFRIEND SERIES

Fake Out
Trick Play
Deke
Blindsided
Hat Trick

Novellas:

Fake Boyfriend Breakaways: A Short Story Collection
Final Play

STEELE BROTHERS

Unwritten Law
Unspoken Vow

ROYAL OBLIGATION
Unprincely (M/M/F)

ACKNOWLEDGMENTS

I want to thank all of my betas, especially Leslie Copeland and Jill Wexler from Les Court Services, Deb Nemeth for development edits, Susi Selva fro line edits, and Kelly from Xterraweb editing for copy-edits.
Thanks to Lori Parks for one last read through.
To all the ninja typos who still got through all of that, you deserve a medal.
Kellie from Book Cover by Design for putting up with my almost never-ending search for the perfect Soren.
And to photographer Wander Aguiar for providing me said perfect Soren.
Lastly, a big thanks to Linda from Foreword PR & Marketing for helping get this book out.

Printed in Great
Britain
by Amazon